Voice in the Wilderness

"You're not from around here, are you?" the voice said.

"Who said that?" I replied, stopping dead in my tracks.

"I can tell you're not from around here. Your clothes are like nothing I've ever seen on a human before," the voice continued. This bothered me for several reasons. The first was that I had no idea where this voice was coming from. The second was that it referred to *me* as "human," as if *it* were not. As for my clothes, I was wearing an old pair of blue jeans, a hand-me-down Wings concert tee shirt from one of my older brothers, and a pair of basketball shoes. This was pretty common casual wear where I came from. The voice went on.

"What's the symbol on your tunic mean? Did you come from Englishland like the others?"

I looked around and tried to find a face to put with this curious voice. "I'm not answering any of your questions until you show yourself."

Just then I heard branches moving apart and leaves crunching. It seemed whoever or whatever was speaking had been following me for a while! For a split second I thought it was the giant monkey, but I was certain that I would have heard such a large creature before now. As I turned around a face popped out from behind a large tree. It was that of a small wolf! Could this really be the source of the inquisitive voice?

"Hello," it said.

I could hardly control myself. I didn't know whether to faint, scream, or run off. I tried my best to speak calmly. "You... you're... you're a wolf cub!"

"I'm no cub!" it responded curtly. "I'm almost a year old now."

"But, but... you can talk!" I blurted out.

"Yes," he responded. "So can you."

"But you're an animal. Animals can't talk," I said.

He cocked his head sideways like a confused dog. I suppose that's precisely what he was. "Can you understand me?"

"Well, yes," I said.

"Then obviously I'm talking," he replied. "Do you mean to tell me animals don't talk where you're from?"

"No. No, they don't," I started shaking a little bit and then sat down rather quickly.

"What's wrong?" he asked sincerely. "Don't you feel well?"

"I'm fine," I managed to say. "...actually I just have... I just never. I, uh..."

"You should get a drink of water, maybe." The little wolf nodded towards the river.

"Yeah. Maybe that is a good idea," I said quietly. I reached over and cupped my hands and took a good long drink of water. Then I washed my eyes and rubbed them vigorously in hopes this mirage would fade.

The Legend of Gwerinatha
Branwen's Garden

by Brad Parnell

A BlackWyrm Book
Louisville, Kentucky

THE LEGEND OF GWERINATHA: BRANWEN'S GARDEN

A BlackWyrm Book
BlackWyrm Publishing
10307 Chimney Ridge Ct, Louisville, KY 40299

Printed in the United States of America.

ISBN: 978-0-9820067-6-4
LCCN: 2009927032
Cover by Brad Parnell
Interior Illustrations by Brad Parnell
Edited by Dave Mattingly and Jason Walters

First edition: July 2009

DEDICATED TO:

My wife Amy,
who believed I could finish the project
and listened to every chapter along the way.

Our sweet little cat Padme,
who was with us for far too short a time.
She was very much inspirational to this story.

Special thanks to:

Simon Ager, for going above and beyond.

Dave and Jason, for making it happen.

Chapter One
The Last Road Trip

I used to get anxious a great deal when I was a teenager. This was mostly due to the fact that I was afraid of the future. I guess most kids go through that. My particular problem centered on a lack of identity which, in turn, led to an unclear desire of what I wanted to be when I grew up. My good grades were no consolation to me. It could be that my problem was that I was overshadowed by my older siblings. I was born several years after they were and spent much of my childhood in the shade of their accomplishments. My oldest brother John had spent several years in the Peace Corps helping families in Asia and Africa. He went on to become a pediatrician. My other brother William had been an Eagle Scout and, by his senior year, was the starting quarterback for his college football team. Then there was my sister, Margaret. She was always volunteering for something. She was a candy striper, spent time ringing bells for the Salvation Army and spent most holidays at a homeless shelter, serving meals. She was also a history buff and spent countless hours tracing our genealogy. In fact, it was one of her discoveries that led to the most amazing adventure I have ever experienced, one that not only changed my life but that send me on a journey of self-discovery few are fortunate enough to experience. Unfortunately, it also took from me my best childhood friend.

Margaret had invited me to lunch so that she could share some of her latest discoveries about our family history. At that time she was living in an apartment across town with a roommate named Candace whom I had a mild crush on. Of course at fifteen I had a crush on a different girl each week: not counting, Marcia Brady, Laurie Partridge, or any other innumerable television personalities. I didn't know it at first, but Margaret had an ulterior motive in mind for me that day. It turns out that, besides the fascinating history lessons, she also wanted to lecture me on my future... or seeming lack thereof. She loved illustrating how learning about the past helped us to shape our future; presumably including mine.

I had just finished locking my bike to her deck when she ran up and greeted me with a hug. I shrugged a bit and, in youthful embarrassment, looked around to see if anyone was watching. "Sorry, little brother. I forgot that you're too grown up for hugs now," she said.

"It's not that," I said trying not to sound too sarcastic. "It's just embarrassing out in public and everything."

"You know, one day you're going to be grateful that you have family members who want to hug you," she told me.

"You're not going to lay a guilt trip on me are you?" I whined. She gave me a look that made me sorry I had asked that question. We went into her apartment where piles and piles of research papers were spread out all over the place.

"Macaroni and cheese okay?" she asked. Macaroni and cheese was pretty much the only palatable dish my sister could make, so I eagerly responded in the affirmative as we sat down to her kitchen table. She added to the plate a garden salad, and some iced tea rounded out the meal. The lack of a meat dish was due to economical considerations rather than any sort of vegetarian ideals.

"You won't believe what I've uncovered now!" she exclaimed.

She sounded more excited than I'd ever heard her. So I tried to act interested while I hungrily wolfed down the macaroni.

"Well, as you know, I've traced our family all the way back to the 1600s. That's when the first of the Moore clan came over from England. Back then they spelled it with just one 'o' though, that tripped me up a little bit. Are you listening?" she asked sternly.

"Absolutely," I stammered. I'd probably seemed a little distant while munching on the salad, but I quickly turned my gaze towards her to get my ruse of attentiveness back on track. We men learn these things young.

"It gets better, I promise," she said. "Anyway, I had recently contacted some distant relatives back east and they sent me a very exciting package."

"Are there cookies in it?" I asked, "Because we could use some dessert."

"Give me a break here," she demanded a bit impatiently. "I've got some chocolate cupcakes I made for Candace when she comes back. You can have one of those." Now she'd really distracted me by mentioning my most recent crush *and* cupcakes. It became increasingly difficult to keep up the façade of interest at this point.

"Now listen," she continued. "This package has a lot of family artifacts in it. When they found out that I was doing all this research, they sent it to me to help me along. They'd like to know more about our roots as well. There are copies of wills and birth certificates. Copies of death certificates. Even some mementos and knick-knacks. They also passed down some stories that have run through our family for generations. There's actually a legend that one of our ancestors just vanished without a trace." I had heard enough to know that was a cue to stop looking for those cupcakes and add to the conversation.

"Vanished?" I said, in a most convincing tone. "You mean like in to thin air or something?"

"Well, yes," she answered. "But I'm sure he ended up somewhere. People don't just vanish. His name was Samuel More and he was supposedly very revered by his community. The weird thing was this difference of opinion he had with his son, Artemis Richard More, who was an early pilgrim. They argued over whether or not the family should immigrate to America. Artemis obviously did since we came from his line, but he never spoke with his father again. The story goes that his son William tried to visit Grandfather More in England, only to find no clue as to his whereabouts." Her face changed from excited to a bit glum. I probably should have guessed what was coming.

"It's sad how some negative things repeat throughout a family's history," she said with a quieter tone. Now I knew what made her change expressions. She was referring to my rift with *our* father. My father, Peter, had split with mom a few years back. All the other kids were already living on their own so it didn't affect them as much. But for me it was a really big deal. I had to choose who to live with and was caught up in a competition for attention between mom and dad. It was terrible and, as far as I was concerned, dad was pretty much just trying to buy my love with trips and gifts. He wasn't really concerned with me any more than I was concerned with Margaret's genealogy search. Throughout it all mom was a rock. I've never regretted choosing to live with her. But at that particular time I completely resented my father and had rejected his attempts to bond.

I leaned over the counter peeking around for those pesky cupcakes which I could smell but still eluded my grasp. "Look, Mags, I didn't come over here to get a lecture about seeing dad. So if that's what—" she interrupted my angry speech with both hands upraised.

"No, no," she said. "I just think it's sad you don't spend more time with him, that's all. I won't mention it again. And the cupcakes are in the last cabinet on the right. I'll get them in a minute. They're not iced yet."

She went over to a box and pulled out what looked to me like some really old dusty junk. "Look here," she said, "I have no idea what some if this stuff even is. There're some key fobs, ribbons..." Her voice trailed off in my mind as my eye was drawn to one of the items she thought was a key fob. It was the strangest looking thing I'd ever seen. It looked like it was made of petrified wood with some really drab jewels encrusted in a metal setting. The metal was like something I'd seen on a field trip to an old-fashioned blacksmith. The wood part resembled two entwined arms that ended in hands of a sort that held the metal with the jewels. They were dark and cloudy, with a reddish hue that hinted of blood. It looked like they may once have been radiant, but were now dim and lifeless. I was so interested in the strange item that I'd actually forgotten about the cupcakes.

I leaned over to examine it. "What's this again?" I asked, this time with sincere interest.

"I'm not really sure," she said with a puzzled look on her face. "But if you're interested in finding out more about it, be my guest. The more information I have on these heirlooms, the better I can put together our family's history."

She was pleased that I had taken an interest. Besides the lecture on dad, I'd feared there was going to be another lecture on my "intellectual laziness," as my sister referred to it. What she was really talking about was my lack of interest in anything other than television, comic books, or cupcakes. My hobbies weren't the type that either bettered myself or helped others, unlike the extracurricular activities of my older siblings. I suppose I seemed lazy to them, but I just didn't share their interests. It didn't help matters that our parental upbringing was different. I know she was worried about my future, but she stopped bringing it up because she knew how much it bothered me. I guess she saw my interest in this family artifact as a chance to get myself into something with a positive spin for a change. And, of course, it was a chance for some family bonding. I told her I would take a look at it to see if I could come up with something. It really *was* fascinating. The more I stared at it, the more I wondered what it was.

After we spent some quality time icing and eating cupcakes, we poured over some of the writings in the package. I found some pages that referred to the story Margaret had told me about concerning Samuel's disappearance. I asked her if I could take them home along with the artifact and, after some pleading and promises that I wouldn't let any harm come to them, she begrudgingly obliged.

That night I poured over the texts I'd gotten from Margaret. The stories about Samuel disappearing were stranger than I had first expected. According to the legends, what William discovered was not only that his grandfather, Samuel, had disappeared but that several other people from the town vanished at the same time. I *had* to know more; but a three hundred-year-old mystery had far too many clues lost forever to the ages. I don't know why, but I was certain that the strange "key fob" had something to do with the vanishings. I'd read nearly everything Margaret had given me. She still had the bulk of the papers, but most of them were just cemetery listings and the copies from various certificates and licenses. There was only one other piece of text that remained: a copy of a really old piece of paper. Well, I guessed that the original must have been old from the way it was written. But I hadn't given it much thought because it wasn't written in English, at least not modern English. Fortunately, there were innumerable books in our library. My dad had always loved to read and his collection had been added to by my siblings. I remembered that there was a book in there about old languages, so I did some quick checking and found it. Sure enough, the words on this old letter were not English but Welsh. Margaret had told me that some of our family was from Wales and, since it was mixed in with everything else, it seemed likely that the original was part of our family's history.

I spent the next few hours trying to decipher what I could of the letter. I was certainly no linguist! But I'd spent a lot of time using code languages. Cameron and I used to go back and forth with ones we'd find in magazines and old books. We even made up some of our own. So I figured if there was enough to go on in the book. It couldn't be too different from deciphering a code, could it?

Since it reminded me of old times with Cameron and I hadn't heard from him in quite a while, I thought he might get a kick out of helping me. I hesitated calling him at first, remembering how we were spending less time with each other and how he might laugh and think of it as kid stuff. Then again, so what if he did? At least I would feel better for making an effort to keep our friendship going. I called to find out he was in fact at home and was bored to tears. He came over a few minutes afterward. I wondered idly whether the fact that he got there so quickly was due to excitement towards the task at hand, or simply having nothing better to do.

It took a little convincing but, after I showed Cameron the artifact, he decided to help me. After a few hours we came to a perplexing conclusion. It seemed that Samuel had believed he'd discovered a doorway into another dimension and was determined to settle in this new world, rather than go to the "other" new world in America. He had written a letter to persuade his son to come with him and had given him the key to get there in the form of this artifact.

After a rather bemusing discussion, we decided to try and use it ourselves... even though there wasn't much to go on in the way of instructions. All we could figure out was that it had something to do with using a natural doorway and the rising sun as a way to open a portal to another world. Of course neither of us expected it to work, but it gave us an excuse for a road trip. We decided to go to the nearest natural doorway we could think of: the rather aptly named Natural Bridge.

Like several other states, ours has a Natural Bridge and a state park to go around it. It's really nothing more than a large hunk of rock with a big hole in it. But this seemed to be absolutely perfect for our needs. Samuel emphasized a natural doorway in his letter to Artemis. I didn't realize until much later that we were making the whole process a lot harder than it needed to be, but that was something that came naturally to me. Needless complication was the hallmark of my youth. But, since we'd been there on a field trip in the fifth grade, Natural Bridge was the first place that popped into our heads. We didn't even stop to think of what we'd have to do once we got there before we started planning the trip.

We sneaked out of the house and managed to get a ride from one of Cameron's older friends. Cameron didn't tell him what we were doing. It *did* sound ridiculous, after all. For my part, I was paranoid because I knew Cam and his friends had done some experimenting with drugs. I worried throughout the drive that this guy might be high. (I was fairly naive about such things.) It turned out I didn't have anything to worry about. I caught a few alarming words of their conversation in between naps – mostly about people I didn't know and things I'd never considered doing – but his buddy got safely us to the park in plenty of time.

Unfortunately, we hadn't figured out exactly what the next step was going to be. We arrived a little less than six hours from sunrise, which is when the letter told us we needed to use the key. We'd thought that would have given us more than enough time to figure out our next move, so we headed off toward the natural bridge: the opening we needed to form a portal to another world. (Or so I quietly hoped.) Then the adrenaline began to wear off from our late night escapade and I began to get sleepy again. Cameron said he'd look out for any park rangers in case I wanted to doze off. I took him up on the offer, and found a nook several yards from the opening where I threw down my backpack and used it as a pillow. Despite the uncomfortable surroundings and the excitement of the morning's adventure to come, I fell into a deep sleep.

The next thing I knew I was being shaken violently. It was Cameron... and he looked quite agitated.

"Dude! Wake, up!" he whispered urgently.

"What's wrong? Did I miss sunrise?" I asked.

"No," he answered. "But your snoring is really loud, man. I was afraid you'd wake up a ranger or a bear or something. Have you always snored like that?"

"No, I... how should I know?" I said grumpily. "I'm always asleep."

"You might want to get that checked out," he offered. "It's pretty bad."

"Yeah, well, maybe," I grumbled. I began to sleepily get my bearings when, suddenly, my attention turned to what we had come for.

"What time is it?" I asked groggily.

"I don't know," he replied. "Don't you have a watch?"

"No. I thought you had one," I told him. It was yet another reminder at how unprepared we really were. I'd thrown what I could into my backpack, but I never was much for watches. We would have to estimate for how long it was until sunrise.

"Well, which way is east?" I asked as if Cameron would really know.

"What do you mean?" he shot back. "I don't have a compass. All I know is the sun comes up in the east. So, until the sun comes up, that question is pretty much moot."

"Great," I said, barely hiding my sarcasm. "So we have to be in position for this thing to work and we're pretty much going to do that by guesswork. That's just great. How long was I sleeping?"

"Again..." he said pointing to his wrist. "No watch. But it couldn't have been more than a couple of hours."

I didn't really trust Cameron's estimate, but I had nothing else to go on. "Well, we'll just have to keep watching the horizon and see where it starts to get lighter. Then we'll make sure we're on the right side of the opening to get the doorway to work." I felt like I had gotten more than a couple hours of sleep and, judging by the sky, it didn't look like we had too much longer to wait.

Even though I didn't really expect anything to happen, as we waited I couldn't help but wonder if there weren't some really important parts to the message we had missed. Could there have been some warnings about what to expect? Maybe there were warnings about wild animals or aggressive natives on the other side. We didn't even know what kind the weather would be like. Were we wearing the right clothes? What were we thinking? We certainly weren't prepared. I shared my concerns with Cameron, but he chalked it up to me always worrying – especially since nothing was actually going to happen. He was right. With nothing but time and silence while waiting for the sun to come up, I'd predictably let my mind run away again.

Why was I even there? The whole thing was crazy. I began to question my own sanity for the first of what would be many times to come. I don't believe I would even have gone on that trip if it weren't for Cameron. By this point I couldn't even remember whose idea it was to come out here. Did Cameron twist my arm? No. But left to my own devices I wouldn't have made the trip. I needed him to make it happen. Without Cameron I'd be too afraid to pursue the whole crazy idea any further than a library. And what of Margaret? Was I just doing this to prove something to her? Did I want to make her think I wasn't a lazy kid without a future? Or did I just need to prove something to myself? Either way, I was here and determined not to back down now, no matter what happened next.

After I'd calmed myself down, mostly by balancing my fears against the more logical thought that nothing was going to happen anyway, I noticed the sun breaking over the horizon. It was time. I yelled over at Cameron, who was standing a few yards away "Cam! The sun's coming up! What should I do?"

He looked at me as if I was speaking a foreign language.

"What do you mean, what should you do?" he asked. He ran over to my backpack, grabbed the key, and threw it over to me. "Hold it up!" he yelled. "Keep moving it around until something happens."

I wasn't really sure what to expect, so I did as he said. I kept moving it around at different angles until it caught the sunlight.

"There!" he screamed, getting genuinely excited. "That's where you want it. Don't move!"

"Now what?" I asked.

"Well, give it a few minutes. If nothing happens we'll give up, go home, and never talk about it again."

If he knew then how accurate the last part of his statement would turn out to be, he might have wished we'd never made that fateful trip. I stood there for what seemed to my aching arms to be several minutes as more and more sunlight inched its way up the key. Then I saw something; or at least thought I saw something. The jewels seemed to get brighter... and then something happened in front of me. I wasn't sure exactly what to make of it. I guess I was expecting some far-out Hollywood special effects with loud hums and colorful, blinding lights. Instead, it was just a subtle difference in the opening of Natural Bridge. The dawn was still too dim to be sure if my eyes weren't just playing tricks on me. I asked Cameron what he could see.

"I don't see anything Bobby," he replied, sounding disappointed. He also sounded pretty certain, so I blinked hard a few times and had another look.

"Something's definitely happening, Cam," I told him, not quite believing the words even as they emerged from my mouth. "I can see something. I'm sure of it."

"What are you talking about? I don't see anything," he said with an exasperated tone.

It was as if I was seeing two places at once. I could see the dirt and rocks on the other side of the opening. I could also see some grass taking up the same space that wasn't there before. There was a slight blur around the grass, like the kind you see from heat waves on the roads on a hot summer day. But they were different too. The blurring was subtler and seemed to radiate in an ellipse. I still wasn't sure, but it seemed as if it were growing larger. I began to see more and more of the grass, and less of the rocks and dirt, than was there before.

"Cam, get over here!" I yelled. "It's happening! It's really happening!"

"All right, all right. Hang on," he said impatiently.

He came rushing over as I pleaded. A quick change came over his voice. "Holy cow!" he exclaimed. "I see it too now. I thought you were just sleepy and seeing things; but something is definitely happening. Who would've believed it?"

I had decided that the portal wasn't visible from other angles and needed verification from Cameron. "Go ahead and step back to the side again." He did so and I continued, "Do you still see it?"

"No! It's like it's completely gone," he told me. He ran back behind me and was able to see it again. "That is the weirdest freaking thing I have ever seen. It's real! The whole thing's real!"

I got a little nervous as the portal began to widen to the point where it was as half as large as a hula-hoop, but slowly getting wider. "So, should I try to step through?" I asked, half hoping he would talk me out of it.

"Duh," he replied sarcastically. "We didn't come all this way for nothing."

"M–Maybe you should go," I stuttered nervously.

"No way, man," he replied. "It's your family's history after all."

That sounded reasonable enough. But I was still quite frightened. Despite the fact that the letter had indeed been written by someone who was supposed to be my distant ancestor, the invitation wasn't really intended for me. And even if the invitation was extended to all of Samuel's descendants, how sure could I be that it hadn't expired at some point over the last few centuries? I tried one more time to get talked out of it.

"Well maybe we should both go," I suggested.

"No way again, dude," he responded. "What if you don't come back for a while? Somebody's got to be here to go for help."

On the one hand, that made perfect sense. On the other hand, it was self-evidently ridiculous. But I wasn't thinking clearly in the excitement. His remark calmed me down: probably because I didn't stop to consider how foolish it was. It was only later that I realized that there hadn't been any way *for* him to get help. Unless park rangers were issued trans-dimensional portal opening devices along with their bear repellent and green pickup trucks I was pretty much on my own.

"All right," I said at last. "I'm going to do it. Tell everybody where I went and that we were right about the letter and everything."

"Don't sweat it," he said. "Just step in and then come right back out."

Step in and then step right back out. I hadn't even considered that. Once again I was glad Cameron was there with me. I had been worried that this may end up being a one-way trip or something; but surely Cameron was right. All I had to do was step in, look around for a couple of seconds, and then step right back out again. I would still have accomplished my goal of proving the other new world that my ancestor had written about existed. There wasn't any reason to be afraid. Then I stared into the portal. By now it was just slightly larger than your average hula-hoop and still gradually increasing in size. I felt the same paralyzing fear I had as a small child testing how far I could leap down a flight of stairs. First I'd take one step, then two, and finally three; but up on that fourth step I just couldn't move. I knew I could make the leap to the floor, but something held me back. The same thing was holding me back now. Just like jumping off that fourth step, I assured myself. I could do it. But it was just a little too much to take in all at once.

I looked back at Cameron. He was motioning for me to go forward. "Maybe I should take my backpack," I suggested.

"What do you need that for?"

"Well, I'm not sure," I answered. "Any number of things."

He stepped behind me to where my pack was laying and reached for it. "Here, just walk through and make sure you can come right back. Then I'll hand you your backpack if you want to go in again."

"Make sure I can come right back?" I echoed. "Now you're not sounding so sure."

"Well, I mean... well, we really don't know too much about this, do we?" he was beginning to waffle. "But it sure looks like you can walk right over there and back again. I don't see any problem with it, really."

I clearly remember not feeling all that reassured. However, I figured that as the sun rose and the portal began to slow in its increase that my time might be running short.

"Hurry up!" Cam yelled. "The sun is almost to the middle of the opening."

"You're right," I told him. "If I'm gonna go and come back, then I'd better go ahead and do it."

"Just stick your arm in if you're scared," he said condescendingly.

This was yet another sensible idea that Cameron had come up with that I may have overlooked on my own. I tried his suggestion, slowly raising my arm and putting first my fingers, and then my hand, through the portal. There was no awkward sensation or anything. I put my whole arm through and waved it around over the grass that was by now every bit as clear as any I'd ever seen, completely masking the dirt and rocks that I knew to be on the other side of the opening.

"Seems okay to me," I said confidently.

"There, see?" he said. "Nothing to worry about. Go ahead. I'll be right here."

At that point I gathered my jangling nerves together, inhaled a deep breath and took a quick, confident step through the portal. I felt no tingly sensations. No weird hum in my ears. No nausea. It was just like walking through a regular doorway. I exhaled with a profound sigh of relief.

Then I looked up and down and saw no signs of the natural bridge.

The terrain around me was quite different from that of the park. I turned around to walk back, but was shocked to see there was nothing to walk back through. I yelled out, "Cam! Cam! Can you hear me?" There was no response. I wondered what he could see and if he was trying to get through to me. I looked up at the sky and down on the ground. I did a complete sweep of the area with my eyes and found there was no trace whatsoever of anything resembling a portal. I looked at my hand, which was still firmly grasping the key. I raised it up towards the sun and maneuvered every way I could think of. Nothing happened. I realized that the sun was no longer on the horizon but, instead, was high in the sky as if it were midday. I slowly looked around again. Wherever I was, I realized to my horror that I was going to be here for a while.

Chapter Two
Another New World

A sense of dread overwhelmed me. I had thoughts of never seeing home again. I thought I'd never again see any of my family or friends. It was possible even that I would never again hear another human voice. My thoughts raced, thick with worry. Only this time there *was* a logical reason for it. I had no idea where I was. No idea of how to get back. For an instant I fervently hoped that the whole thing was a dream, and that at any moment Cameron would wake me up so that we could try to open the portal. I squeezed my eyes shut in an attempt to wake up.

But it wasn't a dream. The portal had opened up and I had crossed through to the other side.

After a while I simply gave up and accepted my fate. What else could I do, really? I was in an unknown land; the other new world my ancestor had journeyed to with his fellow townspeople so long ago. There was no denying it. So I checked myself over. There seemed to be no ill effects from making the crossover. Everything seemed intact and healthy. In fact, instead of a nauseating feeling that I had surmised would take hold of me, I actually felt pretty good. With less than normal sleep and no breakfast I should have been fatigued; but I actually felt remarkably energetic. I took in a deep breath. The air was rich and clean. It filled my lungs like... well, like a breath of fresh air. I don't know any other way to explain it. I'd read somewhere that thousands or millions of years ago the earth's atmosphere was more saturated with oxygen than it is today. I thought this must be what that felt like. After breathing the thick air a bit more, my mouth began to feel tingly. It was like I'd just brushed my teeth with a brand new toothbrush after having used an old one for far too long.

Reassured by all this, I decided that I'd better take a look around and try to figure out what to do about food and shelter. I started walking, slowly at first. My feet felt lighter than normal. I had that 'brand new shoe' feeling. The stress from my worrying began to gradually fade; though the worries themselves didn't fully go away. Despite my newfound energy, I realized I would have to find something to eat before too long. But what to eat, and where to find it?

The grass around me to seem just like the grass from the world I left. The rocks and trees were similar, if not exactly the same. The sky was blue enough. I felt a sweet, flowery-smelling breeze in the midday air. Yet this new world was still somehow different. At first I couldn't put my finger on why. It was just the creeping sensation that things were somehow "not right" in the back of my mind. Then I noticed the first thing that seemed out of place.

At first I thought it was a sponge. As I got a little closer to it, it seemed as though it must be some sort of plant. The spongy part was a golden color and it had a long, green shaft rising from its middle like a cattail. It seemed to jiggle when I knelt down to get a better look. Thinking it must be the wind, I reached toward it when, all of a sudden, it jiggled more violently. The flowery portion at the top of the shaft opened up and squirted a gelatinous substance straight at me!

I quickly darted to the side as the ooze splattered on the ground beside my feet. I surmised it must be a self-defense mechanism: probably poisonous. There were several of these gel-spewing plants spread out over a large area before me, some much larger than others. Simultaneously they all began to start quivering like the first one. Reasonably enough (or so I thought at the time), I took off running... until I tripped over my feet and started rolling down a hill.

My descent was broken by what I at first took to be an old, rotted log; though it had a bright scarlet hue quite unlike any tree trunk I'd ever seen before. It was certainly softer than a log should be. Bruised and startled, but otherwise uninjured by my fall, I stood and looked inside of it to verify that it was hollow. Two large eyes blinked back at me. Startled, I stepped back; but when I did, a tentacle slithered out of it and wrapped itself around my ankle. Then six legs emerged from the underbelly of what I had decided now was not a log and stampeded off, dragging me behind it.

I tried to grab on to something but there was nothing around. The speed of the thing was shocking. I remember seeing spiders that could run fairly rapidly, but something its size shouldn't have been able to move half that fast. I was being battered and bruised by the ground blurring by around me. Then I saw a large mound like a giant anthill. Clearly that was where the creature was taking me.

I knew I wouldn't stand a chance if the "log" were able to get me underground. I had to think fast. I remembered watching trick riders on television that were able to do amazing things dangling from a galloping horse. I would have to try something like that. We were going to rocket past a fairly sturdy looking tree before we got to the mound. I knew I'd only get that one chance. I began to bounce off the ground with my hands and my one free foot until I was able to right myself somewhat. Just as we came under the tree, I was able to bounce up and grab the limb. I swung around as hard as I could and tried to shake the creature free of my foot. The tentacle's grip became tighter, but I wouldn't let go of the tree for anything. I knew my life depended on it.

Using my other foot I began to violently kick the creature, feeling the flesh of its trunk give way a bit under the sole of my sneakers. I was determined that it would not drag me underground to where an undoubtedly grisly fate awaited. Though not a violent young man by nature, I struck at the things with all of my might. Finally, I felt its grip loosen and, with a disturbing hiss, the tentacle was sucked back into the creature. It ran off and slunk slowly, disturbingly down into the mound.

I had encountered my first dangerous animal life on this new world and survived.

If there were plants and animals here, I figured there could very well be human life as well. I reasoned that, if this was indeed the place my ancestor Samuel had come to with his group of like-minded pilgrims, their descendents could have build some kind of civilization somewhere on it. The thought also crossed my mind that Samuel and his group may not have survived. Certainly, this *new* new world contained dangers they would never have encountered back in Wales.

At this point either scenario was plausible.

All I'd seen of this land were lush green meadows and rolling hills. They were all that was visible from where I stood. Pretty, but devoid of food or human life. If I was going to find out if I was alone in the land, as well as sate my hunger, I knew I'd have to start moving. The most pressing question was: which direction should I head? Obviously, I wanted to get as far away from that mound and the creature within it as possible, but beyond that I wasn't sure which direction to go.

I decided to follow the sun. That would give me as much daylight as possible, plus it would allow me to go in the same direction day after day. Also, I wanted to put off the darkness of night for as long as I could. I was afraid of the unknown enough as it was in the light. The thought of nightfall in this strange land terrified me.

I assumed that the direction I was heading must be west. But how could I be sure? After all, this place was clearly not home. Was it somewhere on Earth? Was it in another solar system? Was it even in the same dimension as "my" Earth? Who knew how this place orbited its sun? The only thing I knew for certain was that the sun was setting. I had no idea how much time it would be before disappeared behind the horizon, plunging the land into darkness. And I feared darkness on the open face of that alien land more profoundly than the tree-thing that had just tried to pull me under its surface.

My pace quickened. Precious time passed. But as I walked, the landscape on the horizon began to shift from rolling hills into a welcome jagged tree line. The closer I got to the trees, the more densely packed I realized they were. I was looking into a forest.

At first I couldn't decide if it would be a good idea to enter it or not. On the one hand, there could be some food and shelter within. On the other hand, there could be any number of horrifying creatures there as well. I simply had no way of knowing. I looked around and saw nothing that could be edible in the meadows unless I wanted to take up grazing. So it was into the woods for me.

Cautiously, I crept into a large opening in the trees and tried to keep close to the edge of the forest as I walked. After a while I became surprised, and then intrigued, by the large variety of trees that comprised it. In a fairly short distance I could see at least two-dozen distinct varieties. I figured somewhere in its depths there had to be a tree which produced fruits that I could eat.

Suddenly, there was a rustling in what had otherwise been a quiet canopy. Leaves and branches shook in the distance. The noise became louder and louder. I could see trees swaying closer and closer. I wanted to run, but I didn't. I was afraid to look up, but I did anyway. And when I did, I had my second animal sighting.

It was what I can only describe as a giant monkey. Its proportions were exactly that of a little monkey, like the kind you'd see dancing awkwardly in front of a hurdy-gurdy man. Only this monkey was at least eight feet tall. It made its way rapidly through the trees and, when it got close by me, stopped. I held perfectly still as several leaves fell all around me, hoping its stopping here was merely a coincidence. Then I heard the monkey shriek. The branches above started shaking violently. The noise was deafening, at least in contrast to the quiet I'd known before the monkey's appearance. I stared straight ahead, denying it eye contact and hoping it might ignore me.

By this time all hope of the monkey stopping being coincidental had completely evaporated. I didn't stand a chance on its turf. I thought that maybe I could make a dash for the meadows, where I might possibly be able to outrun him. But before I could move a muscle I was pelted with a large fruit, which knocked me straight to the ground. I decided to play dead. I had no idea how intelligent the creature was, so it was a huge gamble that it wouldn't call my bluff and simply take a bite out of me. As I lay there I heard the monkey utter a few loud, excited sounds that half resembled human speech and then he threw a few more fruits at me. I bit my tongue, trying not to scream in pain since the fruits were large and heavy. But if I was going to fool the creatures I had to keep still and quiet. I heard it get little closer. It swung down a little bit lower, sniffed the air, and let out a few more screeches. Then took off in the direction in which it was originally headed.

Terrified, I waited several minutes after the last screech had faded from my ears before I moved again. Groaning, I slowly rolled over and got to my knees. I checked for any bruises left by the large fruits, but didn't find any. Then I noticed that they smelled quite sweet and I decided to give one a taste. Some of them had erupted into mush when they hit the trees. I picked one of the more colorful ones that hadn't burst. It was nice and round and had a peach-like hue. The size was that of a large grapefruit and it was soft but firm. It seemed as though I could easily break the skin, so I carefully took a small bite out of it. My lips instantly puckered; the taste was quite bitter. But there was also a faint aftertaste that wasn't so bad.

The ones that had opened up smelled very sweet so, after a moment's thought, I decided to rip this one apart and investigate further in hopes of finding something more appetizing closer to the core. When I did this I discovered a sort of bright reddish-orange ripple or swirl like you'd find in ice cream. The center itself was as sweet as I'd hoped. It also had a sort of spicy tang to it, almost like cinnamon or ginger. All in all it was quite tasty. It occurred to me that if I ever found a way back home I should definitely take some of these with me. Unfortunately, the fruits grew on the tallest of the trees. I never would have even noticed them if it weren't for the monkey passing by. I rested for a moment, thanking God for the monkey who inadvertently fed me.

The next question that came to mind was which direction to go next. I could head in the direction after the monkey and see where it was going. Or

I could go towards the direction the monkey came from. In the end it hardly mattered, as I had no idea where I was or what I was doing. I could hardly be expected to know a dangerous direction from a safe one. I simply prayed that, whichever direction I went, I would find someone or something to aid me. I'd already been provided with food. I figured shelter should be next. So that is what I would be seeking.

I picked up a couple of the better fruits, picked out a direction and traveled on. As I walked along I heard what sounded to me like harp music. I looked about but saw nothing that seemed responsible for the sound. Then I heard it again; but this time it sounded more like birds chirping. Up to now I had yet to see a bird of any kind of close in this strange new land. I still couldn't see one despite the sounds. Several minutes went by as those melodic notes haunted my ears. The only things I could see around me were trees, yet that sound had to be coming from somewhere. Then I stopped for a minute and just stared at the trees. When I heard the sound again I noticed a subtle vibration in some of their branches. The trees themselves were making music whenever a breeze blew through their limbs! Certain trees gave off a more whistling noise like the bird sounds. Others sent out stringed instrument sounds; like the harp I thought I'd heard earlier. It was quite amazing and gave a whole new dimension to the term "woodwinds." I felt very relaxed whenever I'd hear the sounds from then on, but I always wondered what it would sound like if the there were fierce winds blowing.

Spongy plants. Music making trees. Exotic fruits. Giant monkeys. I'd realized by now that this place was a little more than just a destination that my ancestor had drawn on a map somewhere. I obviously wasn't anyplace on earth. I wanted to know how he had discovered it – and where it came from. But first I still needed to find some kind of a shelter. And I still needed to be careful. Just because things were looking up with the good fruit and nice music didn't mean I was safe.

I needed to find a place that could keep me protected, from both exposure and any dangerous animals that might mistake me for a meal. I knew that there wasn't much daylight left. I saw nothing that resembled a cave so I thought I might make a lean-to. It wouldn't be much, but if I covered it up well it might at least keep me hidden from predators. I looked around and saw a nice, level piece of ground situated conveniently right next to a large fallen tree. I examined the area around it to make sure nothing was actually living in the tree. I didn't need another surprised creature taking off with my roof! I gathered up as many logs and thick branches as I could, building a makeshift shelter just slightly larger than what I needed for sleeping. I leaned the sticks and small logs across the fallen tree and piled up as many of the smaller branches, twigs, and large leaves as I could across the top, covering it completely. I felt quite proud of it when I was done. I'd seen my cousins make lean-tos in the woods near my grandfather's farm many times. I even helped out with several of them, but this was the first time I'd made one all my own. I was pretty sure it would keep me dry and warm, and that it was just camouflaged enough to keep away any prying eyes, ears and hungry mouths. Or so I hoped.

By the time the work was finished I was getting pretty tired. The sun had almost set, so I decided I might as well get comfortable for the night. I gathered my fruits together and scrunched myself into the lean-to, covering myself up as best I could. But before I was able to fall asleep I began to worry again. The darkness had come, bringing fear with it. I fretted about some animal detecting my scent or the scent of the fruits. I despaired over the fact that I had no idea how long the night would last or how cold it would get. Despite the juice from the fruit, I worried that I couldn't go on too much longer without water. Basically I worried myself to sleep. But sleep did come, and with it the most bizarre dreams, as if my current reality wasn't bizarre enough. I dreamt of talking trees from the Wizard of Oz to the Lord of the Rings to H.R. Pufnstuf. They were all there having some sort of conference over what to do with me, a stranger who had dropped in on them uninvited. The Oz trees wanted me stoned, the Pufnstuf trees wanted me banished, and the Ents didn't care. Then the scene morphed into a cage as I was on display in some sort of zoo meant for monkeys like a bad scene out of Planet of the Apes. Yet, in spite of these bad dreams, I actually slept rather well. When I awoke, the sun was just over the horizon. I was pleased to see that whatever kind of cycle this world was on matched my own. Refreshed from sleep, I decided to eat one of my fruits for breakfast and then begin a new day of exploration.

By this point I really wished I had gotten my backpack from Cameron. It would have made my night's sleep more comfortable. I also would have had something other than strange fruit to eat and, most importantly. I would have had a canteen to fill up with water once I found some. That was my next order of business: to find water. I stretched, yawned quietly, and began looking around for a direction to walk in. I suddenly regretted not following in my brothers' footsteps and becoming a boy scout. Those camping trips and survival lessons would have more than come in handy right then! But I'd never bothered with the outdoors before. There were cartoons to watch and comic books to read. Who had time for scouting? Still, I knew that I couldn't go back into the past and change that, any more than I could go home in the present. It was no time for regret.

So I picked a random direction and started hiking.

I'd completely forgotten which way the giant monkey had gone. I didn't know if I was following his lead or not. Thinking of him again once more, I decided it would be a good idea to pick up a large branch to be used as a weapon. Just in case. I found a perfect one several yards into my hike. It was about the length of a yardstick and four inches in diameter at its thickest point. It wasn't exactly a Louisville Slugger, but it would do.

After an hour or so of walking in the same direction seeing nothing but the same types of trees, I heard what I thought might be running water. At first I wasn't sure that it might not be another tree noise, but there was no breeze and the branches were quiet. By this point I was quite thirsty and, as I got closer to the sound, I prayed that it would be a babbling brook. Sure enough, as I started over a hilly portion of the forest I could hear it clearly. I ran over a small hill and down the other side to where there was a small river. Now I was in business. I knew where I could get some food, as long as I could annoy another passing monkey, and I could even build a shelter. Now I had running water! I was becoming a regular Robinson Crusoe in no time! I reached down to cup my hands and took a long cool drink of water. Fortunately for me there was nothing wrong with the water. I was too thirsty and ignorant to worry about bacteria that could tear through a digestive system like a banshee. I also hadn't considered the idea that animals probably used it for a bathroom. It just felt good to be hydrated again. I thought it would feel even better to be clean. So I washed up as best I could in the river.

Now clean and refreshed I was beaming with confidence. I had survived the night outdoors, and not just any outdoors, but in a wild forest in some strange, otherworldly dimension! I hadn't felt this good about myself since I was seven years old and helped a neighbor who had forgotten their keys get into their house. I hadn't actually volunteered for the job but, since I was the smallest person around, it was decided that I'd crawl through an open bedroom window and go in and unlock the front door. It went fairly smoothly, except for the part where my shirt got caught on the bedpost and I hung there awkwardly for a few seconds until I could free myself. But after that I felt like a hero. Sure it wasn't feeding starving kids in Africa or anything, but in my book it had been quite an event. Now that feeling stirred within me again. The worries of yesterday were like a distant dream. One without talking trees.

It was time to make another decision. I could go back to the lean-to or continue my search for civilization. It was still early in the day, so I figured I'd have plenty of time to make another lean-to before nightfall. So I decided to follow the river for a while. I guessed it would lead to a larger river, or possibly even an ocean! Somewhere along the way I hoped there would be some sign of human life. Either way, I wouldn't be thirsty anymore.

I started walking parallel to the river with a jump in my step and a tune in my head. I decided to sing out loud. *Good Day Sunshine* I think it was. It seemed an appropriate choice for my mood. Then a slight breeze came up, causing the trees began their music again. It didn't go along with what I was singing and I lost the tune. I tried to sing again in between the breezes, but it became too confusing so I stopped. It was then that I heard another voice other than my own for the first time since Cameron had urged me through the portal.

"You're not from around here, are you?" the voice said.

"Who said that?" I replied, stopping dead in my tracks.

"I can tell you're not from around here. Your clothes are like nothing I've ever seen on a human before," the voice continued. This bothered me for several reasons. The first was that I had no idea where this voice was coming from. The second was that it referred to *me* as "human," as if *it* were not. As for my clothes, I was wearing an old pair of blue jeans, a hand-me-down Wings concert tee shirt from one of my older brothers, and a pair of basketball shoes. This was pretty common casual wear where I came from. The voice went on.

"What's the symbol on your tunic mean? Did you come from Englishland like the others?"

I looked around and tried to find a face to put with this curious voice. "I'm not answering any of your questions until you show yourself."

Just then I heard branches moving apart and leaves crunching. It seemed whoever or whatever was speaking had been following me for a while! For a split second I thought it was the giant monkey, but I was certain that I would have heard such a large creature before now. As I turned around a face popped out from behind a large tree. It was that of a small wolf! Could this really be the source of the inquisitive voice?

"Hello," it said.

I could hardly control myself. I didn't know whether to faint, scream, or run off. I tried my best to speak calmly. "You... you're... you're a wolf cub!"

"I'm no cub!" it responded curtly. "I'm almost a year old now."

"But, but... you can talk!" I blurted out.

"Yes," he responded. "So can you."

"But you're an animal. Animals can't talk," I said.

He cocked his head sideways like a confused dog. I suppose that's precisely what he was. "Can you understand me?"

"Well, yes," I said.

"Then obviously I'm talking," he replied. "Do you mean to tell me animals don't talk where you're from?"

"No. No, they don't," I started shaking a little bit and then sat down rather quickly.

"What's wrong?" he asked sincerely. "Don't you feel well?"

"I'm fine," I managed to say. "...actually I just have... I just never. I, uh..."

"You should get a drink of water, maybe." The little wolf nodded towards the river.

"Yeah. Maybe that is a good idea," I said quietly. I reached over and cupped my hands and took a good long drink of water. Then I washed my eyes and rubbed them vigorously in hopes this mirage would fade. When I opened them the little wolf was still there, staring right in front of my face.

"Waugh!" I yelled as I fell backwards.

"Did I startle you?" he asked. "I'm sorry."

"Yes," I answered. "Yes: you startled me. And you're freaking me out too. What were you doing following me?" I said, my tone getting a bit grumpy.

"I've been alone here for a good while and when I saw you I thought you might be good company but then I saw you were an outsider and figured I'd better watch you some before I started talking to you. I heard your singing and thought you must be friendly because only friendly people sing..."

"Whoa, take a breath, Sniffles," I said, referring to the chatty cartoon mouse.

"My name's not Sniffles. It's Louie," he retorted

"Okay. Okay, Louie," I said. I raised my hands in an effort to get him to slow down.

"Listen Louie, I imagine I have as many questions for you as you have for me. So why don't we start one at a time? But first I need to catch my breath. This whole thing is still a bit overwhelming to me."

I sat for a moment, gathering my thoughts. From what I could tell this little guy might have some answers to my burning questions. Whatever I had gotten myself into, it seemed the picture was about to become a little clearer.

Chapter Three
A New Friend

It took a little while to get my thoughts together. Even though I had already experienced some fantastic things – the red log creature, the spongy plants, the weird fruit, the musical trees – I still was about to carry on a conversation with a wild animal. It was going to take some time to get used to the idea. I settled back and breathed in and out with my eyes closed until I felt relaxed enough to continue. When I was ready, the little wolf was staring at me still with bright yellow eyes, waiting patiently for my next word.

"Well, are you rested enough?" he asked.

"As well as I can be, I guess. Do all the animals around here talk?" I asked.

"Mostly all," he replied. "All the wolves in my pack can; but I probably talk more than the others. At least that's what they tell me." Without taking a breath he returned to his questioning. "My turn. Where are you from?"

"America," I replied pithily.

He cocked his head sideways again and said, "I've never heard of America. Is it far from here?"

"Well, that's out of turn. But I guess it counts as a follow-up question," I told him. "The answer is that I have no idea if it's far from here or not. I walked here: so, in a sense, it's must be close by. But my best guess is that it might as well be light-years from here. Wherever here is."

"What's a light-year?" he asked with his bright eyes widening.

"A light year is... am I going to get to ask a question?"

"I'm sorry," he said quietly. "Go ahead and ask a question."

"What is this place?"

"This is Anhysbys Forest," he answered. "This is where I've been banished to!" He sadly turned his head away for a moment. He paused as if he needed me to pursue the issue.

"Banished?" I asked politely. "Why would you be banished? You're young and helpless."

"I am not helpless!" he retorted. "I'm a brave wolf! I've stalked prey all by myself and brought down many deer with no assistance from the rest of the pack!" He went on, "I can run as fast and jump as high as anyone I know! I'm stronger than those who bathe in the green orb's light! Banishment means nothing to me. Nothing!"

"Okay, okay," I tried to placate him and he seemed to calm a bit. "It's just that you're raising more questions than you're answering. I'm not from around here, as you can see, so I need to know as much as I can about this place." I looked pensively around at my surroundings. All the while the little wolf never took his eyes off me. "You knew that I was human. Are there are any other humans nearby?"

"The humans are pretty far from here, but they live all around," he answered. "My grandfather says they've overrun the place."

That last bit didn't sound too encouraging. But I had to know where to find my own kind. Encouragingly, it seemed they would be speaking English, since Louie knew the language. "You say they live all around. Where are the closest ones?"

"I'm really not sure," he said, and then took his eyes off me for a brief moment. "I'm not allowed to go to any of their villages. It's not safe for my kind."

"You're obviously not afraid of humans. You're talking to me."

"Of course I'm not afraid of humans! I could take on a whole pack of 'em if I wanted to!" he responded gruffly. "But that would endanger my family. I wouldn't want them getting hurt. So I stay as far away from their villages as possible."

"Would your grandfather know where to find these human villages?" I inquired eagerly.

"Sure. I'll take you to him," he replied matter-of-factly.

"But what about your banishment?" I asked.

"Oh that," he said and began to roll his eyes. "Well... it was more of a temporary banishment. They'll overlook it if I come home with you."

Though it started off awkwardly, the conversation with Louie put my mind at ease. I'd learned the name of the place I'd spent last night: Anhysbys Forest. I learned from Louie that it was the largest forest in the land... and perhaps the scariest. Louie continued to be helpful. He explained more about the flora and fauna around us. He told me that much of the land he knew outside of his forest was made up of meadows and hills. The hills were all grassy and seemed to go on and on like sand dunes. There were interesting plants in the lowlands in between the hills. Besides the spongy plants I'd all ready seen, there were also some lavender-colored plants that actually had crystals growing out of them instead of flowers. The crystals opened up, showing off brilliant colors as they reflected the sun's light. There were also some dangerous plants Louie told me to watch out for, such as the cornleash vine. These plants had long black vines that resembled giant licorice ropes. They grabbed their prey like a lasso and yanked them toward blue green bushes that were centrally located between several other cornleash vines. The bushes held their victim in place long enough for the vines to slowly wrap around the victim, constricting their prey until they suffocated.

Frightening stuff.

The plant that scared me the most, however, was the picellau bush. This seemingly harmless plant was a bush that had some reed-like plants that grew up from its middle. Inside these reeds are poisonous quills that can shoot outwards up to several yards as a defense. Why anybody would want to actually bother that plant is beyond me. Luckily, we never came across any picellau bushes or cornleash vines on our way to Louie's home.

Besides other wolves, Louie told me that his forest also had deer, rabbits, raccoons and plenty of other animals that seemed like fairly normal forest dwellers to me. Idly, I wondered why there were normal animals in a place that had such bizarre plant life. (I didn't think about the fact they talked.) I assumed there must be some strange animals around somewhere in this alien environment... other than the red log creature, at least. To my horror I would later learn that I was completely right. As knowledgeable as he was, Little Louie was limited to his own environment, which consisted of the forest, the meadows, and hills just outside of it. Therefore, his information on the humans was rather light. I hoped that his grandfather would give me something more to go on. I wanted to meet whatever humans lived in this place. If anyone was going to know how to get me home, I was certain it would be them.

I had a new goal, a new hope, and a new friend.

Louie was quite a character. He wasn't very old, but seemed to be very smart for his age. Then again he was a wolf and, like most animals, they mature much more quickly than humans. It was obvious that he was stretching the truth when he talked about himself. I only hoped that he was talking straight when it came to everything else. He did love to talk, that's for sure. He told me that the name of the place his family lived in was Serenity Forest. It took us a day to get there so, on the way, we talked quite a bit. Actually, Louie talked quite a bit. I mainly listened. Whenever his curiosity would get the better of him, he'd ask me a question. It didn't take long before he'd grow tired of my answer and ramble on over me about some marvelous adventure in which he'd been involved. Or he'd ask another question halfway through my answer. Either way it was fine so long as he got to hear himself speak. I didn't care. I was ecstatic just to hear a voice other than my own.

Louie taught me the name of the fruit I'd been eating. He called it a hewlifruit. Said that they were quite a delicacy. Apparently they were very rare, so my hopes of bringing some home with me began to wane. Besides the fruit, I described the giant monkey that I had gotten them from. He had never heard of such a beast, but had heard stories of wild creatures living in Anhysbys Forest. Of course, he explained, he wouldn't be afraid to meet one of these giant monkeys if one should ever come upon him. That had got me to wondering just how well Louie really knew the area... but he seemed to know where he was going. Though by the time we came out of the forest I'd surmised that I'd been deeper into it than Louie ever had.

Outside the forest was a large meadow with hills and grass as far as the eye could see. This wasn't the same location that I had started my journey from, but the topography was almost identical. I guessed that I was headed back in the same direction. The meadows and hills seemed to go on forever; we went hours before seeing a tree taller than me. We only stopped to rest a couple of times and to get some energy from a honey like substance that came from some rather familiar looking spongy plants. I was too embarrassed to tell Louie that I had feared this same substance as a poison just a day before. It was really pretty tasty. It had the texture of runny Jell-O but smelled like a fruity flower. I really needed something to eat other than fruit or honey; but at least I knew I wasn't going to starve.

Shortly after that we came over a series of high hills. A large group of trees was visible in the distance. I could tell from the excitement in Louie's eyes that they had to be part of Serenity Forest. It looked as if it would just be an hour or less before we'd reach them. I could also see that the sun was about to set. I'd been so interested in learning everything I could from Louie about my new surroundings that I hadn't paid attention to how much time had passed. My old friend worry crept up on me again, as I feared what would happen to us entering the forest just after dark. I asked Louie how much longer until we reached his home.

"Not much longer," he replied. "It may take another hour or two after we enter the forest before we get to my family's den."

With that answer I knew it would definitely be dark before we reached his home. I should have been braver about the situation after my previous night's triumph, but the combination of weariness from the day's journey and the stories of all the dangerous plants made me worry.

"Are there any dangerous plants or animals between here and your den, Louie?" I asked, trying to sound more courageous than I really was.

"I don't think so," he said. "But don't worry. You're with the bravest wolf in Serenity Forest. If anything should happen I'll be here to protect you."

"Of course, Louie. What was I thinking?" My retort fell on deaf ears, as it seemed Louie was completely oblivious to sarcasm. Oddly, his bravado put my mind at ease.

After another ten minutes or so we were only a few yards away from the opening of the forest. There were many more trees visible from this perspective. The forest canopy was illuminated by the setting sun. It was really quite beautiful. We only had to get over one more hill and through some large bushes before getting to the forest's edge. Just as we got to the top of the final hill, Louie stopped short. I almost tripped over him before I stopped myself.

"What's going on? Why did you stop?" I asked.

"Shh!"

"What is it?" I asked nervously.

"Shh!" he repeated, as if I had clearly not understood the first time. He put his face to the ground and began sniffing furiously. He lifted his head quickly and sniffed the air while twisting his head in all possible directions. "Nghuryll," he said quietly.

"What's a nghuryll?" I asked just as quietly.

"It's a bad thing," he replied.

"How bad?" I urgently whispered.

"Pretty bad, trust me."

The nghuryll was one of many of the creatures that I would learn about that I'd wish I hadn't. It resembled something out of a Hiëronymus Bosch painting. Its head looked like a falcon's with small horns like a bull's curving back towards its body. The body underneath that severely oversized head was short and stocky, resembling a man's but without any arms. Its hunting method was simple: it pounced on its victims and pecked them to death with its massive beak. It was fast, deadly, and highly feared by all.

"Is it close by?" I asked.

"I'm not sure," he replied. "I need a moment to figure it out."

Louie kept sniffing. But he began to slowly step forward. "I don't think it's close enough," he said calmly.

"Close enough for what?" I asked impatiently.

"Just keep your head down and run as fast as you can," he replied.

"That's easy for you to say," I told him. "You've got twice as many legs as I do!"

"Trust me!" he whispered again. But his voice got louder and I heard more urgency in his voice. "I don't think it can get to us before we make it to the safety of the forest." He hesitated a bit, looked back at me, took one last sniff, and moved forward again. "On my mark..." he said, "...Run!"

Louie took off down the hill at breakneck speed. I tried my best to follow but even if I'd wanted to, which I did, I could in no way match his speed. It took everything I had not to trip and fall over! Bipeds weren't made to run downhill that quickly. By the time Louie was a few yards from the forest he had quite a lead on me. Even though the sun hadn't completely set, we were covered up by the shadows of the trees that lay ahead. I was barely able to keep sight of Louie. I could feel my heart pumping blood at a feverish pace. My lungs began to burn. I hadn't run this fast in a very long time and, somewhat bizarrely, I began to worry about being sore the next day. As if that were the worst thing that could happen.

As I got near the bushes I heard something. At first it sounded like the rustling of leaves, but then the sound got louder and everything seemed to slow down. The whole world was in slow motion: the sights (what I could make out in the dark), the smells, and the sounds all seemed surreal. Then, competing with the sound of my own heart beating, I made out a rather disturbing low-pitched shriek like that of a bird. I was running around a bush when I saw it: the nghuryll, leaping toward me in what seemed to be even slower motion. I was in full panic mode. There was nothing I could do. The nghuryll had caught me by complete surprise and I was already running as fast I could possibly go. In mere seconds he would be down upon me, ripping me to shreds with his giant beak. I'm not sure but I think I started to scream. But before I could get a noise to even consider emanating from my vocal chords, the already-pouncing nghuryll was violently shoved out of my frame of vision. As the scene shifted back to real time I could make out what seemed to be two creatures fighting in the grass to my left. Then a third figure rapidly joined the melee. I was too dumbfounded to continue running forward. I only realized after Louie had yelled for me that it would probably be a good idea to head for safety.

Without looking back, I got back to top speed and made it to the forest where Louie was waiting. I only turned and looked back once I was under the large trees that formed an impressive doorway to Serenity Forest. With what little sunlight was left at my back, I could just make out two very large wolves attacking the nghuryll. One of them had leapt from nowhere, knocking the vile bird-thing away from me only moments before it would have torn me to shreds. They were doing their best to convince the hideous thing to retreat and, after a few yelps and shrieks, the nghuryll finally relented and took off into the darkness amidst flying clumps of grass and dirt.

The two wolves held their ground for a moment, making sure the nghuryll had truly fled and wasn't just hiding somewhere, waiting to continue the attack. When they were satisfied it wouldn't return they came over to where Louie and I were waiting. I was still trying to catch my breath after what was by far the scariest moment in my young life. When the wolves grew close, they backed off and circled slowly around, unsure whether or not I was a danger to them. Once Louie convinced them I was harmless they calmed down and introduced themselves. The wolf who saved my life was Louie's older sister Wendy. The other wolf was his older brother Richard. They had been searching for Louie most of the day.

"Where have you been Louie?" Wendy scolded. "Grandfather sent us to look for you when you didn't return home after breakfast."

"And none of your silly stories," Richard added impatiently.

"Well, I uh... I had some things to do," said Louie.

"Come on Louie! We don't have time for your games. It's getting late and we need to get back home. I'm sure grandfather is very worried," said Wendy.

"Who's the human and where did you find him?" Richard asked

"This is Robert," Louie proclaimed, happy at the change of subject. "He was wandering blindly through the depths of Anhysbys Forest when I rescued him from a giant ape."

"Only it was a monkey, not an ape. And you didn't even see it," I interjected.

"What were you doing in Anhysbys Forest, Louie?" asked Richard. "You know very well that you are forbidden to go there."

"Aw, everybody's always telling me what I can and can't do," Louie pouted. "I've had enough of everybody treating me like some little kid!"

Wendy chimed in. "Just because you are a yearling doesn't mean you are through learning from your elders! You're too young to go on hunts and you're too young to be wandering in strange places by yourself. And you know none of us are allowed in Anhysbys Forest because it's too dangerous!"

I decided to interrupt again, if only to save my little friend from more scolding.

"Actually, I spent last night there and it seemed safer than out in the meadows." Wendy and Richard stared at me for a couple of awkward minutes before Richard turned his questions to me.

"Where did you come from, human, and what do you want here?" he asked me.

"Well, I come from a land very far away. All I really want is a way to get home," I said. "I was hoping your grandfather would direct me to some other humans so that I might learn from them how to get home." After I finished there was another long, awkward pause. Then Wendy spoke up.

"I don't know if grandfather will help you or not. But we can take you to him, I suppose," she said, not sounding very enthusiastic.

"Thank you," I responded. "I would appreciate that – and thank you very much also for saving my life."

"You're welcome," Wendy replied. "But I wasn't even aware of your presence. We had seen the nghuryll behind the bushes as we were searching for Louie. We were just making sure he didn't attack us first."

"You're lucky indeed, human," added Richard. "That nghuryll had a particularly nasty beak and was obviously hungry. But he'll learn to find a meal somewhere else rather than face the wolves of Serenity Forest again."

"Yes. Well, thanks again in any case," I said timidly. I told Richard I preferred not to be called "human" and he begrudgingly obliged.

The four of us began the long walk to their family's den. I wasn't sure how welcome I'd be, but at least I knew I was in safe hands. (Or paws, as the case may be.) The hike included some more scolding for Louie, which seemed to be a familiar albeit uncomfortable experience for him. Wendy and Richard occasionally glanced look back to make sure the nghuryll hadn't gotten up enough nerve to follow us. After a while they seemed confident we'd seen the last of him. I was getting very tired and was glad we'd be able to rest soon. I could tell Louie was tired as well. Whether due to exhaustion from the long day – or the admonishments of his siblings – Louie actually got quiet. After a pleasantly uneventful and thankfully brief journey we arrived at the den where the wolves' grandfather was waiting nervously.

Chapter Four
Serenity Forest

It looked as if Louie's grandfather had been pacing back and forth for quite a while. He'd worn a pattern into the dirt alongside the den's opening. I stood back a bit as Wendy led Louie to see him. I didn't want to get in the way while Louie got yet another scolding. While Louie's lecture – and probable punishment – was being handed down, I took the opportunity to check out my new surroundings. Unfortunately, it was too dark for me to make much of anything out. I did notice something different about the trees, but I wasn't sure what it was. As I looked around I could feel that I was being watched. It was Richard, who never let me out of his sight. Wherever I went, he was always a few feet away. Which made me a little nervous. Finally, when Louie's chastisement was complete, I heard a loud and powerful voice.

"Who is this, then?" Grandfather demanded.

"This is Robert," said Wendy. "Louie found him wandering in Anhysbys Forest. He's not from here and hoped that you would help him find some of his own kind."

Grandfather walked right up to me and I began to feel even more nervous than I was before. His eyes were bright yellow. I could tell that even in the darkness. They seemed to reflect light like a cat's and pierced my very soul. He was the largest of the wolves, a good bit larger than any I'd seen in any zoo, and was obviously the alpha male. As such he demanded respect. My feet felt as if they were glued to the ground. Even if I'd wanted to I don't think I could've run anywhere. He sniffed all around me and then stared directly into my eyes.

"Yes, you're definitely new to the area. You don't smell quite like the other humans. Where is it you say you are from?" he asked.

"America," I stated quietly.

"Can't say as I've heard of such a place," he replied.

"I'm afraid it may be in another world altogether," I sighed. "As Wendy has already told you, I was hoping that you could help me find other people like me so that they could possibly help me find my way back home."

He spun around, considering the situation in a very dog-like manner. Then he replied. "That is probably for the best." He continued, "It's unusual to have humans as guests in Serenity Forest; but not unheard of. You may stay the night and, in the morning, we will consider what next to do with you."

"Thank you, sir," I said with a faint smile.

I looked for as soft of a place as possible to lie down. I waited for everyone else to find his or her spots first, though. I knew enough about canines to know it was a bad idea to suggest that I was "above" anyone else in the pack! Finally, I found a comfortable enough spot in the dirt between Louie and Wendy, curled myself into a fetal position and waited impatiently to fall asleep. It took a while, what with my nerves thoroughly jangled by the encounter with the nghuryll and, then, with Louie's grandfather. Eventually I fell into a deep slumber even more restful than that of the previous night.

I awoke as the sun rose. I was alone in the den. The wolves had already gotten up and begun their day. In retrospect, I suppose I'd grown used to sleeping in. Or perhaps the events of the previous day had left me exhausted. In any case, I walked outside to find some of the older wolves near the den's opening keeping an eye on some of the younger ones playing nearby. They kept their distance, giving me much more room than I actually needed. I thought this might be as good a time as any to check out Serenity Forest in the daylight. Louie had been playing with some of the pups and came running up to me as he saw me walk away.

"Where are you going, Robert?" he asked. "Breakfast will be here shortly."

"I thought I'd take a look around," I answered. "I haven't seen your home in the daylight."

"I'll come with you," he said eagerly. "I can show you around."

"Thanks, Louie," I responded completely honestly. "I'd like that."

Some of the older wolves glared at Louie and I as we walked around. I wasn't sure how much of that was meant for me and how much for him, since surely he wasn't allowed to wander too far away after his recent misbehavior. With this in mind, I made sure we never got out of earshot of the den. I didn't want Louie getting in any extra trouble on my account.

"I sensed something different about the trees here last night, Louie. But I couldn't make it out in the dark," I commented.

"I'm not sure what you mean, Robert," Louie said with that puzzled tone I had often heard when we originally met.

"Well, I can't be sure," I said. "Let me see..." I was trying to find the specific tree that had given me this feeling the previous night. "There! That tree, Louie. Oh, I think I see it now." I had gotten far enough around the tree to notice little awnings that appeared to grow naturally over small holes inside the tree. "What are those?"

"The little holes?" Louie asked. "Those are squirrel homes."

"Squirrel homes?" I said surprisingly. "Those weren't man-made?"

"Man-made?" Louie said in an almost detestable tone. "Why would a man make a home for a squirrel? Those grow especially in squirrel trees. I'm told they only exist in Serenity Forest."

"Squirrel trees, eh?" I said scoffing. "I don't see any squirrels."

"Well, they may still be sleeping," Louie said. "Let's see..."

Louie took a couple of running leaps over to the squirrel tree and threw his front paws up on the trunk. He was just barely tall enough to get his snout a few inches from the lowest of the holes on the tree. "Archie! Sally! Anybody home?" yelled Louie towards the hole. A couple of seconds later I heard some chattering and squeaking. Then I heard a small voice from inside the tree. "Go away, Louie. I'm not interested in hearing any of your tall tales."

"But Archie," Louie moaned, "I have a real live boy here with me to see you."

"I'm not buying that again, Louie. I've heard this story too many times before," the voice said.

"No, really," Louie pleaded. "It's true this time, I promise!"

"Get lost, Louie!" came the reply. "I'm going back to sleep!"

Louie turned away from the tree and looked up at me with disappointment. "Well the squirrels are at home, but I don't think they want any visitors now."

"That's okay Louie, I understand."

I didn't want Louie to feel any more embarrassed than he already was, so I didn't bring up the issue of his stretching the truth. I was curious about it, though, and wondered if that had something to do with his getting into so much trouble.

Louie took me next to a large garden that was nearby. The flowers that grew in it seemed indistinguishable from those at home. I didn't notice any new varieties or different colors; but, then again, I was never one for studying flowers. They could have been completely alien and I wouldn't have known. The thing that seemed truly odd to me was that wolves would have a flower garden at all. Before I could ask Louie about this, however, a rather large insect that looked something like a grasshopper distracted him. He chased it around for a couple of minutes before it burrowed itself into the ground like a corkscrew, leaving Louie with nothing but a disappointed moan to show for his efforts.

I looked up at the sky, and then took a long, deep breath. The sky was bright blue and the air was fresh. A comfortable feeling washed over me, as if I were somehow at home. Despite some strange-looking plants and animals, Serenity Forest *felt* like any forest you'd find back home. Only better: as if it were an idealized version of what a forest *should* be, as opposed to what it actually *was*.

Of course, the talking animals were always there to remind you that this was anything *but* home!

Some of the other wolves were starting to get a little antsy, darting back and forth in front of the den. I wasn't sure what was going on, but I figured it'd be a good idea if Louie and I didn't wander any further away. Just then some of the hunting party came back with breakfast: mice and rabbits. Most of the rabbits had been brought back whole. Unfortunately, the mice and at least one rabbit were regurgitated for the younger wolves. Usually, I can't stand to miss breakfast; but I suddenly lost my appetite. The older wolves gathered around the front of the den and began to split up the meal. Louie's grandfather motioned me over to join them. "Here now, Robert," he said, "come and have some nice rabbit."

My face pretty much told the story. He could tell from my expression that I was less than interested in consuming raw rabbit meat, especially with most of the fur still attached.

"Oh! Sorry. I guess like most humans, you aren't much for eating the raw meat then, are you?" he asked.

"No, sir. I'm not," I replied.

"Well, we can't have you starve on us." He motioned to Wendy. "Wendy, show our guest to Branwen's garden and maybe he'll be able to find something more palatable there."

Wendy signaled me to follow her. She took me back to the flower garden I'd visited with Louie just moments before, and then departed. For a moment I wondered just how full I could get eating flowers, but then I was surprised to see that behind the flower garden there was much more. Louie and I hadn't gone all the way around the garden. I hadn't seen past its tall flowers and hadn't been curious enough to investigate further. On the other side though were several rows of vegetables: mostly familiar varieties, with a few unfamiliar one mixed in. Wendy invited me to help myself to whatever I wanted. I sampled a bit of almost everything. There were some plants that looked a bit like corn but whose kernels were thicker and had a rather grayish hue to them. I took a small taste, thinking at first that they may not yet be ripe. But they tasted wonderful. Then I saw some carrots and cucumbers and had one of each of those. There was some lettuce as well, which gave me the idea to put together a salad. I've never been big on vegetables or salads, but when faced with a choice of salad or raw fur-covered meat, the choice was pretty simple. After I had eaten my fill of this wonderful bounty I started to wonder: in addition to the flower garden, why wolves would need a vegetable garden as well?

When I returned, the wolves had finished their breakfast and were lying around, enjoying the digestive process. I walked over to Wendy and asked her about the garden. "Why would wolves have a flower garden?"

"That's Branwen's garden," she replied. "She thought it would be nice for us to have some decoration around our home."

"And the vegetables...?" I asked.

"Those are for her and her friends when they visit," she told me. "Occasionally, a rabbit or two will get brave enough to try to steal some of them; usually while we're away, of course."

"So I take it Branwen's not a wolf?"

"Of course not," Wendy replied. "She's human like you. We couldn't have planted a garden ourselves."

"I didn't think so," I nervously commented. "But I thought humans weren't common here in Serenity Forest."

"Well, Branwen's a different case altogether" Wendy said. "She isn't like most of the humans we encounter. She loves the forest and all the animals within it. She's welcome here anytime and, in fact, she sometimes spends days here with us."

"She sounds pretty cool," I said. "I think I'd like to meet her."

At this point I felt comfortable enough to ask Louie's grandfather about the other humans again. I walked over to where he was resting and sat next to him. He looked me up and down, and then sort of frowned. "You're beginning to get a bit to used to us, I'm afraid," he said.

"Pardon?"

"You see Robert, humans and wolves aren't usually found lying about together after sharing a meal. We have a natural, respectful fear of one another. Your approaching me in that manner makes me feel that you're a bit too comfortable here. I think it's time I directed you to the nearest human village."

I fell silent for a few awkward moments. It was my goal, of course, to find some humans that could help me get home, but I was feeling genuinely comfortable around the wolves. I honestly didn't want to leave. But I also didn't want to overstay my welcome. "I only wanted to ask you a few questions, sir," I said.

"That's as it may be," he replied "But I think the time for questions has passed. You can get the answers you need from your own kind. Now where is Richard? He'd be ideal to take you out of Serenity forest and point you to the next village of humans."

Just then it occurred to him that Richard and one other wolf hadn't returned from the morning's hunt. He didn't seem worried as such. I suppose there were any number of reasons for them to be held up. He then gave Wendy the task of escorting me from Serenity Forest. I would have vastly preferred to get some more answers before leaving, but at that point it didn't seem to matter very much. I could tell that I wasn't going to get them. I went over to say my goodbyes to Louie, who seemed as if he'd actually miss me. Then Wendy and I simply walked away from the den. But before we had gotten very far, we heard a commotion just off the trail ahead of us. Wendy told me to stay back and she crouched down as if preparing to leap on some prey, when all of a sudden Richard and the other wolf burst onto the trail.

They seemed very upset and were in a big hurry to get back to the den.

"What's wrong, Richard?" asked Wendy, sounding alarmed.

"It's Branwen! She's in trouble! We have to tell grandfather," he replied.

They dashed back to the den, leaving me behind in their haste. Fortunately, we hadn't walked too far. Within a couple of minutes I caught up to them. Richard and the other wolf were just beginning to tell their story to Grandfather, who seemed none to pleased by what he was hearing.

It seemed that some other humans had kidnapped Branwen, the girl who I'd just learned about from Wendy. She apparently had knowledge of some sort of device they were interested in having. It was clear that Branwen was very important to these wolves. Some of them appeared to even be crying at the news, while others were seething and ready to attack.

My trip was obviously postponed. No one was in the mood to take me out of the forest. It was as if they'd even forgotten I was there at all. In any case, I was getting second thoughts about meeting up with my fellow humans at this point. Branwen sounded great, but if there was a group capable of kidnapping her, then there were obviously some bad apples in the bunch. At least I could hope for another opportunity to get some information out of Louie's grandfather.

Chapter Five
Samuel's Legacy

After a while, things settled down somewhat. Louie's grandfather sent out two groups of wolves to investigate Branwen's kidnapping. They, of course, were hampered by the need to stay far enough away from the humans to avoid getting killed. Unfortunately, most humans in this world were no different in their attitude toward wolves than the ones back home. Most simply assumed that wolves were always dangerous: better to shoot first and ask questions later. This explained why the wolves were so cautious with me – and why Louie's grandfather insisted that I had been getting too comfortable with them. Louie himself seemed comfortable with me, but came from the fact that he was especially close to Branwen. His comfort level with humans was part of the reason he was watched so carefully. It was the unfortunate downside to having a friend like Branwen. Apparently, however, it was worth the upside to them. The garden was only a small part of what she had done for them. Her importance to the wolves was becoming even more apparent.

Louie was simmering with frustration because he wasn't allowed go with either group in search of Branwen. I tried to console him. I walked over to where he sat under the careful watch of a couple of aunts named Sara and Sabra. "It's okay Louie. I'm sure your family will find her," I told him.

"But it's not fair!" he exclaimed. "I should be with them. Branwen needs me!"

"Well, I'm sure the rest of the pack needs its bravest member here at home to protect them with everybody gone."

"Still... my heart is with Branwen," he insisted. "I must help find her!" Louie's tone was getting angrier.

"Look, I understand how much she means—"

"No you don't," Louie interrupted. "She's not just my friend. She is the protector of the whole pack."

"How can one girl protect an entire pack of wolves?" I asked.

Sabra, the older of the two aunts answered. "Branwen keeps certain secrets for us. She knows where the green orb is and teaches us how to use it."

Sara, the younger of Louie's aunts interrupted, "Don't tell him that. He's human!"

"It's all right, Sara," Sabra replied "I sense much compassion for animals in this human. I've watched how he's acted with Louie since he got here. I don't believe there's any problem sharing information with him, especially since he's not from this world. Even if he does join up with other humans, I can't believe he'd harm us."

"I suppose you could be right, Sabra," Sara said cautiously "However, we shouldn't tell him where the green orb is."

"I certainly hadn't intended on doing that," Sabra said.

"What is this green orb I'm not supposed to know about?" I asked.

"Suffice it to say," Sabra answered, "that it is a magical device that helps us defend ourselves."

Sara jumped in, "Not only that, but many of the humans would love to get their hands on it!"

"Yes. More than likely than not that is the motivation for Branwen's kidnapping," Sabra replied.

With that, Louie spun around, sat hard on the ground, and began to moan grumpily. I decided it was best to leave him be for a while and searched out his grandfather to try to get some more answers.

Louie's grandfather was resting. Since he'd sent off most of the hunters in search parties, he was the primary hunter for the immediate future and needed to conserve his energy. I decided this would be my best chance to question him further about the people of this world.

"Sir," I began carefully, "do you think you could tell me a bit more about the humans that live here?"

"I'm not sure what you want to know," he said. "Humans are usually bad news. My father passed down to me tales of the time before humans. It seemed that things were much better back then."

"When did the humans first arrive here?" I asked.

"It's hard to say for certain. Many generations of them have come and gone since then," he replied. "But things got definitely worse once their leader left. That's certain."

"Their leader," I wondered aloud. "Who was their leader, and why did he leave them?"

"Well, now, that goes back a long way," he said. "The way my father heard it from his father was that the humans had a leader who cared for them deeply. He was a kind, big-hearted man. Something I would never have believed about humans until I met Branwen. He was a good leader and for many generations everyone admired him greatly. But things changed over time. The humans had different ideas about how things should be. They began to fight among themselves. At first it was just a little bit of arguing here and there as humans often do. Then it began to get worse with, words elevating to fists, fists elevating to knives, and so on. The humans no longer wanted to follow him and decided to go their own various ways. He tried to stop them, but they just wouldn't listen. Eventually they split up into different factions and he left, never to be heard from again."

"That's sad," I replied.

"It's more than just sad," he said mournfully. "From what I understand when the humans first got here they were much better behaved. They would still kill us out of fear, but they never came into Serenity Forest to attack us directly. Then some of the humans decided it would be a good idea to permanently rid the forest of us. They don't understand our ways and had no intention of trying. That's why Branwen and a few others have tried so hard to protect us."

"A few others..." I parroted. "There are other humans like Branwen?"

"Yes. From time to time Branwen brings a few friends with her. They also know how to use the green orb that helps us fight off the humans who try to eradicate us. Sometimes, when she can't come herself but gets word of an attack, she sends them to our aid."

"Where are these people?" I asked. "Perhaps they could help us find Branwen!"

"I'm not sure what village they're from. They weren't as close to us as Branwen is. Some of them spend time with the squirrels, others with the raccoons or rabbits. They believe that their mission is to protect the entire forest, even though I have the feeling that some of them fear us a bit. And, frankly, that's the way I prefer it. I imagine even now they are searching for her, wherever they are."

"I hope they find her," I said. "She sounds very special."

"She is indeed."

I hated to change the subject when finding Branwen was obviously so important, but I desperately needed to know more about the history of humans in this weird place, and how their history matched the one I knew. I also figured that talking about something else would help to take Grandfather's mind off the tragedy. "Sir, did your father give you a name for the leader of the humans you were speaking of earlier?"

"Yes. I believe he called him Samuel."

I'd suspected as much, but needed to hear it to be certain. I explained to Louie's grandfather what I knew of Samuel's history up until the time he left for this world and that I was his descendant. "I thought there was something different about you," he said after some thought. "If you are cut of the same cloth as Samuel, then you have great potential."

"I wouldn't go that far," I replied with genuine humility. "I'm just an ordinary boy."

"You may be ordinary where you come from. But here I think you could be extraordinary."

I had no idea at the time what he meant. I was simply interested in finding a way back home, and wasn't eager to become a political figure or anything of the sort. I didn't even know what I could possibly do with Branwen's kidnapping. I was still very new to Gwerinatha and didn't know my left from my right. I could hardly have been expected to help with anything more than the most basic labor. Even a task as simple as going for water could end up with my being lost or even killed, what with all the dangers that exist in this wild land.

"Thanks, sir. I think," I said.

"You don't have to call me sir all the time," he replied. "My name is Arthur."

"Thank you, Arthur."

Samuel must have left an impression on everyone here. The moment I mentioned I was his descendant, Arthur's whole perception of me seemed to change. He felt much more comfortable talking with me. He even opened up about some of his personal history. I think part of it was that he needed to talk to get his mind off the current troubles. He explained how he was really too old to be the alpha male and how his eldest son, Brian, had actually been his heir apparent. Brian was the strongest of his generation, and the smartest too. With a chuckle Arthur told me of several incidents in which Brian outsmarted the humans who hunted him. It reminded me of any one of a dozen or so cartoons I used to watch where the main character would always win out and make fools of the bad guys.

Only in this case there was an unhappy ending.

One day when Richard and Wendy were about Louie's age, Brian had been out teaching them hunting skills. Louie himself was just a pup at the time, not yet old enough to have been yet weaned from his mother. Also with them was Brian's son Jack. Jack was from a previous litter, and thus older than Richard and Wendy. They were a good distance away from the den, which was in a different location from the one the pack lived in now. A hunting party came upon them, taking them by surprise. Brian had let his guard down this one time. Maybe he had been too attuned to his children. Maybe it was something else. Whatever the case, Brian didn't sense the humans until it was too late.

Their path home was cut off. The humans herded them towards the meadows with loud gunshots. Once out in the open they would be easy targets. Cornered, with no viable options, Wendy and Richard trembled behind their father, while Jack leapt at the nearest hunter's horse. Brian had yelled for him to stop, but by then he was already in the air. He clamped on to the horse's leg as if it were a deer he'd planned on taking down. The horse reared and the man fell off. Jack stalked over to him and began to growl ferociously. One of the other hunters shot Jack in the head. Brian began to howl for other wolves to come to his aid, but knew in his heart they wouldn't get there before they were all slaughtered. He then jumped up at the man who had shot Jack, and yanked him off his horse. The man fell onto the other hunter who was struggling to get up. Brian then bit another horse on the leg, which caused a chain reaction that resulted in the remaining horses stampeding. In the midst of this turmoil he told Wendy and Richard to make a run for home. They heard some men scrambling and yelling. A couple of shots had rung out, but they never looked back... and Brian and Jack were never seen again.

Arthur believed that Brian took the shots that were meant for his children. It certainly sounded to me as if he would do such a thing. I found myself putting an arm around Arthur as he finished the tale. He welcomed the affection and I tried to hide the tears that were welling up in my eyes.

I used to always cry watching "Lassie" movies where Lassie and Timmy would get separated. I never could make it all the way through "Old Yeller." So the story that Arthur told me felt especially tough to take. Now I knew why Richard had watched me so keenly – and why everyone was so overprotective of Louie. I assumed that the people who wanted to eradicate the wolves were the ones who took Branwen. At the very least, they surely were of the same ilk... and I was beginning to develop a fear of them. But, at the same time, anger was growing in me that made me want to stop them. I wanted to join in the battle to help protect the wolves. I wanted to find Branwen. But I had no idea where to start. After all, I didn't even know where I was.

"If only Samuel would return," bemoaned Arthur. "He could bring healing to his people. At least then we wouldn't have to worry about extinction."

"...*would* return?" I questioned. "Don't you mean *could* return? I can't imagine he'd be alive after all these centuries."

"He's not dead, Robert," Arthur replied. "At least I don't think so. It's said that he went away, but no legend speaks of his death."

"But he'd have to be over three hundred years old by now!" I reasoned.

"My father told me that Samuel was gifted with extraordinarily long life. He'd already outlived many generations of his own people. He could still be alive somewhere."

"I'm sure that's all just part of the legend, Arthur. It couldn't really be true."

"You may be right, Robert. It may be just a lost hope. A fading memory of better times. Perhaps in the midst of all these troubles I've allowed my emotions get in the way of my reasoning. Either way, our struggles continue." He seemed distracted, and then looked away. "Leave me be for a while, Robert. I need some rest. We'll continue our conversation after the evening's hunt."

Frustrated, I went to console Louie some more. This time it would be easier, since I had more empathy for him.

Louie couldn't sit still, but wasn't allowed to stray further than eyeshot from the den. He paced about in circles, pausing only to jump up and down after more of those weird, corkscrewing insects.

I walked towards him and smiled. "It'd be a lot easier if you had a net."

"Only if I had hands!" he snorted. "But I still wouldn't enjoy it as much."

"I understand. You're getting some frustration out," I told him. "I'm frustrated too. There must be something we can do."

"Not unless you can cause some sort of diversion so that I can take off without my elders seeing me," he suggested.

"I don't think that's the best idea, Louie," I told him. "I don't think you'd be much help, giving the pack something more to worry about on top of everything else."

"You don't think I can find her, do you?" he exclaimed.

"It's not that, Louie," I said. "What would you do if you *did* find her? Even *you* couldn't take on a whole band of human kidnappers."

"I could too, if I had bathed in the green orb's light."

"What are you talking about?" I asked. "Just what does this green orb do anyway?"

"The green orb can give you great power," Louie replied. "I've seen some of those who've bathed in its light. They become very strong and fast. Faster than any deer and stronger than even the strongest bear."

"Oh great: they've got bears here, too," I thought out loud. "Why can't we use the green orb, Louie?"

"Oh, there's no way grandfather would let me use it. They have some foolish notion that I'm too young. They're probably just afraid it'd make me too powerful, since I am already the strongest and fastest wolf around," he boasted.

"You don't think he'd let me use it, do you, Louie?"

"I doubt it. But I guess it wouldn't hurt to ask," Louie suggested.

I thought about that for a bit. On the one hand, Arthur had gained tremendous respect for me once he'd learned I was Samuel's descendant. He even saw "great potential" in me, and thus it seemed to me that he might have allowed me to use the green orb if it meant I could help out. On the other hand, I was still a stranger to this land. Even if I had gained the trust of the wolf pack, I still wouldn't know where to begin searching for Branwen. Even if I *did* find her, I wouldn't know even as much as Louie about what to do next. I still had a lot to learn about this world: most importantly to me at the time, where the humans lived, and what kind of society they had.

Chapter Six
The Hunting Party

I walked over to talk with Arthur as he got up and began to stretch. I knew he'd be leaving shortly for the evening hunt, and wondered if I should even bring up the subject of the green orb. But I could even open my mouth another commotion broke out. At first I thought it was Wendy, Richard, or one of the other wolves who were out looking for Branwen returning with some good news. Unfortunately, it was just the opposite. Chattering like mad, some squirrels rushed in to get Arthur's attention. Almost immediately, all the other wolves formed a circle around him.

"They're coming! They're coming!" one of the squirrels cried.

"Who's coming, Archie?" asked Arthur.

"A hunting party!" he exclaimed. "Humans from the Village of Broad Meadows, I think!" he said.

"How much time do we have?"

"Maybe only a few minutes; they're on horseback," replied Archie.

"The forest is too thick for horses to get all the way to our den. They'll have to dismount to go this far in. Still, we'll need to go into hiding." Arthur looked around at the rest of the remaining pack. "Initiate evacuation plans immediately!"

The wolves began scrambling about. I suppose one of the advantages of being an animal is that, if you have to evacuate your home for any reason, you don't have to worry about gathering your belongings together in a hurry. You can just take off like a bolt of lightning, which is was exactly what the wolves were doing. Even though the whole affair looked chaotic, I sensed they knew what they were doing: as if this had happened before. Which undoubtedly it had: with all the human trouble the pack had, I imagine evacuation plans were something they had drilled for, like families back home would have for a fire or a tornado. Unfortunately, I hadn't been in on the planning and wasn't sure where to go. Arthur yelled at me to take cover somewhere and not to worry. Being human, he assumed that I wouldn't be harmed if the hunting party did find me. I looked around... but everyone was gone in a flash. I suppose I lingered a bit too long trying to think of a hiding place, but I was shocked by the whole experience. And once again my worries began to take control. I feared for my life when I needn't have feared at all.

I couldn't see anywhere that made sense as a hiding place. Then I thought of the garden. The flowers were tall enough to hide the vegetables growing behind them. Surely they were tall enough to hide a boy as well! I ran as fast as I could, but before I could reach them I heard the rustling of leaves and creaking of branches. It was too late! I'd made it to the large flowers and had crouched down behind them before I saw anyone. Voices shouted. Two men appeared, yelling something about the green orb. They didn't seem interested in the wolves. Despite the anger in their voices I started to feel my tension lessen a bit. After all, these were the first people I had seen since coming to this world, and it was my sincere hope that they could help me get home. I knew I was going to meet with them sooner or later, so I made what I thought at the time was not such a bold decision to get their attention.

I stepped out calmly from behind my insubstantial hiding place and addressed the strangers. "Hello there. What's happening?"

One of the men pointed at me and shouted, "You there! Who are you and what are you doing here?"

I walked a bit closer and said "My name is Robert. I'm new here." Before I could say another word they rushed toward me and grabbed my arms behind my back, like police officers holding a criminal. "Hey! What's going on here? What do you think you're doing?"

"We'll ask the questions!" one of them barked.

"What is your business in Serenity Forest?" the other demanded.

"I'm lost," I said, only half-lying.

"People don't just get lost in Serenity Forest," the first man said. "What are you doing here?"

"I told you: I'm lost," I said, clearly getting frustrated. "I'm not from around here and I have no idea how to get home."

"Maybe he's telling the truth, Urien," the second man said. "Look at his clothes. They are unlike any I have ever seen."

"You may be correct, Haydn," the first man replied. "In the moment I had not noticed, but his clothes are certainly different. Where did you get such odd garments?"

"Uh… at home?" I said – risking the fact that sarcasm was likely to get me hurt in the position I was in.

"Where *is* your home sir?" Urien asked, his tone now showing his irritation.

"Here we go again…" I mumbled. "I am a citizen of the United States of America… and you're going to tell me you've never heard of it."

"America?" Urien questioned. "Haydn, where have I heard that name before?"

"I'm not sure," Haydn responded.

"I've not heard of any United States; but I'm sure *America* is a name I *have* heard. I just can't quite place it."

Well this was a change for the better I thought. Maybe we were getting somewhere. At least the name seemed to ring a bell no matter how faint. "Please," I begged. "I've done nothing wrong. Unhand me." They looked at each other and then again at me.

"He appears unarmed, Urien," said Haydn.

"Yes," replied Urien. "Go ahead and let him go. There's no reason we can't be civilized about this." Haydn then let go of my arms and I thanked him ever so politely.

"You will tell us what you were doing here… what did you say your name was again?" Urien asked.

"Moore. Robert Moore," I replied feeling not-at-all like James Bond. The thought struck me that they wouldn't recognize the reference anyway.

"Yes, well, Robert Moore: you will be entertaining us with an account of your presence here soon enough, but for now there is still the business we came here for. And that is to search for the green orb. You wouldn't happen to know anything about the whereabouts of the green orb, would you Robert?" asked Urien.

"I can honestly say I do not," I replied. "Nor do I fully understand what the green orb is."

"Nonsense!" yelled Hadyn. "He's obviously lying. He's probably one of those forest defenders."

"Possibly…" replied Urien, "But I've certainly never seen him before. Maybe this strange outfit is a new uniform of the defenders." He then addressed me. "If you are a forest defender and are hiding the secrets of the orb's location, we *will* get the information from you."

"What is it with you people and this green orb business?" I responded. "Listen, I'm not even from your world. If my clothes aren't clue enough for you, my accent and speech patterns should tell you I'm a stranger."

In just the few short moments I'd had to listen to them I could tell there was a huge difference between our dialects. I couldn't quite put my finger on it, but their accent was vaguely familiar… though I knew I'd never heard it before. They could indeed be descendants of the original followers of Samuel More, in which case their English accents would have become differentiated in the same way that we Americans and the Canadians and Australians who were of English ancestry had developed different way of speaking. It sounded sort of like a mish-mash of South African and Irish accents, with a bit of Canadian thrown in for effect. Their dialect wasn't that different from what the forest creatures were speaking, but I had been so astonished at animals actually speaking I hadn't really noticed it that much.

As far as their clothing being different... well, that was an understatement. I don't know what I had expected them to be wearing, but I had never seen anything in any history books or encyclopedias quite like what they had on. If I had been more interested in history or fashion, I'd probably be better able to describe them. The best way I can put it is that their clothes were like costumes designed for an alien civilization on Star Trek. It made me think of 18th and 23rd Centuries colliding. I suppose the material was something similar to cotton, but it didn't look it breathed as well. It reminded me of felt. They had no buckles or buttons, replacing them with more straps than seemed practical. They wore their leggings tight and their shirts loose fitting. The colors were mostly earth tones; good for hunting, I surmised. Their boots were dark and wouldn't have been out of place on a character in a swashbuckler movie.

What caught my attention more than their clothes or accents, however, were their weapons. Each man was armed with a good-sized knife and wore a pistol at his side. The guns looked like something pirates would have had: flintlocks, only a little more advanced. They weren't automatic weapons and didn't look as if they could hold particularly powerful ammunition. I was sure they were deadly, nonetheless. I certainly didn't want to find out what they were capable of at as close range! I decided it'd be best to keep my tongue and be as cooperative as possible.

They discussed what to do with me for a bit, finally deciding to take me back to their village for further questioning. I walked with them as Urien searched for clues that would reveal the green orb's secret hiding place while Haydn watched me like a hawk. After a few minutes of kicking around rocks and leaves, Urien found nothing to his satisfaction and decided to get back to the rest of the party. I'm not sure who had the most surprised look on his face when I met the rest of them. They were as shocked by my clothing as I was dumbfounded at the "horses" they had brought into Serenity Forest. The beasts looked like Clydesdales from the neck down, but had a bird-like head reminiscent of the nghuryll I'd encountered at the edge of the woods. They were hairless, with large black feathers where a mane should be that contrasted with their light-grey bodies. Their tails were similar to an eagle's; again, with black feathers. The hooves were cloven, more like a goat than a horse, sort of like a cross between a hoof and a talon. Their large size had it obvious why they couldn't have gotten too far through the thick brush. It also didn't look like they could move that swiftly; but there was no doubting their power. They had very strong musculature to go along with a fierce visage that sent shivers up my spine.

I was introduced to the other men as a "guest," but I took it to mean a guest with very few privileges. I was helped onto the back of Haydn's horse. Then Urien led the men out of Serenity Forest. Urien was obviously their leader, as he kept barking out orders and no one seemed to question him. He also had a very confident appearance. I hoped that he'd end up being someone I could talk to without being too intimidated, but his gruffness offered little promise of that.

The hunting party took me to the nearest village of humans outside of Serenity Forest. Oddly, it was exactly where I'd planned on going just the day before, but now it was the last place I wanted to be. I'm not certain how far away it was from the forest. We were traveling on horseback, and I had been walking everywhere else up until then. It was only an hour or so before we entered the town rather accurately named the Village of Broad Meadows.

Fortunately, we arrived at suppertime. I was beginning to get hungry. The hunters went into a large building that seemed like a mess hall of sorts. Haydn took me to a smaller building, which looked more or less like a small town jail. After a bit he brought me a plate of food. I certainly wasn't expecting a feast in my honor or anything, but it would have been nice sit at a table and eat with everyone else! By now I had figured out that this green orb business was serious stuff. It was obvious by this time, between what the wolves had told me and how the hunters were treating me. At least they'd let me eat before they started drilling. And the meal wasn't half bad, either. I wasn't sure what anything was, exactly, but it included a piece of well-cooked meat. I was at last getting some kind of protein. There was also a mixture of vegetables with some odd-smelling, but not at all bad tasting, sauce that pretty much poured over everything. I wasn't sure if that was the way it was meant to be served, or if it came from being thrown around a bit before it got to me. I didn't really care, either. It was palatable and kept me from starving. Based on this, I reasoned I wasn't going to be tortured or anything, which was reassuring and kept my usual doubts from setting in.

After I finished eating, I peered out of the window to get as good a look as I could at my new surroundings. The Village of Broad Meadows was a good-sized little place. It was centered, aptly enough, in a broad meadow. I don't remember seeing any hills in between the forest and the meadow, despite the fact that there were many hills in the meadows where I first arrived. The village was made up of sturdy-looking little buildings that reminded me of what you might find in an old western town in the 1800s.

I didn't see many of the townspeople when I first arrived. It seemed, however that all eyes were upon me while I was being thrown into my comfortable "suite." Of course, I was an unexpected guest. There wasn't time for a red carpet or anything.

They gave me plenty of time to wait between supper and my inevitable questioning, which sapped away some of my confidence. This was undoubtedly the idea: they wanted to make me nervous before grilling me. Then again, I was a late addition to their agenda, and they might have been busy with other things.

Not long after the sun went down Urien came with Haydn at his side. They were unarmed, which made me breathe a little easier. But I knew they weren't coming in for a tea party. They suspected I had information they needed, and I wasn't going to be able to give it to them. I braced myself for unpleasantness.

Urien sat down at the small table across from me. Haydn stood over in the corner with his arms across his chest. He looked me up and down and began sneering. "These garments," he began, "...they are simply dreadful. It's as if you were going to some fancy dress party or something. What mad tailor did you get these from?"

I decided to act every bit as confident as I didn't feel.

"Look Urien: let's cut to the chase. As distracting as they are, we both know you didn't come in here to rag on my threads." It was, perhaps, a bit too insolent.

"I'm not exactly sure what you just said," replied Urien cautiously. "But you're not in any position to take a casual tone with me. That's especially unheard of for someone as young as you. How old are you, anyway?"

"I'm fifteen," I answered.

"You're nothing but a lad! Why in the world were you in Serenity forest all alone?"

"I told you already: I'm not *from* here. I'm not even from your world at all! I came from America, which is in another dimension apparently, and I got lost in the forest because I don't have any idea where I am." I wisely omitted my entire experience with the wolf pack, not to mention my knowledge of Branwen's kidnapping. At this point I had no idea whose side these guys were on, but since they were searching for the green orb, I had a pretty good idea they weren't intending to help the wolves. I knew that I couldn't trust them; or at least not yet.

"That tale is indeed hard to take, young sir," Urien suggested.

"Well, take it or leave it, that's exactly what happened. If you have any idea how to get me home or could take me to someone who might help me, I'd be greatly appreciative," I added.

"Your appearance and strange language gives me reason to believe your story," he said. "I have many questions for you, but you may prove of even more interest to my uncle, who is the governor of Gwerinatha. I shall cut short my hunting trip and we shall return to the city in the morning. I'm sure he'll have a plethora of questions to add to my own."

"Fine," I said. "That sounds just fine. Just a quick question here: what is Gwerinatha?"

Haydn began to chuckle in the corner. I looked at him like he was an idiot to counter the look I knew I was about to get for asking what was undoubtedly a very stupid question.

"Gwerinatha," Urien said, "is the name of the land you find yourself in. My, you are a strange traveler, aren't you? If only I could remember why this 'America' place sounded familiar to me..."

He looked at me thoughtfully, but by that point it was late and Urien made it clear he was in no mood to answer any of my questions. So with that it was off to sleep. I can't say as I slept too well that night in my new surroundings. But when daybreak came I was as eager as anyone to start traveling again. Though, I must say, I wasn't looking forward to getting on the back of one of those horses again.

I was pleased to discover that I needn't have worried about that. After breakfast there was a small caravan of horse drawn carriages loaded up and ready to take the entire hunting party off to the city. What city it was I didn't know yet, but of course it really didn't matter. I had no knowledge of the geography of Gwerinatha. I was just glad to be going somewhere that held some hope of getting me home. I was also pleased to find that the carriages were quite nice. I guessed that being the governor's nephew had some perks. Not that I objected. We were traveling in style! At least as far as I could tell with what I'd seen so far. To me it was like heading off in a limo compared to the ways I'd traveled up to that point. The seats had plush, comfy upholstery, and there were nice little brass frames around the windows. There was lots of leg room, too; which was nice, because it was a bit crowded inside with me as an extra passenger.

I figured there were about eleven guys on the trip, counting the ones who were driving. The carriage interior would comfortably fit four, so I found myself squished in between Haydn and some other guy who I hadn't been introduced to as of yet. Urien and another of his aides sat across from us. I smiled as much as I could and tried to refrain from asking too many uppity questions. Urien was nice enough to offer up a good bit of information without my prodding, however. It seemed he really did believe my story about being from another world and was doing his best to help me out.

He explained the city we were going to was called New London, the capital of Gwerinatha. First, however, we'd make a stop in a town called Dinas Rhyddid, which was much closer. There we would have some lunch and separate from most of the hunting party, who lived there. Dinas Rhyddid was a few hours from the Village of Broad Meadows and quite a bit larger. I was happy to see it when we arrived. Finally, I was in a civilized bit of this strange world! I was glad to see a lot of people, even if they were all strangers. If the village of Broad Meadows resembled an old western town from the 1800s, then Dinas Rhyddid would be its eastern counterpart. It had several buildings over three stories in height and a good-sized population. We had put away the horses and the carriages and had lunch at a nice restaurant with menus, a wait staff, and everything. I was quite excited by the experience, despite the fact that it was nowhere as near as modern as any 20th Century Earth town. After all, just a few days earlier I was living under branches eating what fruit I could find on the forest's floor!

It was clear from all the mumbling and whispering that my appearance was causing a bit of a stir. I didn't get bothered by anyone, however; due in no small part to Urien's presence. He was apparently quite well-known and respected. Thus everyone left us alone.

After lunch we walked out into the street where an even newer-looking carriage with twice as many horses was already waiting for us. These horses had fancy decorations on their bridles and even more colorful feathers than the ones that had brought us into town. I thought for a minute that I could get used to this sort of treatment, but then started thinking of home and remembered I didn't truly belong here. Urien must

have detected the longing in my eyes as I stared out of the window, with
Dinas Rhyddid rapidly disappearing in the background.

"Homesick young, sir?" he asked.

"Yes," I said. "You've been very kind and everything – and I appreciate
the nice treatment – but I do miss home."

"Hopefully someone in New London will be able to find a way back to
America for you," he replied. "My uncle is a fair and wise ruler. I'm sure
he'll be able to help you."

"I hope so, too," I replied softly as I rested my arm outside of the
window.

The rest of the trip was fairly quiet. Urien sensed I needed time to
reflect and did little talking. I enjoyed watching the countryside through
the window seat. It was also much more comfortable with only three of us,
Haydn being the other passenger. New London wasn't that much further
away and, with twice as many horses, we made good time. We actually
arrived with plenty of time before dinner. New London was definitely a city
and not a small town. Again, the technology here wasn't what I was used.
There were no cars, planes, or telephones. But from what I could see this
would have been a modern, competitive city in the 19th Century. I was told
the population was three times that of Dinas Rhyddid and that it was the
largest city in all Gwerinatha. The architecture was certainly very
interesting. While Dinas Rhyddid had the look and feel of an old west's
eastern counterpart, New London seemed like something out of Dickens. I
half expected to see David Copperfield, Oliver Twist, or the Artful Dodger
come running up to meet us when the carriage stopped.

Urien set me up in a nice hotel room that was down the street from the
capital building where his uncle worked. It was a far cry from the little hole
I slept in the previous night. I wondered for a moment if there was room
service. Then I started wondering if I was going to have to pay for anything.
But that was absurd under the circumstances. Left alone for a few moments
before dinner, I finally had a moment to reflect. I'd been so overwhelmed by
all I'd seen that I had completely forgotten about the wolves' plight in
Serenity Forest – as well as Branwen and her kidnapping!

Chapter Seven
The Lords of Wisdom

Sometime later Urien returned with some clothing for me. There was a pair of dark grey pants something like dress up slacks; not nearly as tight as the leggings the hunters wore. Then, of course, there was the ubiquitous white, billowy shirt. I don't know what the deal was with the loose-fitting garment, but it was obviously the latest fashion trend. Everybody seemed to be wearing one. He also gave me a pair of fancy shoes that didn't quite fit. I decided to continue wearing my sneakers, which were comfortable and in fairly good condition. The native shoes were a little bizarre in any case, festooned with strange laces and worn unnaturally high to my way of thinking.

Urien suggested I destroy my own clothes for some reason. I flatly refused. My clothes definitely needed cleaning after a few days of running about in the forest gathering dirt, but I certainly wasn't going to get rid of them. He dropped the subject and showed me where I could get cleaned up. As distracting as my native attire was to Gwerinathans, their clothes would be equally so back on my world. I also felt the need to hold on to some sense of identity in the face of this bizarre new world which I found myself in. My clothes were the only thing I still had from home.

So far I was feeling more comfortable in New London than anywhere else in Gwerinatha. I suppose of all the places I'd been, it was the closest to home. That, and the bit of homesickness I'd felt on the journey there, caused to think about home for the first time in a while. I hadn't really considered what my mother and the rest of my family must have been going through. I imagined they were worried silly about me, since I'd vanished days ago without explanation. The worst part was that they had no idea where I was. They were probably imagining that God-knows-what had happened to me. Whimsically, I wondered if they would have been even *more* worried if they knew where I actually was. It was then I first realized that I would never be able to tell anyone about my adventure, because they would never believe any of it.

It was while I was thinking this that Urien came back to get me for dinner. We went outside the hotel and around the corner to a pleasant restaurant; much nicer than where we'd eaten lunch. In fact, it made the restaurant in Dinas Rhyddid seem like a small diner in comparison. We were seated at a table that could easily sit twelve, so I wondered just how many people were going to be joining us. I was also glad that Urien had given me a change of clothing. This particular restaurant seemed too upscale for a t-shirt and jeans. It was also nice not to have people staring at me all the time because of what I was wearing... though I did get a few odd glances from the people who noticed my shoes.

I hadn't had much time to study the menu when the governor and his entourage arrived. The restaurant staff treated them with the type of attention and courtesy you'd expect such august personages to receive. Urien introduced us. "Robert, this is my uncle Padrig Baylies, the honorable governor of Gwerinatha."

I stood up and shook his hand. "Pleased to meet you, sir. My name is Robert Moore."

"How do you do young man," the governor said. "My nephew tells me you are from America. Is this true?"

"Yes. Yes it is sir," I replied.

"Well... sit down and tell me all about how you got here, son," he said, motioning me to sit back down again. "This should be a most interesting tale indeed."

We sat down to eat and, over the first couple of courses, I explained as best I could about my sister, the genealogy search, the letters from Samuel to Artemis and the key which I used to enter Gwerinatha. Once again I left out my encounter with the wolves in Serenity Forest. They seemed quite taken with my tale. In particular, they were excited to talk to me about home. It turns out they had indeed heard of America. Urien hadn't remembered the story well because, for most Gwerinathans, it is a subject they touch on only very briefly on in adolescent history classes. It is mentioned in their histories as another destination for their pilgrim ancestors.

They were also intrigued to hear that I was a descendant of Samuel More. Samuel was almost a mythological figure it seemed. I was told how, in their earliest school years, they all learned about how he brought their people to Gwerinatha. He was a bit like George Washington in that sense. I was just as interested in hearing about him as they were about America. I hoped there would be plenty of time to learn their history before I returned home again. They were anxious to see the key, which I hadn't thought about in days. I got it from a pocket within the billowy shirt; a far more comfortable spot, actually, than the pocket in my blue jeans where I had been keeping it. I showed it to them, provoking a series of 'oohs' and 'ahhs.'

"About this key," I asked. "Does anyone here know exactly how I could use this to get home?"

"Unfortunately, no," Padrig said. "Legends say that Samuel fancied himself an alchemist; and, apparently, he was. They also say that he used some very odd methods to come up with his discoveries. It will be difficult to figure out precisely what he did to find this place, let alone how to open a door back to your world. He didn't leave any sort of information about how he got our ancestors here, and I don't believe he ever had any intention of anyone ever leaving."

At that my face fell. The governor reached over and put his hand on my shoulder. "However, if there is anyone in Gwerinatha who can figure it out, they will be here in New London." He went on, "You see son: we have a lot of bright people here. In fact, we New Londonites are also known as the Lords of Wisdom. That's not just a political name. We'll put the word out and see what we can come up with. Perhaps with your key to study someone will be able to decipher this grand mystery."

I didn't feel too encouraged by this promise. Despite the wonders of this city, it still appeared kind of backward to me. Then again, Samuel had made his discoveries in a far less technologically advanced time as this, so who knew what could be accomplished? Governor Baylies invited me to stay with him over at the governor's mansion for a while so that we could have more in-depth discussions about my experiences. Shortly thereafter, I retrieved my few belongings from the hotel room and settled in.

The mansion was luxurious in what I imagined to be an early Victorian manner. I decided that I was getting to like it in New London, despite the backwardness of the place. In any case, I certainly preferred the oil lamps of the city to the candles of places like the village of Broad Meadows! They might not have been light bulbs, but they were a definite improvement. Still, I wondered why in all these years no one had discovered how to tame electricity? Unless time was different for our two worlds, they should be at least three hundred years advanced from the original settlers. And, even if it wasn't, they were clearly several generations past Samuel's time. From what I understood, he'd brought just a few people with him, not an army. This many people couldn't have come from so few in just a hundred years or so. I hoped that I'd get some answers from the governor.

The next day I was invited into a large den, where the governor and a couple of his attendants were sitting among musty tomes in the back of the room. I explained as much as I could to them about our history and technology. They were particularly interested in our advances in weaponry and, at the time, I wished I could explain things in better detail. But I only knew so much myself. I didn't even bother mentioning things like electronics or aviation, which I had little chance of explaining at all.

Soon enough, the time came for me to learn about their history and culture. The governor told me how Samuel had discovered Gwerinatha and brought with him six likeminded couples to begin a new colony. Their names were forever inscribed in the history books: Seth and Humility Winslow, Jacob and Mary Tinker, Edward and Constance Barker, William and Desire Baylies, John and Elinor Wellington, and Bartholomew and Katherine Collins. All the citizens of Gwerinatha had descended from them and, as such, had one of those six surnames or a hyphenated version of any two. That is everyone, of course, except for the native Gwerinathans.

There were no more true natives left, he said. This he glossed over, making it sound like that part of the book of Genesis which few preachers ever seem to talk about: the section were the demigod-like giants who originally lived on the earth mated with humans, and then they all left for parts unknown. So there were some not-fully humans lurking about who had been descended from these unusual pairings. I'm not sure how much of that he actually believed, because he went over it very fast, and quickly changed the subject when I questioned him on it.

From there it was on to a basic geography lesson. Gwerinatha had a fairly simple topography. There were the many meadows and hills of which I was familiar. There were also four different forests, two of which I had been to in person. The largest forest was Anhysbys Forest to the far west.

Nothing much was known of it, as it has always been considered too dangerous for human investigation. This, of course, I had surmised from my earlier lessons with the wolves. Further east, past the meadows Louie and I had traveled, was Serenity Forest. Here, humans could hunt for food, but it wasn't done too often because there were some dangerous creatures there as well. I didn't know if he was referring to the wolves or not, but I let that pass, since I still wanted to get as much information as I could before revealing what I already knew. Beyond Serenity Forest a little to the east was the Village of Broad Meadows, with which I also was quite familiar. Then to the east of that village was a large section of land divided up into several different cities. I was told that this was the heartland of Gwerinatha where most of their civilization lived. Besides New London and Dinas Rhyddid, there were other large cities named Winslow, Baylies Crossing, Barksburg, and Sibridale. All other human habitations were suburbs, or "country townships," as they preferred to call them. To the north of this land was Hunoliaeth Forest, where most of their hunting was done. This was a smaller forest that was much closer to civilization than Serenity Forest. To the south of the land was Didoriad River, which ran straight through the middle of all Gwerinatha and, as I had seen, Anhysbys Forest as well. To the south of the river was a small mountain range called the Ochneidio Mountains. On the southern side of those mountains is another large block of land which he didn't want to talk about very much. He said there were various cities there, mostly of which were controlled by a rival faction called the House of Fates. South of that was yet another forest. There were also a lot of tiny villages scattered about both to the north and south of the mountains. They were all technically under the rule of the Lords of Wisdom, but the House of Fates had more control over the ones in the south.

Then, back towards the west in the very southernmost part of Gwerinatha, was something called the Unfinished Lands. When I pressed, he didn't want to explain much about them to me, either. He made it clear that the Unfinished Lands were off limits to humans who valued their lives, and that it was clearly the most dangerous place in all of Gwerinatha.

Since exploring the subject of the Unfinished Lands seemed to be especially taboo, I decided to press him on the previous unpopular topic of the House of Fates. He relented a bit, seeing both how curious I was about it and that I wasn't going to let *every* subject slide! The Governor explained that the House of Fates ruled alongside the Lords of Wisdom over all Gwerinatha. There was a lot of tension between the two groups, however, as their opinions on how to run things differed. He didn't want to go into too much detail about what the differences in the two groups were, however. It seemed to me that these were the factions that Arthur had spoke of when he told me his father's tale of what had happened to Samuel Moore.

"You'll find those in the House of Fates are quite intolerant of our beliefs and way of life," the governor explained. "They are closed minded, and constantly interfering in our attempts to do what is needed for the people of Gwerinatha. They cannot be trusted, what with their lies and deceptions about our government to the people."

"I'll keep that in mind," I said. "But I'm really not that interested in politics."

"That's probably for the best," he said.

Before we could get to another subject I brought up the issue I was most curious about, the green orb. "Pardon me sir, but could you tell me what the green orb is?" I asked. "Your nephew and his party seemed very intent on finding it the other day."

"The green orb... yes. I suppose you would be interested in that. The orb is something that, at its heart, is nothing more than legend. Legends say that it is very powerful..." he paused, and then continued. "Do you believe in magic, Robert?"

"A little more than I did before my arrival in Gwerinatha," I responded.

"The reason I ask is because you will need to be in the right frame of mind in order to understand just what the green orb, and its sisters, are all about. From what you've told me it seems there's little or no magic in the modern world from which you come."

"Not more than just illusions from stage magicians. You know: parlor tricks, sleight of hand, and the like," I told him.

"Yes, well, here in Gwerinatha there are certain items that some consider to be have magical properties. Others argue that are creations of science and logic crafted by an earlier, more advanced – but sadly now lost – people. The glowing orbs are just such artifacts. If they are indeed real and not simply legend, it could very well be that they are not exactly 'magical' either, but the science of their origin is simply so far beyond us that we have yet to figure it out. Either way, they are supposed to be very powerful objects." Then he continued, "The story goes that there are three magic spheres of ancient origin. They are metal, with panels that when slid away reveal glowing orbs inside. It is said that the green orb gives anyone who bathes in its light powers of a physical nature, including enhanced speed, strength, agility, and heightened senses. There is also a sphere that houses a red orb which increases the power of the mind, granting those who bathe in its light limited telepathic and telekinetic abilities. The last sphere's orb is blue. It gives anyone in the presence of its light power over emotions, such as empathy and the ability to change the way others feel. The powers that come from the orbs are temporary and need to be recharged frequently, though the person using them becomes weak if he uses the orbs too often. However, it is said that if the three are united, they glow together a great white light that gives anyone the powers of all three permanently."

"Wow, that's really something," I said. I couldn't help but notice that Governor Baylies seemed to know a great deal about something that was simply supposed to be a legend. "Well, your nephew sure seems to think the green orb is real."

"Yes," he replied. "In the past few years there have been stories coming out of Serenity Forest of creatures and even some humans who have abilities that could be described has having been augmented by the green orb. Urien is the head of our security forces here in New London, and has been investigating with some of his staff. That's all."

"I see," I said, trying not to reveal any more curiosity in my voice. I had gotten the sense there was more than I was being told. It would probably be wise not to ask any more questions about the subject. But now I knew there were three orbs. Since there was more than enough circumstantial evidence for me to believe that the green orb was for real, I didn't doubt the existence of the other two.

During the course of this discussion the governor's attendants left to go about their various duties. As it was getting late, one of them came in to see if I needed anything before retiring. I explained I was fine and headed off to the guest room to get ready for bed. As I was walking up the stairs, I heard someone knocking loudly on the front door. It sounded urgent, so I decided to hang around close enough to hear what was going on. After the valet opened the door I heard a lot of loud and nervous yelling. The governor rushed in to see what the disturbance was all about.

When the men calmed down long enough to be coherent, I couldn't believe what I was hearing. The governor's daughter had been kidnapped! She'd been thought to be staying with relatives in another city, but word got back that she never arrived. After a lot of questioning and sifting rumors from facts, it turned out that she had been kidnapped by a fringe faction of the House of Fates. I kept listening to make sure I got the name right and that this was no coincidence. It wasn't. The Branwen whose kidnapping I had already been aware of was Branwen Baylies, the governor's daughter.

Chapter Eight
A Nice Place to Visit

The next morning I woke to the sounds of people rushing about. It was clear the news of Branwen's kidnapping had sent the mansion into a frenzy. At the breakfast table I met some more of Governor Baylies' family, unfortunately at a most inopportune time. The governor explained about the kidnapping and how it would obviously alter any plans we had for the day. Instead of going over more of the history and technology of my world, I'd be seeing the sites and sounds of New London with another of the

Governor's daughters, Seren, who was closest to my age. It was hoped that giving her something to do would keep her mind off of worrying about her sister.

Seren was just barely fourteen, two years younger than Branwen and thus closer to her than any of her younger sisters. She showed me around the mansion after breakfast. I saw some family paintings and was able to pick Branwen out without anyone showing me. She was as pretty as I had imagined her to be. I'd always wondered if you could fall in love with someone without ever seeing them. After all I had heard about her, I was sure she was someone special and, after seeing her image, she immediately replaced Candace as my latest crush. I think Seren could sense my appreciation for Branwen, as I stared her portrait at little too long.

"She's really pretty, isn't she?" Seren commented.

"Yes, she is," I replied shyly. "I hope you find her soon."

"Me too," she said, her voice trembling slightly. "I know my father's very upset. But I..."

"But what?" I asked.

"Nothing," she said. "I'm supposed to be keeping my mind off all this, so I'd rather just not talk about it. What would you like to see in New London first?"

"That's all up to you I guess. I have no idea of what there is to see," I told her.

"Well, in that case," she said, her voice lifting, "we can go shopping."

I rolled my eyes a bit and geared up for a shopping trip with a teenaged girl in a backward, alien world.

Our first stop was the marketplace. I wasn't sure what to expect, but it was mostly comprised of street vendors selling food; quite like a farmer's market back home. We passed through that area very quickly, even though I was interested in seeing what was available. Seren didn't care too much about it. I surmised that, being the daughter of the governor, other people bought her food for her. She made a beeline for the area of town that had clothing stores. At this point I knew I was in trouble. We probably spent at least two hours in various clothing shops. She was most interested in the new fashions that had come in from a place called Dyffryn Heul, which was a city to the south of the Ochneidio Mountains and was one of those places Governor Baylies didn't want to talk about, since it was firmly planted in House of Fates territory. Apparently, the honorable governor wasn't too hip to these types of clothes, and would be very disapproving of Seren even looking at them, let alone buying any of them. Personally I couldn't tell much difference in the clothes myself, but it was obvious Seren did. She went on and on about how exciting they were.

After a while she could tell how disinterested I was, but she wasn't quite ready to leave the garment district so she decided to see about buying me something. "That shirt you have is dismal, you know," she stated.

"Thanks," I replied. "Your cousin Urien picked it out for me."

"That figures," she said. "He hasn't got the best taste in the world."

"He particularly hated the clothes I arrived in," I added.

"I thought they were *outrageous*," she squeaked in an excited tone.

"Wait a minute. Where did you see my clothes?" I asked.

"When I heard about a boy from another world coming for a visit, I was naturally curious."

"Naturally," I mimicked.

"So, I did some snooping. I followed the help down to the laundry and took a gander when they were doing your wash last night."

"And outrageous is good?" I questioned.

"Absolutely!" she exclaimed. "They're choice!"

"Really?" I said with a tone that tried unsuccessfully to hide my approval.

"Yes, but you need something..." her voice trailed as she looked around the shop we were currently in.

"Aces!" she yelled. "A belt, I think. Here's just the one." She walked over to a rack that had what I'd refer to as sashes rather than belts. Seren pulled out a deep purple one with a rather tacky pattern to it and held it up to my waist.

"I don't think it goes with these pants," I said.

"No, no. Not these. But it'll look smart with those blue ones you have. I've never seen blue pants before," she added. "Not even in south Gwerinatha. Is that color common where you're from?"

I chuckled a bit, which drew a scowl from Seren. "It's very common actually. In America, blue jeans are everywhere."

"Wow! I'd love to hear more about America," she said. "In school they just barely mention it. They said the natives were savage. Aren't you afraid of them?"

"Uh, not really." I decided the story of what happened to the Native Americans would be better left for another time. If at all. "Probably no more than you are of the natives here."

"Yes, well, you don't really see any natives in the city," she replied. "They'd all be in the Unfinished Lands or there about."

"Your father wouldn't tell me much about the Unfinished Lands. Do you know anything about them?" I inquired.

"Only to stay away from them," she replied. "Unless you're interested in suicide. The nasties of that place stay away from the cities, we stay away from them, and that's just the way we'd like to keep it. I don't know how those people in the south can stand living so close to them."

"That's something else your father wouldn't talk much about. The lands to the south of the mountains."

"Aw, that's just political stuff. I don't much get involved in that," she explained. "I just like to look at some of the stuff they send us. It's really nifty, don't you think?"

"Yeah, swell," I answered with a less than subtle hint of sarcasm.

Just then a couple of teenage girls ran up to us. They were apparently friends of Seren's. They exchanged pleasantries, and then consoled her about her sister's disappearance. Once they could tell she wasn't in the mood to discuss it, they shifted their attention to me.

"So who's the stranger, then?" one of them asked.

"Just a friend visiting from the south," Seren replied.

"Oh, he's quite a boykie, Ser," the other one chimed in.

"Stand off, Nesta! I'm just showing him around town. He's a guest of my father's."

"Well, bring him to the show tonight Seren. I'd like to see him again."

"Oh, that's right. I was going to see the Barmies tonight outside the Broken Tower."

"What do you mean *was*?" one of her friends asked.

"I'm not sure if I can go now," she replied. "I mean, what with the kidnapping and showing Robert around today, I may have to change my plans."

"You don't have to change your plans because of me," I jumped in. "I mean, if you were going to do something, go ahead. Seeing a show might help to keep your mind off your troubles."

"C'mon then. Don't let us down. Bring your friend here tonight," said Nesta. "Branwen would want you to go."

Seren relented. "All right, I will. What time are you going to rock up?"

"The show starts at seven. We want to be there by then to get up close," the other friend said.

Just then Nesta saw someone else she knew, made her quick goodbyes and she and her friend ran off down the street.

"Close friends of yours?" I asked.

"I guess so," she said unconvincingly. "It's hard to have really close friends when you're the governor's daughter. They're mostly pretty shallow. Branwen's the closest friend I have." Her voice trailed off as she began to worry again about her sister. Changing the subject, I asked why she told her friends I was from the south.

"My father made it explicitly clear that no one was to know of your origins," she explained. "He doesn't want there to be a big to-do over it, in case it starts a riot or something."

"A riot?" I wondered

"Well, you know, in case some people might think you're an advanced scout for an invasion or something," she said.

"I guess I can see how people might think of it that way," I responded. "I am an alien here, after all. If word got out about my advanced technology and my evil plan to take over the world, it could become quite chaotic."

She stared at me wide-eyed for a minute. Then, when it hit her that I was only joking, she playfully nudged me away.

"Let's go for lunch," she said.

I was pretty happy to get out of the garment district. Clothes shopping had never been a favorite activity of mine, and shopping for clothes with girls is akin to watching paint dry, only with a scratchy soundtrack playing in the background. As far as lunch was concerned I was getting pretty hungry. I asked Seren if she had a place in mind. "Oh yes," she said. "I know a place a couple of blocks away where they make a grand dog butty."

"Whoa!" I said with my hands held up. "Please tell me you people do not eat dogs around here."

"What?" she exclaimed. "No! Don't be silly. A dog butty is a corned beef sandwich. There's a small place ahead that makes all kinds of great sandwiches."

"Okay. I'm not into corned beef, but you can't believe how relieved I am that we're not having Fido stew."

We went to a restaurant that looked somewhat like a cross between a New York delicatessen and an old English pub. We sat at a table near the back and a waitress came over to ask what we wanted. Seren ordered her dog butty and patiently waited for me to find something. "There sure is a lot of meat on this menu," I noted.

"We have a great blind scouse, if you're so inclined," the waitress said.

"A what?" I asked with a more than confused look on my face.

"That's a meatless stew," she added.

"Oh that's fine," I said. "I'll have one of those and a Coke."

"What's a Coke?" Seren and the waitress said almost in unison.

"Sorry," I replied sheepishly. "Forgot where I was for a moment. Tea, please." The waitress left with our orders and I leaned over to Seren. "You guys have got to get a bit more variety in your beverage menus." She didn't seem to notice I'd said anything but stared off out the window.

"Seren. What's wrong?" I asked. "Is it Branwen again?"

"Yes. I'm sorry," she finally responded. "It's just that she always gets blind scouse when we come here. She never eats meat because she loves animals so much. Because I've always loved this place, she comes here with me even though it bothers her."

"Back home we call people who don't eat meat 'vegetarians.'" I said. "Or 'vegans' if they don't eat any animal products at all, like dairy or eggs."

"What funny words," she replied. "I don't know of too many people around here like that, though Branwen does have some friends who thinks like she does."

"Do you suppose they're out looking for her too?" I asked.

"I'm sure they would if they could. But I really don't want to talk about that anymore."

"Sorry," I said. We didn't talk much more until after we were finished eating.

Seren brought up the subject of America again. She was naturally very curious about where I came from and how different it was from her world. I told her some of the same things I'd told her father, but I knew she'd be less interested in the technology and history and more interested in the culture. I told her a bit more about music and television and movies. She was especially interested in film. I imagined her sitting in a movie theatre, jaw dropped to the floor and eyes unblinking at the spectacle on the screen. It was amusing to shift my perspective this way. While watching her expressions, I regaled her with my everyday experiences, imagining that I was seeing it all through her eyes. I didn't want to cause too much more culture shock than I already had, so didn't tell her about big budget action movies or science fiction films. Star Trek or *Star Wars* could be more than someone who had never even heard of a telephone or an airplane could handle.

She wanted to hear more about America, and I was just glad not to have her brooding about Branwen any longer, so she suggested we go somewhere for 'afters,' which was her way of describing dessert. I hoped for an ice cream parlor, and the place we went to did sort of have that look and feel to it. But, unfortunately, it didn't have the key ingredient: ice cream. But she did introduce me to something she referred to as snot pudden and sticky lice. At first I was almost as squeamish as when she mentioned the dog butty, but she made me promise to taste it without telling me what it was. I decided to trust her, and was rewarded with the most flavorful treat I'd had in Gwerinatha since my introduction to the core of a hewlifruit. The snot pudden was actually a version of tapioca pudding, and the sticky lice were actually licorice roots. She grilled me a bit more about my world while we ate, and I tried my best to ease her into it without overwhelming her too much.

The day went by fairly rapidly from there. We shopped a bit more and she took me down a street which contained some sidewalk performers that were rather enjoyable. After the long walk back home, we retired to our separate rooms until dinner. Dinner itself was uneventful. It seemed that the governor was in his office and not to be interrupted; presumably working on communications with either the people who had kidnapped Branwen, or the people he had searching for her. He'd sent word to us that we were not to discuss anything about the case outside the mansion, and to go on as if everything were normal.

On that note, I asked Seren if we were still on for the Barmies show that night, to which she replied in the affirmative. The Barmies I'd found out were a musical group that was quite popular in New London. They'd been out of town for a few weeks performing in other cities; tonight was to be their first concert in New London in quite some time. I looked forward to hearing what music must be like in Gwerinatha and was getting almost as excited as Seren.

After dinner we headed over to the Broken Tower, which was a pub that had an adjoining outdoor café. The café had a nice sized stage where the Barmies were scheduled to perform. We got there early enough that we could get fairly close to the front. Seren's friends weren't far behind. Soon the band came out and was introduced to a crowd who apparently knew them well. Some in the crowd were even chanting the names of the band members: Trevor, Clive, Ian, and Nigel. Capriciously I began wondering if I were at an alternate reality Beatles concert. But the crowd wasn't nearly that lively. Still, they were far more energized than I had expected, which made me anticipate the music even more. The band was made up of the aforementioned quartet with what appeared to be a guitar, bass, mandolin, and fiddle. There was also a lute and a lyre on stage behind them, as well as some other instruments that I'd never seen before.

We listened to the first couple of songs. Though impressed, I wasn't as knocked out as I had thought I would be based on the crowd's reaction. Then with the third song I was totally enraptured. They had obviously been together a while as they were very tight. The melodies were catchy and surprisingly up-tempo for the laid-back society I had encountered that far. The closest thing I could compare them to from home was something like an acoustic version of Jethro Tull with a bit of old-school Irish folk music thrown in. Just as I was really starting to get into the band, I noticed that Seren had gone missing. I looked around through the crowd and didn't see her. Then I made my way to the edge of the crowd so that I could get a better look. She was across the street leaning on a gaslight pole, crying.

I ran over to her, knowing immediately that it was silly to ask her why she was crying. "Do you want to talk about it?" I asked quietly.

"That last song was one of Branwen's favorites," she responded. She turned to me with her wide eyes streaming. "I can't just sit around and act like everything's all right like my father wants. I can't just sit around and do nothing."

"I get the feeling you're father isn't telling us everything he knows," I suggested. "You were going to say something earlier when you said you knew he was upset, but never finished. Can you talk about it now?"

"That's part of what's really wearing on me, Robert. I was going to say that I think my father is more worried about his political standing than his own family."

"What?" I asked, unbelieving.

"It's not that he's not fond of us or anything. He's very strict and old fashioned; a lot of fathers are like that. But it's not that. I think sometimes we children get in the way of his career. You see, Branwen does a lot of things which she thinks are important, but that father is totally against."

"Like helping the animals in Serenity Forest?" I asked.

"How did you know about that?" she cried.

"I've spent a day and night with the wolves in Serenity Forest. I've seen Branwen's garden."

"Her garden!" Seren exclaimed. "She's told me about it so many times. She wanted me to go see it, but I was too afraid of father getting mad at me if he ever found out. I don't care what he thinks any more. I've got to know what's happened to Branwen!"

She reached out, threw her arms around me, and began crying even harder. Maybe it was the music in the background. Maybe it was an all-to-human reaction to having the arms of a grief-stricken young girl encircling you. Maybe it was simple masculine bravado. Almost of their own volition, my lips opened and these fateful words sprang forth:

"Don't worry Seren. I'll help you find your sister."

Chapter Nine
Back to the Woods

Once again I had jumped in deeper than I had ever intended. I didn't know the first thing about trying to rescue a victim of kidnapping. I didn't even know where to begin to look for her. Fortunately, Seren had an idea of where to start. Whenever I had mentioned Branwen's friends, who were apparently a group of wildlife defenders, Seren had gotten a bit distant. It turns out that those friends who could have helped Branwen most had been arrested. Seren said they were caught breaking into some shops and looting. This had seemed strange, since they had never done anything like that before. They all had clean records, except for a few civil-disobedience type offenses. In fact, in their defense they all had stated that they didn't seem to be in control of their own minds at the time of the break-ins. They couldn't explain it, but they were in fact caught red-handed. Seren believed that her father had something to do with it.

More of the story poured out of her. The governor was fed up with Branwen's activities in Serenity Forest, which made him look bad to the other Lords of Wisdom. Many of the Lords wanted the wolves and other dangerous animals in Serenity Forest eradicated in order to make hunting safer. More so than safety, Seren believe they needed to get rid of the main competition for their favorite prey, the deer. Hunters had all but wiped out the deer population in Hunoliaeth Forest to the north, and needed to expand their hunting to feed an ever-growing human population. Correspondingly, the groups that wanted to keep Serenity Forest free of hunters were at odds with those in power. More than once Branwen and her friends had embarrassed Governor Baylies. Seren wasn't sure how, but she was convinced that he'd brought the hammer down on them to put a stop to it. Branwen was visiting relatives in Baylies Crossing at the time and learned about the arrests too late to do anything about them. When she returned home, she became furious at her father, who sent her back to Baylies Crossing. But, as we knew, she never made it back there.

Seren and I left the concert and went over to the jailhouse to talk to Branwen's friends. He hoped to ask them where they thought Branwen could be. Somewhat surprisingly to me, we were granted an audience with them by the jailers, who seemed sympathetic when Seren explained what we wanted to do. We were told by a man named Reece, who was the oldest of the wildlife defenders, that Branwen did come to see them before she left New London. According to him, her plan had been to head out towards Baylies Crossing and, when she was far enough away, double back to the south towards Sibridale. Then from there she would take the southern route to Serenity Forest. It was decided that Seren and I would take off the next morning on that very route to see if we could find any clues left by Branwen. This would be a little easier said than done, however, as the governor was having his children watched very closely. Understandable, under the current circumstances.

My fourth evening in Gwerinatha was the most difficult night's sleep yet. I was accustomed to a full eight hours of sleep, and got nowhere near that with all the tossing and turning I was doing. I was more than a little anxious about the day ahead and, if I'd a clue as to what lay ahead of me, I would have slept even less. It didn't help any that I was no longer able to trust Governor Baylies after adding Seren's suspicions to my own.

After breakfast we had told everyone that we were going to head to the stables to go horseback riding. At Seren's request I dressed in my regular clothes, with the exception that I wore one of those billowy, white Gwerinathan shirts over my t-shirt and the purple sash she bought me going through my belt loops. The white shirt was meant to cover up my modern American clothing and nothing more, though I admit it was starting to grow on me a bit. Seren wore an outfit that was fairly typical for horseback riding, I was told. She had on long, tan riding pants, which was the first time I'd seen a girl wearing anything other than a dress since I'd left home. She also wore long, forest-green boots with more laces than I could count. Fancy laces seemed to be a popular aspect of Gwerinathan footwear.

We were driven to the stables by a couple of the governor's aides, who were supposed to go with us on our ride. Once at the stables, my uncomfortableness with the native "horses" flared up again. It wasn't just that they were so different, with the feathers and everything. It was the beaks that really unnerved me. They simply had a naturally menacing look to them. Coupled with their massive frames they really gave me the creeps. Seren told me to relax and assured me that my ride was particularly safe. Chosen for me was an older-looking grey steed with a black beak and matching feathers. Seren's mount was white with red feathers and had black and tan zebra-like markings all over it.

We decided to head south towards Sibridale, but we had no intention of continuing on in that direction. Our first order of business was to lose our chaperones. After about a half an hour or so we came upon a place to stop and water our steeds. It was there that we decided we had a good chance to make a break for it. The place was a little like a general store you'd see in small country towns. Since it was a common rest stop, it had ample troughs for the horses to drink from out in front. We got off our horses first and Seren asked the aides to hitch them up for us while we went in. While they were doing that Seren looked for a familiar face inside. She found a man named Dylan she knew as a sympathizer of the forest defenders and asked him for a favor. After a quick explanation of our intentions of helping to rescue Branwen, he eagerly obliged. We exited out of the back with a couple of Dylan's friends providing cover. Then we slipped around to the front, where we unhitched the horses and sent the aides' mounts off to the south towards Sibridale. Without missing a beat we mounted our horses and took off towards Serenity Forest. I looked back just before the little store disappeared from view to see we had not been followed. Dylan and his friends had obviously done their job of stalling our chaperones. When they came out they would find two sets of tracks – and no horses with which to follow either.

We were now on our own.

It wouldn't take us long to get to Serenity Forest on horseback. I was anxious to see my friends the wolves again, and hoped to hear some good news about their search for Branwen. My time in Gwerinatha had gone from an adventure to a vacation, and then back to an adventure again. Only this time I wasn't alone. I was sharing my adventure with Seren. As we rode along at a brisk pace I looked over at her and gave her a big smile, which she returned. Even though she was a bit younger than me, I could see us hanging out together back in my world. At least I could until I imagined what she would be like in a shopping mall. Then reality quickly kicked back in.

I had started to loosen up the billowy shirt, which was slowing me down in the wind. "Well, I guess I won't need this shirt to hide my identity any more. I thought since you didn't like it I could get rid of it," I said to Seren.

"I don't know," she pondered. "It's not as bad as the one my cousin gave you." She looked at me again with an odd look on her face. "Something about the way that "W" peeks out from underneath... it kind of twitches my dodgy."

"Okay. The shirt stays, I guess." I was too embarrassed to ask her just what she meant, but I understood it to be a compliment of sorts. I actually did like my new look that combined the styles of Gwerinatha with my own American tastes. But, of course, I was only fifteen, so my taste was questionable.

We rode on for an hour or so until we could just make out the outline of Serenity Forest in the distance. From this vantage point, I wasn't quite sure where the best place to enter would be to get us closest to the wolves' den. My best guess was that we were heading toward a part of the forest that was about halfway between its southern edge, where I had entered with Louie, and the Village of Broad Meadows, where I had spent the night with Seren's cousin. If that was the case, we should be just a little south of their den. I wasn't sure just how much I was going to recognize from the outside looking in, even though I had just been there a few days earlier. I looked over at Seren and she seemed nervous. I realized suddenly that I was going to have to be brave for both of us; even though if she hadn't been there, I'd have been too frightened to continue on myself! But with her needing me to be strong, I couldn't very well act afraid.

Then again, if she weren't along, I wouldn't have made this crazy trip in the first place.

"There's Serenity Forest up ahead, Seren," I said. "It shouldn't be long now."

We rode a bit further, where I found a spot that looked large enough for the horses to enter. After making our way through an opening in the trees, it wasn't long (much to my surprise) before I got my bearings enough to recognize which direction we should be headed. I even recognized enough of the forest to figure out that we were not at all far away from the den. Soon we came upon the very spot were I first met the odd-looking horses of Gwerinatha for the first time. It was the same place where Urien and his hunting party had parked their horses while they were searching for the green orb.

"This is it, Seren," I said. "We need to find a place to tie up the horses, because the rest of the trip will have to be on foot." We tied the horses up to a couple of very large trees and headed over to where I thought the den should be. I saw no sign of any wolves anywhere. I was a bit anxious at first, and then I remembered their rapid evacuation. Surely though, I had thought, they would be back by now. Then I saw the garden. Seren saw it too and was already making her way to it.

"It's wonderful!" she exclaimed. "Just as I imagined it would be."

She stood there crying for a minute, just staring at the flowers in Branwen's garden. I felt awkward. I didn't know if I should just leave her alone or run over and hug her. I certainly didn't know what to say. After a few more awkward seconds I walked slowly over to her and put my arm around her. She then turned to me and wept for a little while. I said nothing and, in a few moments, she pulled herself together, remembering why we came. Her resolve seemed to strengthen. "Okay. What's next, Robert?" she asked.

That was a good question, and one to which unfortunately I had no answer prepared. "I'm not sure." I said quietly. "I had thought the wolves would be here and could help us. Maybe they haven't come back from the other day yet."

"Well, no matter what happens from here on out, I'm glad to have come here," Seren said. "Branwen wanted me to see the wolves, but she knew I was scared. I think though I was more afraid of father's reaction than the wolves."

"Just the same, the wolves don't need a lot of people poking around," I said. "It's better for them and your people to let them be."

Just then there was a rustling in the fallen leaves and brush behind us. I quickly moved Seren behind me as I faced the direction of the noise.

"What is it?" she cried.

"I don't know yet; but stay back, just in case," I replied.

The rustling became louder and, from behind a large tree, I noticed some movement. It was small enough that I wasn't too alarmed... and then I hoped that it would be a familiar face which I was getting ready to encounter. Sure enough, little Louie popped his head out from under a bush.

"Louie!" I yelled. "Where is everyone?"

"Most everybody has scattered to our designated emergency hiding places," he answered.

"Then what are you doing back here?" I asked.

"You have to ask, Robert?" he said, puzzled by my question. "I've come to look for Branwen."

"What of the others who were searching?" I asked. "Has there been any word?"

"No," he answered. "No one has come back. I got worried and sneaked off. I know I shouldn't have, but I had to find out what happened to Branwen!"

As Louie and I were talking, Seren came forward. I began to introduce them but Louie interrupted. "You must be Seren," he said. "Branwen told us about all her sisters, but she mentioned you most often."

"Yes, I'm Seren. It's nice to meet you Louie," Seren replied. "I've heard some nice things about you from Branwen, and Robert spoke very highly of you during our ride out here."

"I hope he didn't embellish my adventures too much," Louie replied. "I have quite the reputation, of course, but it can be somewhat embarrassing."

This comment drew rolled eyes from me. Seren looked over at me with a big grin on her face. I had indeed told her a lot about Louie, and didn't fail to mention his braggadocio.

We decided that it would be safer for Louie to travel with us on our quest. Frankly, I needed somebody who knew the land. And, of course, I enjoyed the little fraud's company. Louie told us that there was no reason to search Serenity Forest any further. From the information he had gotten from the squirrels, Louie believed that Branwen had been taken to Dyffryn

Heul, a city on the other side of the Ochneidio Mountains in the southlands. The fact that some of his pack had gone in that direction already and hadn't been heard from was disconcerting, to say the least. There were any number of explanations as to why they may not have returned, not the least of which was that they may have been captured or injured. I didn't want to fall into my old habit of conjuring up needless doubts, however, so I shifted my thoughts to the task at hand. We needed to figure out what path to take to head towards the southlands. And keep our eyes and ears open for any clues along the way that might lead us either to the other wolves or Branwen.

From where we were now, we would need to head south past a couple of small villages towards the Didoriad River. At some point we'd have to cross the river and head around the foothills of the Ochneidio Mountains, before heading to Dyffryn Heul to see if the animals were right. I trusted their instincts and, frankly, I didn't really have any other options. I was in it this deep, so as far as I was concerned, there was no looking back now. I asked Seren if she knew of any place to cross the river, and she wasn't sure. Neither she nor Louie had been this far south from their respective homes. We would pretty much have to play the whole thing by ear. I couldn't help but remember that was how I got into this whole mess with Cameron in the first place: by not planning ahead at all. At least Seren and I had packed some food, and a few odds and ends. So I was far better off this time than the last. And I wasn't alone. I had companions. That feeling made all the difference in the world to me, especially since I wasn't in the world I knew in the first place.

Chapter Ten
Two-Mouths

I was worried that Louie might spook the horses or vice versa, so we walked carefully back to where we had tied them up. Louie walked very slowly around them, sniffing them cautiously as if he were trying to make up his mind about them. Seren's mount had been on many hunting trips and was familiar with the sights and smells of other animals. Mine seemed to be more nervous, but after a period of getting acquainted both horses seemed to calm down. Louie's nervousness slowly lessened, which was just as well, as we thought it might be a better idea if he rode with us rather than run alongside, since he wouldn't be nearly as fast as the horses. So with great trepidation he climbed up in front of Seren, where she could hold onto him as well as the horse's reins. At first this was awkward; but, after a good deal of wiggling and scrunching about, we finally got it to work. It looked rather silly but, later, it became almost natural for all of us.

After a quick look about to get our bearings, we began the journey south towards the tip of Serenity Forest. From there we could head further south towards the Didoriad River. I didn't want to head back too far to the east, as that would bring us back to Anhysbys Forest, and I still had very bad memories of that place despite my brave first night of survival. We also wanted to steer clear of a couple of villages between here and there that were independent of the government of Gwerinatha. Seren didn't know enough about them to be sure if they would be friendly or not, so we decided we'd be better safe than sorry.

As we made our way past the tip of Serenity Forest, I was startled by a rush of memories of my encounter with the nghuryll. We were just west of the path where the ghastly event took place. I couldn't help but wonder as we started our way through an area of large hedges if another nghuryll might not be lurking behind one of them, waiting to pounce on us. Since I didn't want to frighten Seren I made no mention of it.

Fortunately we made it through just fine, with the only casualty being my shattered nerves as I looked back and forth, expecting one of the horrible creatures to pounce on us at any time. Then we were through, with nothing but pleasant hills and meadows ahead of us for miles. Still, I kept an eye out for the strange plants Louie had warned me about earlier, but saw nothing out of the ordinary. Or at least what was ordinary for Gwerinatha.

Finally, as we were getting close to the river, we saw a strange sight. It was even odd even by Gwerinathan standards. Coming towards us from the west was a figure. At first I thought it might be a small man on a little horse but, as it got closer, I saw that it was not. The figure was an animal of sorts, but one like I'd certainly never seen before. It looked something like a horse but, unlike the ones we were riding, it had no beak. It did have a few dark feathers jutting from the back of its head in a sort of strange hairstyle. Its nose, however, was like that of an Earth equine. As it got closer it seemed to be more reminiscent of a mule. It had two bags lying over its back and, as it walked slowly towards us, it called out. "Hello there, travelers!"

"Hello," I replied.

"Would you mind if I inquired where you were headed?" it asked.

"I suppose not," I answered.

It walked directly up to us and, as it did so, we all noticed the single oddest thing about the creature: it had two mouths instead of one. There was a mouth on either side of its face and they were closed off from one another in the front. I could tell that it was the left mouth that had been addressing us. "What is your name?" I asked it.

"I am called Gefell," he answered with the left side. "Yes, I'm Gefell, all right," the right mouth added for emphases.

"Pardon my staring, Gefell," I said. "I've never seen an animal with one face but two separate mouths before."

"I get that a lot," Gefell's left mouth said. "It doesn't bother me so much any more" the right mouth added. "All the same, could you tell me where you're headed?" the left mouth asked again.

"We're headed south," I answered. "We're on a quest to rescue someone."

"Oh dear," his left mouth said. "You wouldn't be looking for Samuel, would you?" the right mouth added. "That's who I am looking for."

"Samuel?" I exclaimed. "Not the same Samuel who first brought the humans to Gwerinatha?"

"The same."

"How could he possibly still be alive?" I wondered aloud.

"He is very long lived I am told," his left mouth said. "He's very much alive," the right mouth added.

"Why are you searching for him?" I asked.

"I am looking for the mystery behind my origin," the right mouth said. "I need to know where I came from," the left mouth added. "And Samuel holds the key."

"Why would he hold the key?"

"Because," the left mouth said with an incredulous tone. "He knew the Originators of Gwerinatha."

"The Originators?" I questioned.

"Yes," his left mouth replied, "those who created this world. It's said that Samuel met with them many times before they departed and that they passed much of their wisdom on to him." His right mouth continued, "If there is anyone on Gwerinatha who would have a clue as to why I am the way I am, he would be the one."

"And you think you know where he is?" I asked.

"If I knew where he was I wouldn't still be looking for him, now would I?" the right mouth responded. "I think I may know where he *might* be," the left mouth added. "That is to say that where he may be is someplace I might not have looked yet: and, in that case, he could still be there."

"Are there two of you in there?" I asked.

"Why, whatever do you mean?" the left mouth said. "Two of what in where? I'm not sure I follow," the right mouth interjected.

Louie and Seren had been listening to the conversation with understandable curiosity. While I had been talking to Gefell they had been debating whether he was a mule or a donkey. However, neither of them being entirely sure what a mule or donkey was, since they'd never actually seen either creature. "Are you a donkey?" Louie blurted out.

"I am not a donkey!" Gefell's left side replied. "Don't insult me by calling me a donkey."

"I'm sorry. I had no idea that would be an insult," Louie apologized.

"Why on earth would that be an insult? After all, my mother was a donkey," Gefell's right mouth replied. "Or was it my father? I never can remember. I'm fairly sure one of my parents was a horse, though. The other had to be a donkey. Not that there's anything wrong with that."

"I have to admit you are the strangest looking creature I've encountered yet in Gwerinatha," I told him. "...and that's saying quite a lot."

"Well, you're the mostly strangely dressed creature I've ever encountered in Gwerinatha," his left mouth said.

"Surely your mother doesn't know you're out in public dressed like that," the right mouth added.

"I'm not from this world," I responded.

"Have you come from where the Orignators are?" the left mouth inquired.

"No," I replied. "I am a descendant of Samuel who has come from his world."

"Samuel's descendant!" the right mouth exclaimed.

"Surely then you'll want to seek out Samuel with me?" the left mouth inquired.

"That might not be a bad idea," I said.

After consulting with Seren and Louie, we all decided that it couldn't hurt to merge the two quests into one for the moment. We could easily separate later should the need arise. In the meantime Gefell would at the very least add to our number, which might help to frighten away any danger we came across.

Besides that, he would make for interesting company.

So now our party had increased. Seren and Louie rode on one horse while I rode another, closely followed by Gefell the Mule. At least that's how we all came to think of him. I was still wondering if he had two distinct personalities. There were times he'd have a complete conversation with us with both mouths and they would stay consistently on the same track. Other times, we'd be having a conversation and one of his mouths would interrupt, or even try to argue with him! It was futile to try and ask him about it. He didn't understand what was happening any more than the rest of us did. However, his bizarre personality made a good distraction. We were all worried about Branwen, and his unusual chatter kept us amused, if a little off center. We all felt less worried with Gefell around.

As it was, a little worry would have done us some good. It was soon apparent that we had no idea where we were going. The hours had raced by before we noticed that we were heading in the wrong direction. "Excuse me," Gefell's left mouth said, "but didn't you say that you were heading south?"

"Yes," I responded. "Why? Aren't we headed that way?"

"Well, we were when I first joined up with you," Gefell's left mouth said.

"But at some point," his right mouth continued, "it seems we began to tilt a good ways to the west."

"Now, it's not so much that I am not fond of the west, but..."

"But if we keep heading west, we'll end up in Anhysbys Forest!" I interrupted. Then, a bit idiotically I added. "Does anybody know which way south is?"

"Well if this is east," Gefell's left mouth said as he pointed in the direction he assumed to be east, "Then that would be south over there." He pointed in what would logically be south, considering that we were, in fact, headed east. After stifling a giggle at the odd appearance of a mule standing on three legs pointing with one of his hooves, I gathered myself together and led the party back towards the south. I hoped wouldn't be too far off the path we had started for Dyffryn Heul.

We were going to need to water our horses soon and I hoped we weren't too much further from the river. Sure enough, after several more minutes of heading in the correct direction, we could see the Didoriad River in the distance. We decided to take a break at a nice flat spot near the water. We had a pleasant rest, ate some of our rations, fed and watered the horses, and even shared a joke or two with Gefell. He really did make a difference in everyone's moods. Then the time came when we had to get back on the road again. The big question ahead of us now was where to cross the river.

Fortunately, Gefell knew of a bridge we could cross. He wasn't completely certain, but thought it to be just a few miles to the west of where we took our break. It turned out he was correct. In just a couple of hours we caught sight of a bridge. Had we not veered off course, we would have come right to it.

The bridge was just wide enough for a small carriage to cross, so we should have no problem with our little group. However, Gefell mumbled something under his breath about dreading to cross it. At first I couldn't see the problem. The bridge seemed safe enough. Then, as we got several yards away, I saw it. There was a small booth under the bridge just above the water.

"What's that under the bridge, Gefell?" I asked.

"It's a troll booth," his left mouth responded.

"A troll booth?" I mocked. "And just what, pray tell, is a troll booth?"

"A troll booth is where we need to pay money to get across the bridge safely," Gefell's left mouth replied.

"It's a scam set up for trolls who won't get real jobs," the right mouth added.

I looked over at Seren. "Is this something you think we should worry about?"

"I don't know. I've never heard of a troll booth before," she said.

"I don't see anybody in there," Louie added.

"Look, Gefell," I said, "I'm not sure if there's anybody in there or not."

"Oh, he's in there all right," Gefell's right mouth said.

"And he probably hears us right now," his left mouth added. "Trolls have very good hearing, you know."

"They've got hideously huge ears, of course," the right mouth blurted out.

"Well, why don't we just run across quickly?" I wondered. "I think we could all make it on these horses."

"You may do things differently on your world, but here we don't just break rules just because they're silly," Gefell's right mouth said.

"Besides, he's a lot faster than he looks. Trolls have been known to tear people's legs from their bodies," his left mouth countered.

"So how much is this troll booth going to cost us?" I asked.

"Depends on his mood, I reckon," said Gefell's right mouth.

"Hopefully it's been a good year for trolls in the south and he won't need to charge us too much," his left mouth said.

Much to my dismay it was decided we'd encounter the troll and pay him what he asked to get across a bridge we could just as easily run across. No one wanted to argue the point. So I went with the 'when in Rome' adage and led the party up to the booth.

Slowly I approached the small doorway. "Excuse me," I said. "Hello. Is anyone there?" As I turned to the others to tell them no one was there and that we should consider going over the bridge anyway, I heard a creaking. Without turning around I could tell by the frightened looks on their faces that the troll booth was opening up for business. I slowly turned my head to see a creature that was about three times larger than the doorway standing in from of me. To this day I have no idea how he got his giant frame through that door, but it helped to explain my friends' jaws hitting the ground.

The troll was roughly about seven feet tall and had a mane similar to that of a lion. His face was deep and full of crevices. He had the kind of a face that would scare itself if ever it saw its reflection. He wore a bright green tunic and tattered, burnt orange breeches. His arms were each twice the size of my legs. I could understand where Gefell's trepidation about running across without paying him came from. He moved with the speed of a sloth; which, unfortunately, allowed me plenty of time to stare at him.

"Grumble, mumble, forsooth," he started. "Who wishes to approach my booth?"

"Uh... hello," I said. "I'm Robert." I waved my arm behind me towards the others. "These are my friends. We'd like to cross the bridge."

"Grumble mumble, you don't say. And what's the price you expect to pay?" the troll replied.

This storybook crap was getting to be too much.

"You really work on those rhymes there don't you, troll?" I said, forgetting that my sarcasm had yet to be welcome anywhere in Gwerinatha.

"It's tradition, boy," the troll bellowed. "But, to be honest, I'm not in the mood today. Where on Gwerinatha did you get those shoes?"

My sneakers had completely distracted the troll. "Nowhere on Gwerinatha, as you thought," I said. "'was K-Mart where these shoes were bought!" The troll stared at me insensitively for a long, awkward moment.

"Sorry. I couldn't resist," I admitted sheepishly. "Look, can we cross the bridge or not? We've got places to go and people to save..."

"You haven't told me the price you expect to pay!" the troll grumbled.

"Well," I said thoughtfully, "Let's see: there are two of us humans, a wolf, a couple of horses, and a mule sort of. So, two bits apiece for the people, a quarter bit or so for the animals... how's about five bits for the lot of us?" I finally asked.

"So!" the troll screamed. "Five bits you expect to pay in order to cross my bridge today!"

"Yeah; that's what I said. I thought you were too tired to rhyme!"

"I prepared that one in advance," the troll informed us. "I always use it after my question gets answered."

"So are we crossing the bridge or not?" I scowled.

"Yes, yes, five bits is fine. I'm sorry," the troll said as he collected the five bits I acquired from Seren. "This whole troll booth thing is getting old. I should have listened to my inner voice and been a bouncer at that bar in New Berkshire. But no, mum said 'Man your father's troll booth. It's a decent living,' she said. 'No troll of mine is going to go gallivanting off to the city.' she said. 'Be a good troll and collect money from travelers...'"

The troll's voice tapered off as he squished himself back into the booth. We were on our way over the bridge.

Chapter Eleven
The Village of Idiots

Moments after crossing the bridge we noticed a village in the distance. I asked Seren if she knew which village it was. She was aware of a village under Gwerinathan rule just past the river before the foothills of the mountains. According to her the place was called the Village of Idiots.

Naturally, I did a double-take at the name.

The village wasn't made up entirely of actual idiots, she explained. Apparently, both the Lords of Wisdom and the House of Fates placed undesirables in this village to keep them out of mainstream society. They weren't criminals, exactly; more like social outcasts and misfits. It was an attempt by both groups to weed out their undesirables. She reassured me that, despite the village's odd name and its origins, it would be a perfectly safe place to spend the night. Of course, it was either that or we slept out in the open someplace.

So we made our way into the Village of Idiots to find a place to bed down. Not too far into the town we found an inn of sorts. It had a nice place to keep the horses and Gefell over to the side. Seren got a fairly good sized room to herself, and I passed Louie off as my pet dog so he could stay in a smaller room with me.

While signing into the rooms I spoke with the clerk and a villager who happened to be loitering on the premises.

"You actually call your town the Village of Idiots?" I asked the clerk.

"Well, we tossed about different ideas," he replied.

"Retardville seemed too offensive," the other villager said.

"Yes, and Intellectually-Challenged-Town wouldn't fit on the sign out front of city hall," the clerk added.

The villager who was hanging around stared at my shoes intently. You'd think I would have gotten used to this by then, but it was still a little unnerving.

"Those are some mighty fancy shoes you have there, mister," he said. "We can't have shoes like that here in our village."

"Oh, you can't, huh?" I said, hoping to end the conversation and get back to my room.

"No sir. We've got a village ordinance that only allows slip on shoes here," he replied. "There were too many accidents with all the fancy lace shoes: tripping and such." He went on, "But your laces aren't as fancy as those I've seen most everywhere else."

"You've been around a lot of other places?" I inquired, assuming they weren't allowed out and about much.

"Oh, yes," he said, his voice getting more excited. "I've been to New London, Sibridale, the village of Shallow Creek, the village of Hollow Creek, Dyffryn Heul..."

"Dyffryn Heul?" I interrupted. "My party is headed to Dyffryn Heul. Do you think you could direct us there?"

"I suppose so," his voice wavered. "But it would be easier to take you there."

"Now, Borb!" the clerk exclaimed.

"What's the problem?" Borb asked the clerk. "He needs a guide to Dyffryn Heul. I'll take them there and back in a day or so and then I'll return."

"Just be careful," the clerk cautioned.

"Is there a problem I should be aware of?" I asked the clerk.

"No, no," he slowly replied.

"I mean, he knows what he's talking about, right?" I asked. "He *can* get us to Dyffryn Heul, right?"

"Oh, yes. Borb can get you there," he replied.

The clerk gave a stern look to the man, as if there was something unspoken being said between them. Despite that, I asked Borb to meet us back there in the morning so we could make arrangements for him to guide us to Dyffryn Heul. I told him that we wanted to get started as early as possible. Borb's last name was Feargrinn. Like many of the people in the Village of Idiots, he had a different surname from the original six that had come in with Samuel. I was told by Seren that it had something to do with their wanting to separate themselves from the rest of the country, but I wasn't sure if she knew the answer or was just regurgitating some propaganda she'd learned.

Borb's vocation, it turned out, was that of a tree tuner. He was supposed to check on the musical trees I had run into much earlier and keep them from sounding too sour. How this was done I could only guess but, as I was told later, it was pretty much a sham profession that was quite common throughout the Village of Idiots. Most of their occupations were meant to placate them and keep them from interfering with the lives of everyone in the larger towns, rather than to produce something productive.

Just then another villager burst through the front door screaming. "It's Lyndon and Renny! They've had another falling out."

"What is it this time?" the clerk said with a tired look on his face.

"Renny," the excited villager responded. "He's on the ledge at the library and says he's going to jump." There was a pause and then he continued. "Well? Are you coming or not?"

"I suppose," the clerk said begrudgingly. "C'mon, Borb. Maybe you can help too."

Being naturally curious and, with a newfound interest in helping others, I thought I'd tag along to see if I could offer any assistance. I was quite surprised when we got to the library to see that it was only one story, as were pretty much all the buildings in the Village of Idiots. I looked around to see where the fuss was coming from and noticed a small crowd of people to one side of the library. As I edged my way around the few people in front of me I saw a man, presumably Renny, standing very cautiously on the window ledge. The ledge was no more than three feet off the ground. Behind him, in the library on the other side of the glass, was another man, presumably Lyndon, acting as if he could care less about the whole situation. As I didn't see anything to get upset about I decided to watch and listen some before commenting.

"Get down off the ledge Renny," one villager pleaded.

"No. I'm going to do it this time. I'm going to jump," Renny said.

"Don't do it!" another villager cried out. "It's not worth it!"

"I don't care," Renny replied. "I can't deal with it any longer. I'm going to end it all."

This scene continued on for several minutes, with Renny threatening to jump from the ledge and the onlookers trying to talk him down. Not wanting to offend anyone I held in my chuckles. It was all quite absurd. Finally, after a few more appeals from the crowd and a few oddball faces made by Lyndon inside the library, Renny took a desperate leap off the ledge. At once the entire crowd stepped out of the way as Renny landed on his feet, eyes closed and fists clenched as if he was expecting a terrifying collision. He opened his eyes slowly, first one then the other, only to see the crowd filing away shaking their heads. Inside the library Lyndon cackled up a storm.

I followed the clerk back toward the Inn. "What was *that* all about?" I asked, bemused.

"I assume Lyndon and Renny had another argument," he answered.

"He didn't really think he was going to get hurt jumping from that window, did he?"

"It's hard to say what he was thinking," the clerk responded. "Renny's a bit unstable. He may have thought he was going to die. But then he was probably just trying to get attention. That's why I was hesitant to go out at first. I hate encouraging him."

"This sort of thing happens often?"

"Oh, yes," he said. "They have been friends for over twenty-five years now and they tend to have arguments on an almost weekly basis. I don't even ask what they fight about any more. It's usually over something trivial. Renny misunderstands something Lyndon says or does and then overreacts – with occasionally humorous results." The clerk giggled, remembering some particular event. "Once, as I recall it, Renny agreed to meet Lyndon at his house for lunch. When he arrived Lyndon wasn't there. He'd been busy sorting out new gnomes in his garden and was so intent on his work that he'd lost track of the time. Renny waited outside Lyndon's house for forty-five minutes, just standing by the door. Lyndon eventually finished his work and, remembering the lunch date, went to the front door to see if Renny had arrived. Upon seeing Renny, Lyndon greeted him, but before he could apologize about the time Renny turned and walked away. They're always carrying on in this fashion."

Just then Borb caught up to us. "I found out what it was all about," he said. "Renny and Lyndon entered the library together. Renny pointed out a new book to Lyndon and was apparently very excited about it. Hours later, Lyndon pointed to the same book and asked Renny if he'd seen it. Renny got all out of sorts, shrieked 'I can't take it anymore!' and opened up the window and climbed out on to the ledge."

"Well, at least it's all over now," the clerk replied.

"I'm just happy no one got hurt," I chimed in mischievously.

"Nothing but Renny's pride," the clerk responded. "However, that was damaged beyond repair years ago. I think it's time we all retired for the evening before anything else ridiculous transpires."

With that, we all went our separate ways. I quietly reminded Borb of his promise to guide us to Dyffryn Heul in the morning and went off to bed. Louie was already asleep when I got back to the room and I assumed Seren also was asleep in her adjacent room. I got to sleep fairly quickly considering all that had happened that day. Still, I couldn't wait to leave that crazy village, and welcomed sleep like never before.

The next morning Seren and I went to breakfast at the inn's restaurant. We overheard some of the villagers complaining about the river flooding. It seemed that, once or twice a year, the river rises above flood level and causes enormous amounts of property damage. For many years the village's representatives had tried to get the government to build a dam with floodgates to help alleviate the problem. However, every time those involved tried to vote on the issue, someone somewhere stalls it in committee. I spoke with the unhappy villagers and quickly learned what was causing their continued dam-less-ness. In simple terms: politics. While both the House of Fates and the Lords of Wisdom agreed that there should be a dam on the river as a solution to the village's flood problem, neither wanted the other to get the credit for building it. So, anytime one group had the upper hand over the other, there would invariably be some sort of addition to the proposal that would cause it not to get voted on. Rather unsurprisingly, the people in the Village of Idiots were completely frustrated by the whole mess.

Seren had been listening to our conversation. Being the governor's daughter, she knew all too well the frustration of politics. Many times, she recalled, her father came home upset because of some stalling tactic that the House of Fates had used to keep him from passing some legislation. It hadn't dawned on her that the Lords of Wisdom did same sort of thing to keep the House of Fates from getting *its* way. But, after thinking about it for a while, it made perfect sense to her. As we got up to leave she leaned over to the villagers and in a very matter-of-fact manner said "You know you should probably just build your own damn dam."

The reaction from the villagers was mixed. Most were incredulous. But some were obviously giving it deep thought. As deep a thought as these particular villagers could muster, in any case. I thought her comment a bit rude: but let it slide, since her haughty upbringing was obviously to blame for her poor understanding of other cultures. She was just trying to help, after all, and I did not want to interfere with the process.

Well, it was that and the fact she was right.

By this time I figured Borb would be waiting and knew the others wanted to get going as well. So we got went to the inn to gather our things for the journey to Dyffryn Heul. Once we were ready to go, Borb Feargrinn came around the corner with a little bundle tied on a stick, like a hobo or a little boy running away from home. The bundle only added more humor to an already humorous image. Borb was slightly overweight and had a rather unruly reddish hair. His clothes didn't quite seem to fit: his shirt was too tight and his pants seemed a bit large. Though his outfit was mostly matched in all earth tones, his slip on shoes were a bright red, and thus were more noticeable even than mine.

"Is that your suitcase?" I asked, holding back a chuckle.

"It is what it is," Borb curtly replied. "And it's all I shall need."

"Okay," I said promptly dismissing any further conversation on the subject. "Are we all ready to go then?"

"I think so, Robert," Seren replied. "Louie is going to ride with me again I think, right, Louie?"

"If it's all the same to you," Louie answered. "I enjoyed riding with you Seren. It's almost like being with Branwen again."

"Aw, that's so sweet, Louie," she told him.

"You ready Gefell?" I asked.

"As ready as I think I can be," his right mouth answered."

"Why shouldn't I be ready?" his left mouth butted in. "I haven't even unpacked my bag. I've most certainly been ready."

"Okay, okay," I replied. "Let's mount up then. Where's *your* horse Borb?"

"I don't have a horse," he replied.

"Well, you can't very well go on foot with us on horseback," I said. I looked around, trying to find a solution. My gaze stopped at Gefell.

"What are you looking at me for?" his right mouth said. "Oh, I get it. Ride the mule, he won't mind. He is a pack animal, after all."

"Well, do you mind?" I asked.

"I suppose not," his left mouth answered.

"Why should I mind? I'm just a beast of burden. Why not burden me with that fat fellow?" his right mouth shot back.

"I'm not fat!" Borb blurted, obviously hurt. "I just have slightly larger than average size bones, is all. No need to panic. I'll not hurt your back."

True to his word, Borb managed to mount Gefell with no problems other than a few more sarcastic remarks from Gefell's right mouth. I'd almost forgotten what sarcasm was like, since I had heard very little of it in Gwerinatha. Gefell was unknowingly giving me a little taste of home, since that was the way most of my friends back there talked. I didn't know that I'd even missed it until then. I suppose my sense of humor was lost on most Gwerinathans, but I felt like I could be more like myself around this misfit crew. Even Borb who was new to the group seemed like someone I could get along with. It was nice to feel like part of a group again. I didn't feel like so much of a stranger anymore.

Soon we were well on our way out of the Village of Idiots and on towards Dyffryn Heul. Borb led the way on Gefell and we followed close behind. I hoped we'd be in Dyffryn Heul by lunch time, as breakfast didn't quite fill me up like I'd hoped. Unfortunately, hunger was about to become the least of my problems.

Chapter Twelve
A Change of Course

After a few hours of riding in the warm Gwerinathan sun and seemingly getting nowhere, I asked Borb how much longer before we'd see Dyffryn Heul. He explained that it would still be a while, as we were still a day or so away. I hadn't counted on the journey being quite that long. Frankly, I wondered how well our guide actually knew the route. Soon I was getting hungry and asked if there would be anyplace for us to stop and eat. Borb replied that the next stop was just minutes away. We'd been riding parallel to a large creek that flowed from the river, eventually leading into the Village of Hollow Creek. This village, Borb assured us, wasn't more than a day's ride from Dyffryn Heul and would give us ample opportunity for lunch.

We arrived in Hollow Creek less than an hour later, just as Borb had told us we would; and there were indeed many places to eat lunch. We hobbled the horses in a nice little glade near a brook that came off the creek. After some discussion, we decided that Borb and Louie would stay with Gefell and the horses, while Seren and I got everyone's food.

The marketplace in the village reminded me of a food court at a mall. We were able to pick and choose different items from each booth. We split up to cover more ground. I soon found myself with the same spinning head I always get at the grocery store in the cereal or ice cream aisle. Those were always the toughest two rows for me as far as decision making goes! I decided on some nice sandwiches for Seren and myself. I wasn't sure what kind of meat was in them, but the other folks that had just purchased the same sandwiches seemed eager to bite into them. I was sure Louie would appreciate them too; though naturally he wouldn't be as interested in the bread and garnishments. The next task was to get something to drink. The booth I got the sandwiches from didn't seem to have anything other than water to offer, so I decided to look elsewhere.

Before I took more than two steps Seren grabbed me from behind. She was clearly frightened.

"We've got to get out of here," she exclaimed in a hushed but urgent whisper. "They're looking for us!"

"Who's looking for us? What are you talking about?" I asked.

"The Southern Guard!" she whispered. "They're here. And they know about us. We've got to leave now."

"What's the Southern Guard?" I asked.

"Shh!" she said, as she motioned me back towards the glade. "We don't want to be noticed. Let's get back quickly but not like we're running. I'll explain on the way,"

Seren explained as we made our way back to the glade with what food we were able to get before the interruption. She'd been getting some chips from a booth when she overheard some men talking right next to her. They were Southern Guardsmen: basically the police force of the southern part of Gwerinatha, with *force* being the operative word. Being in the southern area they were also heavily influenced by the House of Fate. In fact, over the years the Southern Guard had become so closely tied into the House of Fate that they'd become a sort of a royal guard for the members of the government. They took it upon themselves to be judge, jury, and in some extreme cases even executioner for the House of Fate. They had no jurisdiction north of the Ochneidio Mountains and were rarely seen far from the City of Wellington, which is where the House of Fates ruled the south.

Seren had seen a uniformed member of the Southern Guard only once before. He had been imprisoned in New London. He was a renegade who took it upon himself to bully some villagers in the south just outside of House of Fate territory. He'd been extorting them much in the same way the mafia extorted shopkeepers in New York or Chicago back in the early 20th Century. The Gwerinathan Guard, who is basically the federal peacekeepers for the entire country, had brought the man to justice after an intense investigation. Seren was only a small child at the time, but she remembered seeing him in chains brought before the courts in New London. Mostly, she remembered the bright powder blue uniform the man wore. It had white trim with gold epaulets and long white boots and gloves: the same uniform worn by the two men standing next to her at the chip booth.

They'd received word from the north that the governor's second daughter, Seren, had vanished and that she was in the company of a strange boy. The governor hadn't wanted the news to get out for fear of another kidnapping, but somehow word had gotten to the men from the Southern Guard. Seren went on to say that they were quite interested in capturing her in hopes of a reward or, forgoing that, a ransom. The

Southern Guard had no love lost for anything having to do with the Lords of Wisdom and would jump at such a chance to make them suffer.

I was having a difficult time understanding the government of Gwerinatha as it was, before being introduced to the concept of the Southern Guard and how a group of one political party could get away with crimes against another. But such was the case in Gwerinatha, where the government had splintered into two distinctly different parts of the same whole. It wasn't anything like America during the Civil War; but, still, that is the closest comparison I can make. For the most part relations between the north and south were pretty civil; but later I would learn that there were factions on both sides were more than capable of violence.

We returned to the glade and explained the situation as best as we could to everyone. Lunch was more or less postponed until we could get safely away from the Southern Guard. We knew they were looking for a boy and a girl, so we hoped our larger numbers would be helpful in hiding our identities long enough for us to get out of the village. We had Borb lead us out, since he was the only one of our party who knew the area. Unfortunately, he didn't know it as well as he let on. He did indeed lead us to a safe hiding place, miles away from the village of Hollow Creek, where we were able to peacefully eat our lunch. But afterwards when we decided it safe to move on, it turned out that he was lost. I suppose I should say that *we* were lost, since the former had led inexorably to the later.

Borb knew of an unnamed village to the south of Dyffryn Heul where we thought we could stay until we figured out our next move. It sounded like a good idea to the rest of us. Even both of Gefell's mouths thought so. Unfortunately, being lost proved to be the monkey wrench in that plan. After some long consideration, Borb thought we should move towards the south in hopes that new scenery would jog his memory. So we set out from wherever it was we were to the south.

Before very long I began to get worried. I'd been glancing over at Borb from time to time to gauge whether he had any idea where we were or not. Not once in the hour since we'd had lunch did a confident look appear on his face. On the contrary, a couple of times he looked more perplexed than usual. Which was a saying something. Too much time had gone by for us to be going in a wrong direction, so I spoke up.

"Borb!" I said sternly, "Do you have any idea where we are?"

He hesitated for a moment and then looked up at the sky, turning his head first one way and then the other. "Well..." he said, hesitating even more, "it would seem that we are quite some distance from our last location. You know, the one that we left not more than two hours ago..."

"You don't know where we are," I said flatly.

"Of course he doesn't know where we are!" Gefell's left mouth said.

"I can't help being lost any more than the rest of us because I'm only going where he tells me to go," Gefell's right mouth added.

"I'm starting to get worried," Seren said.

"Don't worry!" little Louie piped up; "I'm here! I'll make sure nothing happens to us until we can find our way safely home."

"Calm down everybody," I said. "I've been paying close attention to our route and, if we don't spot anything familiar soon, I can at least get us back to where started from. Maybe Borb could get reoriented back there."

"Look up ahead," said Gefell's right mouth.

"I see it!" exclaimed Louie.

"What is it?" I asked. "What do you see?"

"It's a gateway!" said Gefell's left mouth.

"Well, of course it is," said Borb. "We'll just head towards the gateway. I know I'll be able to remember where to go next."

"You'd better be right," said Gefell's right mouth.

"Oh, no worries! I'm sure I'll be able to figure this out soon," Borb said. "Let's go."

We headed towards the gateway. As we approached it became clear that it was, indeed, a gateway; but there wasn't any fence to speak of. That is to say there was a bit of a fence on either side of the gate, but not enough to be of any practical use. The whole thing reminded me of the landscaping signs you see at the entrances of subdivisions back home. But this wasn't a sign because there were no words on it anywhere. The gate itself was roughly eight feet tall. I'd guess that the fence, what there was of it, was maybe 3 feet long on one side and maybe four and a half or so on the other side. It was made of dark red wood and the gate was metal, possibly brass. I wondered why it was so tall, being that it seemed to be a gateway to nowhere for no reason.

We all agreed there was no point in trying to open the gate when it was much easier to just walk around it. So we walked on around and went past. At first there wasn't much different in the area beyond the gate. But then I noticed that the ground felt a little strange. Instead of the hard terra firma that we had been walking on, the ground got softer and sort of spongy. It was like walking on fresh sod that had been rained on all day. That wasn't so strange in and of itself – especially by Gwerinathan standards – but then Seren noticed that the sky had changed color. Instead of the bright blue it had been, the sky was now more of a dark green color. I thought maybe a storm was coming, but I was told storms as I had described them were a very rare thing in Gwerinatha. Louie noticed a difference in the smell of the air. I hadn't been noticed it, but I would definitely trust a wolf's nose over my own. He said something was odd with the odor, something he couldn't explain.

Before we knew it we'd traveled a couple of miles past the gate. Then it dawned on me. "Borb?" I asked.

"Yes?" he replied.

"Which direction did you choose to go after we had lunch?"

"Why, south I believe," he answered.

"Un huh," I said curiously. "And are you sure that we did head south?"

"Of course," he said.

"Not to second guess you or anything, but under the circumstances I hope you don't mind if I get a second opinion," I said.

"We headed south," Gefell's right mouth said.

"Absolutely, south," Gefell's left mouth added.

"Not sure if that counts as a third opinion or not, but it seems we all agree," I commented.

"Just what are you getting at Robert?" Seren asked.

"Well, I don't know too much about your land, so I may just be whistling in the dark here but..."

"Oh my word!" Seren screamed. "The Unfinished Lands! You don't think that's where we are, do you?"

"Well, you guys would know better than me, but..."

"If these are the Unfinished Lands we find ourselves in..." Gefell's left mouth began.

"We are in some serious trouble," his right mouth finished.

"I think that's the first time I ever heard you finish one of your own sentences Gefell," I said, amused despite the circumstances.

"It's a rare thing. However, it does seem to happen..." his right mouth said.

"...when I am highly stressed," his left mouth finished.

"We can't stay here! It's death for us all!" Seren screamed.

"Now just calm down..." I said trying hopelessly to diffuse the situation.

"She's right, my boy," said Borb. "If these are indeed the Unfinished Lands we have no choice but to leave or d-d-die!"

"Okay, okay. Calm down," I said, trying to keep myself from freaking out along with them. "Maybe this place isn't as bad as you've heard. I mean, I spent the night all by myself in Anhysbys Forest and that place wasn't nearly as bad as I've been told."

"No. You don't understand," Seren told me. "This is not the same thing as a forest. We've got to get out of here! Now!" She screamed again.

"All right. Let's go: but I don't think screaming is going to help," I said.

"You're all forgetting that a brave wolf is with you," Louie exclaimed. "We'll be all right."

"Louie's right," I said, trying one last time to calm everyone. "We'll be fine. Let's just turn around and quietly go back the way we came. There's no need to panic."

As we turned around and headed back the way we came the phrase "famous last words" came to mind. I had never seen anyone so afraid in all my life, either in America or Gwerinatha. Whatever the Unfinished Lands were they had this group spooked like nobody's business. I just hoped I wouldn't have to experience any of the things that had given the Unfinished Lands their reputation.

Alas, that was not to be the case.

Chapter Thirteen
The Unfinished Lands

Even as we turned around the sky began to grow darker. I was certain that it wasn't that close to nightfall and assumed that a storm was coming. At first I didn't see any place that looked like a good refuge from a storm but, on further examination, a cave appeared to the east. I motioned for the party to make a run for the cave, but they resisted. At the time I assumed that they didn't have much experience with storms and simply didn't know what to expect. Later, I learned that they knew instinctively that, no matter how bad the storm may have been, it was preferable to staying even a moment longer in the Unfinished Lands. But moments later the skies really opened up. Rain fell in torrents such as had never been seen in the rest of Gwerinatha. Accompanying the rain were large, marble-sized hailstones that began to float in what was now inch high water, looking for all the world like a frosty breakfast cereal. At that point no one cared about the risks of hypothetical danger over the current, actual danger. I herded the group into the cave with minimal protests.

We shook off the excess water, hunkering together in the darkness while the rain and hail thundered outside. "We can't stay in here for long," Borb insisted.

"I don't think this storm will last too much longer," I said.

"There is no telling what kinds of dangers lurk in this cave," he continued.

"We'll stick together. If anything happens we'll face it as a group," I stated flatly.

"You worry too much Borb," Louie piped up. "I'm not worried."

Borb leaned over to Louie and, with a serious face I had never before seen him use before, very quietly said, "You should be."

"All right," I said, my patience beginning to wear thin, "That's enough of that kind of talk. You're starting to scare everybody."

"I believe we were all quite frightened even before we entered the cave Robert," Gefell's left mouth said.

"Being trapped in the Unfinished Lands is more than just frightful," his right mouth added.

"Who said anything about being trapped?" I wondered aloud. "We'll be on our way as soon as this storm moves out."

Minutes after, but long before we could completely dry out, the storm began to slack off. When it did, the sun started to shine through the clouds, illuminating our hiding place. There were strange markings on the cave wall, but it was still too dark to make them out. I thought they might be some kind of cave paintings like I had studied in school. I could see the floor of the cave a bit better in the dim light, however. It was a reddish color. It was actually changing as I stared at it from a brick red to a pinkish gray!

The next thing I knew the cave floor started vibrating and then what seemed to be cracks began appearing. The floor either gave way or turned into a large mass of overly large earthworms. It was impossible to say. They were wriggling almost in unison. Seren shrieked and the horses started getting restless. Unlike earthworms I was familiar with, these seemed to have large mouths with rows of tiny, piranha-like teeth. They started nibbling at our feet, which instantly drove the horses go berserk. Before we could stop them, they bolted from the cave.

"The horses!" screamed Seren. "We'll never get them back!"

"Don't worry!" I yelled back. "I'll get them!" I took off out of the cave as fast as I could go. Fortunately the rain had ended, but there was still a lot of standing water to splash through. I got close enough to Seren's mount to grab the pack that held most of our food. It slipped free and I fell to the ground with the pack in my hands. Stunned, I looked up to see both steeds running off at a speed too fast for any of us to catch.

I looked back to see everyone running out of the cave towards me. Seren helped me to my feet.

"Well, now what do we do?" asked Seren.

"Don't look at me," demanded Gefell's left mouth. "I'm not about to carry any more weight than Borb here."

"Well, we're all going to have to hoof it now," I said calmly as I wiped the mud from my clothes.

"At least you rescued our food," Seren said. "We're definitely going to need that."

"We're going to have to find our way out of here quickly," Borb reminded us.

"The fact that you, our guide, said that gives me no confidence, Borb. I said.

"He's right, though. The less time spent here talking the better," Seren said.

With that, we began walking at a brisk pace northwards in hopes of exiting the Unfinished Lands. Everything had changed since the rain had started. It wasn't just the worms in the cave. Everything all around us seemed odd. The trees themselves began moving. They were actually moving around on the ground.

"Look out!" Gefell's left mouth cried as a tree just brushed past us.

Then we were bouncing around, trying to avoid trees like rubber balls in a game of dodge ball. After some careful observations, it seemed that the trees were moving around us in circles. It was like they were planted on a disc of earth that rotated around a single point. Each tree had a different axis to move about and, once a pattern could be determined, they were easily avoided. But it was slow going.

Then Seren shrieked again. "The worms!" she cried out.

The worms had followed us from the cave. They were able to catch up to us during the distraction caused by the rotating trees. Then I saw a patch of ground ahead that had very few trees in it. I gestured for the party to head towards it.

"Quick everyone!" I yelled. "Get up in one of these trees! I doubt worms can climb. We'll wait them out!"

"That's great for you humans – but mules weren't made to climb!" exclaimed Gefell's right mouth.

"Wolves weren't either; but I'm going to try!" said Louie.

"Seren, help Louie into that tree over there!" I yelled pointing to a sturdy looking tree close by that I thought she could easily climb. "Borb and I will help Gefell."

Borb and I got into a very large tree that had branches low enough that we could lift Gefell up to safety. We stayed in the trees while they continued to rotate for what seemed like an hour before the worms finally disappeared back into the ground. Then we waited for several minutes after the worms had gone, and slowly got out of the trees as they began to slow down their rotation.

"I think I'm going to be sick," Seren said, trying to regain her balance on the ground.

"We should be all right now," I encouraged. "Hopefully that was the worst the Unfinished Lands has to offer. I've been through far worse back home."

"There are worse storms than this in America?" Seren asked quizzically.

"Oh yes," I responded. "We have earthquakes, tornadoes, electrical storms, ice storms, and even hurricanes. All of which make this little hailstorm look like picnic weather."

"Ice storms?" said Louie with his head cocked almost parallel to the ground.

"Yes, *ice* storms, Louie," I replied. "Blizzards too. Some parts of America get covered up with great amounts of snow all winter, even."

"Unbelievable. There's nothing like that in Gwerinatha," said Seren. "The only snow we have here is on top of the Ochneidio Mountains."

I'd only intended to calm the group down by letting them know that the storm hadn't frightened me, and thus shouldn't have frightened them. But instead I got them worked up even more. Now they were worried about me returning to what they perceived to be an inherently dangerous place. It was touching, but after a while I finally convinced them that the storms I mentioned don't all happen in the same place nor with a frequency that should cause them any alarm.

There was still reason enough for us to worry about getting back to safety, though. The Unfinished Lands were entirely unpredictable. None of my party knew the extent of the dangers that lurked there. I had already seen dangerous plant and animal life in other parts of Gwerinatha. Hearing that the creatures of the Lands were even more fearful made me more than a little nervous. I tried to hide it as best I could, considering that I had somehow fallen into the role of leader of our little group. I knew they were counting on me, so I had to put away my fears and focus on getting everyone to safety.

The challenge now was to try and figure out which direction to go in. The storm clouds had reformed, covering the soon-to-be-setting sun. To make matters worse, all the spinning around in trees had seriously disoriented us. We were *fairly* sure of the direction we had been going when the storm broke, but no one was certain. Still, there seemed little choice but to pick a direction and go in it.

Not far ahead we saw some tall grass. As we got closer it seemed it was in front of a bog.

"Does anybody remember passing a bog before?" I asked.

"I'm pretty sure we didn't," Borb said.

"What about you, Gefell?" I asked, trying not to seem as if I was ignoring Borb's limited contribution.

"There was no bog, that's for certain," his left mouth said. I kept looking at him, waiting for the right mouth to say something.

"I've nothing to add on that score," his right mouth chimed in.

Since we were all sure that we hadn't passed by the bog, we thought it best to backtrack a little. So we turned around and started heading back in the direction of the once-spinning trees.

While walking back, Louie noticed some bones along the trail. They were rather small and had been broken into pieces. Some of them still had bits of fur and ligaments attached.

"Hey, look here!" he exclaimed. "It doesn't smell very old."

"Eew!" Seren exclaimed. "That's grotty."

"What do you make of it, Louie?" I asked.

"Smells like rodent of some kind," he replied. "Rat maybe. Or young gopher."

The last response drew another exclamation from Seren, who by now really was getting ill as this new visual added to her motion sickness.

Apparently, something had been eating small animals and leaving remnants of them all over the place. This was disturbing enough as it was.

But it got worse when a bump in the ground began shaking and a softball-sized beetle came bursting through, grabbing one of the animal remnants. He just about had it in his mandibles when another, equally large beetle burst forth to fight him for it. We didn't stick around to see which one of them won the unsightly prize.

Just then we heard a disturbing sound. As if any sound in these parts was anything *but* disturbing. It was a guttural sort of noise that seemed almost like a growl... and it came from nearby.

"Did you hear something?" Borb asked nervously.

"Was that you growling, Louie?" Gefell's right mouth asked quietly.

"No," Louie calmly responded. "I'm not big enough to growl that loud yet."

We saw some movement from behind a tree in the direction of the noise. But before any of us could take more than a couple of steps backward, the creature that was responsible for that sound jumped out from behind the tree.

"Aaahhhh!" Seren screamed. And rightfully so.

I stood frozen in fear for a second at the sight of the horrible monster. Seren jumped behind me and I slowly moved my arm up to cover her. Borb leapt behind Gefell and began cowering.

The creature had a reptilian head like that of an alligator, but not as broad. Its body was clearly that of a short, stocky man. It wore ragged clothes that were torn in more places than they were whole. Despite the reptilian head, it had a shock of dark brown hair and its arms were almost as hair covered as an ape's. The thing had just finished making a meal of another rodent. Or so I guessed. There wasn't enough of the animal left to be sure exactly what it had been. Drool oozed from the side of its mouth as it began licking its lips with a large, grayish-purple tongue. It sized us up with its oversized yellow lizard eyes. I couldn't be sure what its intentions were, but none of the three hundred and fifty guesses I came up in a split second had pleasant endings.

I had no idea how quick the creature could move, but I knew instinctively that we had no choice but to run. I yelled for us to split up in hopes of confusing it. Seren and I ran off in one direction, Gefell and Borb went in another. Louie took off by himself. I didn't have the time to think about what a bad idea it was for the party to be separated; or how hard it would be for us to get back together later. I only knew the immediate danger outweighed the consequences of thinking too long about it.

That seemed to be an unfortunate reality of late.

Unfortunately, it turned out the strange beast could run pretty fast. It decided to follow the slowest prey, which turned out to be Borb and poor Gefell, who could hardly get up any steam with Borb's weight upon him. I am certain the thing would be on them in no time, so I told Seren to keep running while I went back to help. I hoped to create some sort of a diversion to keep the monster off their trail. I made as much noise as I could, screaming and yelping, whooping and hollering and throwing sticks and rocks into the air. And I succeeded, too... if you want to call it a success.

The thing stopped and turned its attention toward me. As I hoped, Borb and Gefell didn't even look back. They just kept running.

Unfortunately, the grisly creature shot back toward me with a speed I can only call miraculous. The only thing I could think of was to run in a zigzag fashion, as that was what you were supposed to when being chased by an alligator. Or so I read somewhere. Of course, this wasn't exactly an alligator and its legs weren't really that short. But I didn't really have much time for formulating a better strategy.

I dashed up a hill that had a large group of trees on its far side. The first tree was very large, with a very strong lower branch that I could easily climb up into. Hoping the thing following me couldn't climb, I jumped up and started scampering upward. Then I noticed that it was quite easy to get from the tree I was in to the next one. As if by instinct, I found myself swinging effortlessly from one branch to another until the next thing I knew I'd left the lizard thing far behind.

It was strange, but I wasn't complaining.

After finding my way back to the ground, I began circling back in an effort to discover where everyone else had gone. Before long, I heard Seren yelling my name. I'd ended up in front of the very direction she'd been running. She'd seen me in the trees and even yelled up to me, but in the excitement I hadn't heard her. She greeted me with a big hug but, before we could even catch our breaths, we both realized that the sun was almost below the horizon. We would have to find shelter quickly.

We both wanted to find the others but, knowing that everyone had gone off in separate directions, it wasn't going to be safe to search in the dark. As much as it pained us, we knew we'd have to start looking for them at daybreak. We hoped possibly that we might run into them while looking for shelter, but either way we needed to find some place to hide.

And quickly, for night had come to the Unfinished Lands.

Chapter Fourteen
Dark Night

We could barely make out anything around us in the rapidly darkening night. So we simply headed in the same direction Seren had been running. Our steps were slower and more cautious now. We stayed close to one another, mostly out of fear. Then we noticed some hills surrounding a hollow. Venturing into the hollow we found another cave. The Unfinished Lands seemed to be filled with them.

We approached this new cavern cautiously, not knowing what if anything might be lurking inside. Our previous experience with the worms forced us to careful. I went in first to make sure it was safe. The cave entrance was smooth. It was almost too smooth, like glass. Just in case I wasn't alone I didn't go too far inside. So I looked around, feeling the walls and floor for just a couple of yards or so inside of the entrance. I sensed nothing dangerous and called for Seren to follow me.

"Are you sure it's going to be safe in there?" she asked.

"I'm not sure of anything around here," I replied. "All I know is it certainly isn't safe out there. We won't go in too far in, just in case we need to run out."

"Well at least we'll be safe from rain," she said. "But I don't know how safe we'll be from anything else."

"Look," I told her, "we're going to have to tough it out tonight. We'll stay in here until morning. Then we'll go and look for the others. Before you know it we'll be back on the trail to Dyffryn Heul and looking for Branwen again."

I had tried to sound confident, but I'm afraid my voice shook a little. I couldn't hide my fear from Seren. But I think I did show just enough bravery to give her confidence in me. I was just as scared as her, of course, but I tried to hold it together.

I took out one of the blankets we had from the pack and laid it on the cave floor. I then sat down with my back to the cave wall and let Seren lie down on the blanket with her head on my lap. I could feel that she was very tense at first. I did what I could to get her to calm down so she could get some sleep.

"Why don't you tell me more about Branwen?" I asked her. "Would she have been comfortable exploring caves like this one?"

"I think so," Seren responded. "But I don't think she's done much cave exploring. At least I know she wouldn't be afraid. Branwen's never been afraid of anything."

"Then, wherever she is now, I imagine she's not afraid," I said.

"Probably not," Seren added. "She always seems to be in control of any situation, even when she isn't. Comes partly from being the oldest I suppose."

By having her focus on her sister, the subject of our quest, I distracted Seren from her fear of the unknown. I had an ulterior motive for picking that subject, however. I wanted to hear more about Branwen and what she was really like from the one person who knew her the best. She talked about Branwen in great detail and all the while I kept becoming more and more enamored with this incredibly special girl. Obviously, she wasn't perfect, and Seren did mention a few of her faults. But I paid little attention. To me, Branwen was simply amazing. I knew that I had to meet her. I knew that we had to save her. It wasn't just for Seren and her family. It wasn't just for Louie and the wolves. I knew it was selfish, but I wanted to know her for myself.

Eventually Seren grew tired of talking and nodded off. On the one hand I was glad, because I wanted for Seren got some sleep. On the other hand I wanted to hear more about the ever-fascinating Branwen, and wished she could have stayed awake and talked some more. I began to get sleepy myself, but I knew I needed to stay awake to protect Seren in case anything happened.

Still, I dozed off and on throughout the night. Every little noise kept me awake. I heard what I thought to be insects and small animals running about in front of the cave. I kept looking around for the Gwerinathan equivalent of bats, but saw none. So, rather typically, I began to worry. I fought it hard because, this time, it wasn't just me alone in a forest. I had Seren to think of as well. I knew I had to stay strong for her. I also didn't want to lose sight of finding our friends and getting back on to Dyffryn Heul so that we could locate Branwen.

Thinking of Branwen put my mind at ease. Though I was upset by the fact that she was in danger, I had a gut feeling that we'd find her. I can't really explain it in words. I just knew she'd be all right. I also secretly hoped that by rescuing her she'd be so grateful that she'd fall madly in love with me. I don't know what I was thinking there, but the mind of a fifteen-year-old boy is strange like that. As absurd as that thought seems to me now, it comforted me then and allowed me to drift off to a peaceful – albeit brief – sleep.

I awoke to a muffled sound in the distance. I wasn't sure what it was at first but, being that I was just barely awake enough to realize where I was and that I should be on guard for just about anything, I quickly decided to get up and have a look around. In so doing I had jostled Seren enough that she too woke up. Unfortunately, she was fairly groggy and, in the midst of discovering where she was, she began to panic.

"What is it? What's going on?" she screamed. "We've got to get out of here!"

"Calm down. I just woke up and I accidentally woke you too," I told her. "There's nothing wrong. Everything's all right." Just then the noise I had heard before became a bit louder and less muffled.

"What's that?" she screamed again. "Someone's there!" She got up and grabbed the blanket over her head and took off towards the cave entrance.

"Wait!" I screamed. But to no avail: she was off quicker than I could scream "Wait!" – which I just had. I ran off after her and, just as I got through the cave door, that odd feeling of slow motion came over me again. Just as it had when the nghuryll attacked me, it seemed as if time was slowing down. I felt an eerie sensation on my back, as if hot nails were being driven into it. I fell down to the ground and ended up with a mouthful of dirt. I tried to roll over to see what had knocked me to the ground, but I was pinned fast. Seren had turned back to see what the commotion was and, as she lifted the blanket from her head, I heard her scream again. It was bone chilling. Even as I lay there unmoving I remember thinking that she would be great in a horror film. Then I realized that I was actually in a position much like a victim in a horror film, and I wanted to scream myself. But all I could do was spit the last of the dirt out of my mouth.

Then I heard a voice shout out. "Halt!" it shouted. "What goes on here? Who is this then? My word! A human being! Beevel get off that man this instance. Dost thou not see he is a human like your ancestors?"

With that the tightness that held me to the ground released and I was allowed to roll over to at last see what had me pinned down. "Oh man!" I exclaimed. I looked up to see a creature with large thick birdlike feet, a short stocky body and the head of a man with large black eyes and a dull look on its face. "What in the world is that?" I yelled.

"Why, you are not but a lad. What are you doing in my cave?" the voice asked. The voice was that of a very old man. I thought I recognized it as the sound that had awoken me.

"Wh-wh-what is that?" I stuttered, staring straight at the strange monster.

"Why this is Beevel, son. He won't hurt you," the man replied. He then pointed up above the cave and looked towards Beevel. "Back, Beevel! Go on!" With that, the monster leapt up and hopped away over the side of the cave and out of our sight. His movements were like that of a small bird and, if it weren't for the eeriness of his human- like head, it could have been comical.

"And this girl," the man went on. "Who are you, dear?" he said, gesturing to Seren with an open hand. Seren said nothing as she was still shivering from the sight of Beevel with the blanket held up close to her face. "Now what were the two of you doing in my home uninvited?" He looked around, first at Seren, then at me and then at the blanket Seren was clutching. I could see the wheels turning in his head even as a scowl came across his face.

"What indeed hath the world of Gwerinatha come to whilst I was away?" he said. "I hope the two of you were not using my cave as a place to quench the burning fires of youth!"

He stared intently at me as if waiting for a response. "Uh..." was all I could muster. Seren, however seemed to be shaken out of her fear by the accusation which had apparently gone over my head. She threw down the blanket and walked toward us.

"That's not at all what was going on here!" she barked. "As a daughter of the governor of Gwerinatha, I demand an apology for your insult!"

"This is not at all an appropriate way for a young girl to speak to her elders," the man responded. "If an apology is due you, it will be received in proper fashion. Until then you may speak to me in a tone befitting better manners."

Seren looked down at her feet. I could tell she was embarrassed. Although she'd lived a privileged life, Seren wasn't particularly snooty and realized she had come off sounding impudent. I figured that something the man said had hit her close to home.

"Here now," the man said as he began to help me to my feet, "why don't the two of you join me for my morning meal and we can straighten everything out."

He didn't have to ask twice. Knowing anything could happen to us in this dangerous place, I was eager to get to anything remotely resembling shelter. I shook the dust and dirt from my clothes and reached back for Seren's hand. We walked behind the man and followed him deeper into the cave than we had been before. We were both amazed as we turned the corner to see what looked like a living room in a nice house with a doorway, in what appeared to be a dining room, and beyond that a kitchen. This strange old man had the inside of this cave, which was lit with many lamps, looking better than most homes I'd ever been in.

"What is it that has caused such surprised looks on your faces?" he asked. "Have you never seen a cave decorated so?"

"I should say not!" Seren replied. "This is absolutely amazing! Did you do all this yourself?"

"Mostly," he answered. "It took quite a long time; but then I've been away for so long, you see."

He started setting the table and began slicing up some fresh baked bread while he talked with us. "I don't have much I'm afraid," he told us.

"I'm used to eating alone. I suppose I've been in this cave for several decades or so now. I'm not at all sure. I really have lost track of the time."

"That's all right," I told him. "We have some food of our own left in that pack back by the cave door."

He began to spread some jam on the bread and passed it around. It had a very fruity aroma and tasted familiar. I had to think on it for a while but then it hit me. "Hewlifruit!" I yelled.

"Why, yes it is," the man replied. "'Tis rare I know; but I have found a supplier of sorts who swings by every now and then and drops some off for me. Do you like it?"

"Yes I do, thank you," I said.

"Now, perhaps while we all enjoy the bread and jam you may speak of what brings you to this most dangerous of places."

"Well, you see..." I said, trying to make sure my mouth was empty while talking, "Seren's sister has been kidnapped and we hope to find information in Dyffryn Heul that would help us locate her."

"And you I assume are Seren?" he said looking in her direction.

"Yes," she said. "And this is Robert Moore. He's from America."

At that the color, or what there was of it, drained from the old man's face. "America," he said, slowly and quietly. "America," he repeated even more slowly. "It can't be. How long could I have possibly been away from Gwerinatha?" He spoke so quietly that it seemed he wasn't even talking to us. He just kept looking around the room in a confused, distracted manner. Finally, put his face into his hands and began to cry. "Have you news of my son, Artemis?"

I felt my jaw drop as my eyes widened as far as they could. I was looking directly at my ancestor, Samuel More, who should have been dead for at least three centuries. "Samuel?" I stuttered.

"Yes. Yes. I am Samuel Goodwin More," he answered. "Are you related to my Artemis?"

"Man, have we got a lot to talk about!" I said.

Chapter Fifteen
Samuel's Lament

After the shock wore off that I was sitting across the table from one of my ancient ancestors, dozens of questions came pouring to my mind. I had no idea which to ask first. Fortunately, Seren started the ball rolling for me.

"How can you be Samuel More? You should have been dead for centuries!" she exclaimed.

"Well, I can assure you I am indeed Samuel More. I have been gifted, if one can call it a gift, with extraordinarily long life by the Originators," he answered.

"Who are the Originators?" I asked.

"The Originators are those who created the world of Gwerinatha," he replied. "They are supernatural beings that I used to think were fallen angels of our Lord. Now, I am not so sure," he said, his voice trailing off. "Nevertheless, they were beings of great power 'tis certain, and they revealed themselves to me some time after I brought my people here from England. They have long since left Gwerinatha for some unknown place."

"The stories are all true then," I said.

"I cannot be sure of which stories you have heard, but certainly that which I have told you is true. And it is more than apparent I am real and in the flesh before your very eyes," he said. "Now, about you, young sir, the look on your face when I asked about your relation to Artemis should have answered my question, however I must hear it with mine own ears. Are you... my relation?"

"To the best of my knowledge sir," I began, "I am your descendant of many, many generations."

Samuel sat back in his chair and a look of wonder came over his face. "This is a most wondrous thing indeed. How in the world did you arrive in Gwerinatha?" he asked.

"Well, that seems like a long story itself," I answered. "But I guess really I came across your letters to Artemis and your key and the next thing you know, here I am."

"My letters..." Samuel wondered. "If I can but make an attempt to remember that long ago... I believe I had written them in Welsh: the language of my late wife. I wrote in Welsh as to limit the number of people who could read it, should it get misplaced. Can you read Welsh, then?"

"Not really," I said. "But a friend of mine and I figured it out with the help of some old book of my father's."

"This is most amazing. Most amazing indeed," Samuel said. "A very descendant of my Artemis." A tear came rolling from his eye and he reached out to hug me. I was reluctant at first. It's not every day you get hugged by a nearly four hundred year old man. But, understanding who he was, I returned his embrace.

We spoke for several minutes thereafter, with Samuel and I asking many questions of one another. Seren remained as patient as she could in such a situation. She was as floored by the whole thing as I. We learned that when the Originators arrived, the whole world was uninhabitable. They molded it into someplace where the beings they created could live safely. However, they never completely tamed the whole land, and left one area unfinished before departing. That area was, of course, where we found ourselves: the Unfinished Lands.

We also learned that when the English first arrived in Gwerinatha there was peace. Samuel's followers were God-fearing pilgrims who practiced Amish-like tolerance and passivity. However, after many generations had passed, certain problems arose. The seven deadly sins, as Samuel referred to them, began to creep into their society. Those first few who had been guilty of such violent crimes as rape, murder, and the like were cursed by the Originators and turned into hideous creatures. These creatures were banished from the village of the English settlers and, unfortunately, intermingled with some of the other denizens of the new world. Their offspring became just as hideous and cruel. They became known as the Abominable Ones. Some of the creatures that descended from the unnatural pairings them wound up living in the Unfinished Lands.

The nghuryll I'd encountered on my trip to Serenity Forest was one of these creatures. I could never be as certain as Samuel which ones were actually descended from the Abominable Ones and which were piecemeal, unfinished creations of the Originators. Not that it really mattered. They were all pretty gruesome as far as I was concerned. Samuel, having lived in self-imposed exile in the Unfinished Lands, had gotten so lonely that he befriended and named some of them. Beevel – the big-headed, bird-footed man – was one such creature.

I described the lizard-like creature that had chased us in his direction, causing our group to be split apart. Samuel recognized who I was talking about instantly. "Oh yes," he said, "I call that one Nestor. He is dangerous to some extent, but his bark is far worse than his bite. I hope he didn't put too much of a fright into you and your traveling companions."

"Actually, he scared us half to death," Seren replied.

"He was pretty frightening," I added. "You don't think there's much of a chance he harmed our friends, do you?"

"Well, now, that all depends," he said.

"Depends on what?"

"How recently he has eaten," Samuel answered bluntly. "His interest in your friends is explicitly culinary, I'm afraid. But if he's eaten recently, then he may do nothing more than keep them around until he gets hungry again."

"Hopefully they all got away," Seren replied with a shudder.

"Yes," Samuel said. "All the same, I think that you should find them quickly."

"Indeed," I responded with complete honestly. "But I have a quick question for you first: why did you decide to become a hermit here in the Unfinished Lands?"

"That certainly was a quick question! But I'm afraid the answer won't be nearly as quick," he replied. "Still, I'll attempt to explain myself while we're looking for your friends. As I'm sure you know by now, this isn't a safe place for them."

We helped Samuel clean his table. He then began gathering things together. He got out an old cloak and wrapped it around himself. Then he reached for his walking stick and we headed out the door. Although Samuel had been granted unusually long life, he had still quite aged. Though he didn't look three hundred and sixty-four years of age, which is what I had guessed him correctly to be, he was still very old and needed a walking stick to help him get around. The strange thing about this stick, however, was the opossum in a fearful pose that decorated the end of it.

"Is that what I think it is?" I asked him.

"Well, if you're thinking it is a petrified opossum, then yes: it is what you think it is," he answered. "I have few living friends as it is, you know, and will befriend almost anything these days."

We were only a few steps away from the mouth of the cave when Samuel paused and looked around. He motioned for us to stay back as he checked the area. When he felt it was safe, he motioned us forward and we began walking back in the direction Seren and I had come from the previous night.

"You can never be too safe in these parts," he said. "Stay close to me and I will make sure we get around safely."

"Now, about my question..." I said.

"Yes, yes: I know. I promised to *attempt* to answer, did I not?" he said. "Well, I'm unsure as to how satisfactory it will be to you. It isn't always satisfactory to me. Not long ago... or maybe it was long ago, now that I think about it... hmm... either way, some deal of time in the past after the Orignators had long since vanished, my followers had grown restless. They'd grown significantly in number over the years: something in the water, perhaps. They began to spread out, populating portions of the land which had before been unfamiliar to us. After a few more generations had passed, they had even spread out beyond the mountains. With everyone dispersed so far apart I began to feel as though I was losing touch with them. A more sinful human nature began to make its presence known. Since the Orignators were long gone, no one feared being punished with monstrosity anymore. I do not wish to give you the wrong impression. These were good people. They were nothing like the people in Noah's day, for example, but things started to get a little out of hand. Oh, I tried being firm and setting rules and everything: but the people didn't want to hear it. They'd begun to feel less and less like I was their leader; and more and more as if I were simply an annoying parent. After a few more generations like this passed I began to believe my gift of long life from the Originators to be a curse."

"Finally, I could take no more. Since the people would no longer listen to me and had no more desire for me to be their leader, I decided to leave them. One day I just got out of bed in the morning, packed a few things, and began walking. I didn't stop until I reached the cave you found me in. And I have been there ever since."

"That's an amazing story," Seren said. "But you are highly revered in our history lessons. They say nothing of the people wanting you gone."

"That would make sense," he responded. "Those who write the history do not always wish to include everything. Especially the things that would make them appear less than perfectly righteous."

"I don't think you understand," Seren said. "You're legendary. I'm not sure how much of what is written about you is true, but because you led everyone to Gwerinatha, you are considered our father figure."

"You're a regular George Washington," I said.

"George who?" Samuel replied.

"Oh, right," I said feeling dumb once more. "How about Moses?"

"Oh no," Samuel said, sounding exasperated. "I could not possibly be compared to such a great man. True, there may be some similarities in our lives, but I cannot be held in that high a regard."

"You are a very humble man," I said. "You should hear the way these people talk about you. I've only been among them for several days and I've already heard a great deal about you and your mission to bring your people here. They have a great deal of respect for what you built."

"That is indeed hard to believe, considering the way I was treated just before I left," he said sadly. "I would have thought that few had noticed I had even gone."

"I can't speak for them," said Seren, "but I'm certain the people of Gwerinatha today would welcome you back with open arms." She paused for a moment. "...well, most of them anyway."

"What do you mean by 'most of them' Seren?" he asked.

"Gwerinathans are divided today. Did you have the House of Fates or the Lords of Wisdom running things in your day?"

"No. I have not heard of these groups," he responded.

"Well, they have the government in quite a mess, I'm afraid," Seren said. "These two groups spend so much time fighting with each other that things aren't getting done for the people."

I smiled when I heard Seren say that. It seemed she had been paying attention after all. She'd been thinking about government from a new perspective since leaving the Village of Idiots. I could sense a strong desire within her to change things. I also sensed a new hope in her after she learned who Samuel was.

"I pray my actions have not led to the trouble of which you now speak," Samuel said.

"But it's all right now, don't you see?" she begged. "You can come back and make things right again."

"I don't know, Seren," he replied. "It's been such a long time."

"I think she's right Samuel," I butted in. "Maybe we ran into your cave for a reason. Maybe there's a bigger purpose for you than just helping us find our friends."

"I shall dwell on this in due time, but for now we must concentrate on that very task," he said. "And, if I am not mistaken, we may be getting somewhere. Look!" Samuel pointed ahead to a large bag in some tall grass close to the bog we had been by earlier. I reached down to pick it up.

"It's Gefell's pack," I announced. "And there are claw marks on it like it was ripped off of him or something."

Samuel looked around and then down at the ground again. "From the looks of things..." he began, and then paused.

"Nestor may be planning his next meal."

Chapter Sixteen
No Free Lunch

Samuel tried to calm us down. But the thought of our friends being eaten by that horrible creature nearly made us hysterical. The fact that Samuel had given him a name, no matter how mild mannered it sounded, hadn't changed the fact that he was a bloodthirsty creature that seemed to take pleasure in tormenting his prey.

We had to know if Nestor had taken our friends. We had to know if there was any chance of saving them. So we devised a plan: Samuel would distract Nestor while Seren and I would go into his home to see what we could find.

We marched through the bog for several yards. At times the water was deep enough to reach my waist. The place stunk of wet fur and the stench of rotting flesh was heavy in the air. Nestor was obviously a slob; that much was clear. As we got close to his cave, Seren and I split off from Samuel. We went around to the back of the cave and hid behind a clump of trees. Samuel waited for a few minutes until he knew we were settled into place. Then we heard him approach the cave entrance.

"Nestor!" Samuel cried out. "Nestor! Are you there?" Only silence answered his call. I began to worry that we were too late and that he may have gone to sleep after making a meal of our friends. Then the silence was

broken by an all too familiar growling noise. Nestor crawled out of his cave
and began sauntering towards Samuel like some confused Sleestak from
that old *Land of the Lost* TV show. "Nestor!" Samuel called again. "Nestor,
have you seen any strangers in the Unfinished Lands recently?" The thing
just kept walking towards Samuel, not making a sound other than an
occasional gurgle. Samuel threw his hand up in the air. This was the signal
for us to make our way towards the cave.

"Nestor, are you listening to me?" Samuel asked. The thing paused. "I
know you can't speak as humans do. But I know you can understand me. If
you've seen any strangers come by here recently you have to let me know. It
is very important, Nestor." Nestor started to move towards Samuel again;
slowly at first, but then he began to speed up. Apparently this was part of
Samuel's plan. He knew that Nestor would try to go after him, as he'd done
countless times before. He'd also been able to get away from him on every
other occasion and knew this would be no different. Since Samuel was
obviously alive, we had confidence that he knew what he was doing. We
began our part in the plot.

Seren and I crept around the trees towards the front of the cave. We
sneaked in, then immediately covered our noses. "Eew! What a wretched
stench!" Seren exclaimed.

"You think it's bad over there!" a voice cried out from further back in
the cave.

"Gefell? Is that you?" I cried out.

"Yes. It's me," Gefell said.

I had begun to recognize the subtle differences in the voices of Gefell's
left and right mouths. It was the left mouth speaking.

"Gefell, Seren and I are here to rescue you," I said as we made our way
through the muck, growing closer to the sound of his voice.

"Be careful," Gefell's right mouth said. "There's no telling what's on the
floor around here. It's absolutely disgusting."

"Where are the others?" I asked.

"Borb is here beside me," he replied. "We don't know what happened to
Louie."

Seren and I found Gefell and Borb tied together in a corner near some
small jars and bottles of what appeared to be spices of some sort. "He's
going to eat us!" Gefell's right mouth said.

"I don't want to be eaten," Gefell's left mouth added.

"It's all right," I said. "We're going to get you out of here. What's wrong
with Borb? Has he been hurt?" Borb's head was hung over as if he may have
been unconscious.

"He fainted is all," Gefell's left mouth replied.

"He's a right coward that one," chimed in Gefell's right mouth. "If it
weren't for him slowing me down we wouldn't be in this mess."

"Now, now. That's no way to be," Seren told him. "We're going to get out
of here, all of us."

Seren and I managed to untie Borb and Gefell. Then we shook Borb
violently in hopes of waking him. "Borb! Wake up!" I shouted. "We have to
get out of here. We need you to wake up." He started moaning and
shuffling. Then I dropped him to the floor with a thud. The jolt startled him
awake.

"Wha-what's happening?" he cried out. "Are we away from that awful creature?"

"Not yet I'm afraid," I responded. "We have to get out of here as quickly as possible."

We gathered ourselves together and headed back towards the cave entrance. Gefell was able to walk on his own, but Borb was nearly limp. He needed to lean on both Seren and me to make it out of the cave.

Once outside we looked around for any sign of Samuel. We couldn't see him anywhere. "Let's head back towards Samuel's cave like he told us," Seren suggested.

"Not so fast," I told her. "We have to make sure the coast is clear." Strangely, I had always wanted to say that even though I never actually wanted to *need* to say it. Nevertheless, it seemed a more than appropriate cliché at the time. We looked around a few times and saw no sign of trouble. We then got ourselves up out of the bog and headed towards Samuel's cave.

We reached it a short time later. There was no one around. We went in and waited, hoping for the best.

"How long should we wait?" Seren asked.

"As long as it takes," I said.

"We can't stay too long," she said. "We still have to find Louie and get ourselves out of the Unfinished Lands."

"I realize the urgency of our situation," I told her. "However, Samuel is our best chance to get out of here safely. So we're going to have to give him a few more minutes at the very least."

We waited for several more agonizingly slow minutes. Despite the comfortable surroundings of Samuel's posh pad we were on pins and needles, wondering if he were able to shake Nestor yet one more time. One more time is all he needed and then we'd be on our way. But nothing happened. I'm sure we waited there for less than an hour. But at the time it seemed as entire decades were gradually oozing away. I couldn't get the thought out of my mind that Samuel's luck had run out and that his long life had finally come to an abrupt and painful end. I looked over at Seren and could tell by her face that similar thoughts were crossing her mind. Gefell and Borb were just glad to be out of Nestor's horrible cave and in some place safe and clean. During our wait we explained to them how we met Samuel and how fortunate we all were to have him aid us.

Soon my nerves got the better of me and I couldn't sit still anymore. Fidgeting was doing me no good, so I got up and went to look outside. "No!" Seren cried out. "Stay in here with us."

"It's all right," I replied. "I just want to see if he's out here."

"A watched kettle never boils, my boy," Gefell's left mouth said.

"He's right you know," Borb said.

"Of course I'm right," Gefell's right mouth responded. "And I'll tell you one more thing..."

"Shh!" I yelled back. "I think hear something."

I had indeed heard something: a rustling of leaves and creaking branches off in the distance. Someone was coming. Was it Samuel? Or was it Nestor? Since I wasn't sure, I decided to run back into the cave to be safe. "Someone's coming!" I cried out.

"Get back in here!" Seren yelled.

I ran back into the dining room where everyone else was now hiding. Borb and Gefell were underneath the table and Seren was behind a chair. I got behind the chair alongside her. We sat motionless and silent, waiting breathlessly for the approaching party. Hoping it was Samuel. I heard the sound come into the cave and knew that whoever was there was getting closer. Seren reached out and grabbed my hand tightly. I could hear the noise getting closer, but couldn't see anything. Had it been Samuel surely he would have called out to us by now. I couldn't see anything over the table, but the noise of footfalls was getting closer and closer. I glanced over to see Borb's eyes shut tightly and Gefell's teeth were clenched. Both sets of them. Just as the anticipation was getting to me, there was a loud thud on the table and a familiar face was staring right at mine.

The visitor was Louie!

He stood on the table with that ever-inquisitive look on his muzzle. "What's everybody doing in here?" he asked.

"Louie!" I screamed. "Where have you been?"

"My question first," he demanded.

"We're waiting for Samuel," I told him. "He lives in this cave. He helped us get Borb and Gefell free from the lizard creature."

"Oh," he responded flatly, as if he were disappointed. "I was working on a plan to free them myself. I just hadn't had a chance to get it started, is all."

"You knew where we were and didn't come for us?" Borb asked indignantly.

"I told you," Louie said. "I was working on a plan. It would have been no use barging in and getting myself eaten as well as you."

"You're a predator," Gefell's left mouth said.

"He wouldn't have eaten you," Gefell's right mouth added.

"I can't be sure of that," Louie responded. "Did you see his teeth? He looks like he would eat just about anything to me."

"Never mind all that," I snapped. "Now that we're all back together we need to get out of the Unfinished Lands. But not without Samuel."

"I don't know how much longer we can wait on him," Seren said. "He said himself not to wait too long if he didn't come back."

"I don't want to leave without him," I said. "It's not safe."

"How safe is it to stay here?" Seren asked.

"I don't know," Gefell's right mouth said. "It looks pretty safe to me."

"Yes," Borb butted in. "I think I could get quite used to staying in a nice place like this. It's nicer than anything I've got back home."

"Until you remember this cave is in the Unfinished Lands," I reminded.

"Yes... that does put a bit of perspective on it, doesn't it?" Gefell's left mouth responded.

We waited a few more minutes. Then we decided that we had to get moving again. We weren't sure how much more daylight we'd have since this place was so unpredictable. We could encounter another freak storm at any moment, not to mention that any number of bizarre creatures that could be waiting around a bush or tree to ambush us. So we all walked slowly out of the dining area and back towards the foyer of the cave.

Before we could get a foot out of the cave, however, I heard a screech like that of a pterodactyl from a B movie. A figure leapt down from above the entrance of the cave, screaming and advancing toward us. Everyone ran back further into the cave as the creature continued slowly towards us. I recognized the odd walk as the birdlike hop of Beevel.

"Beevel?" I called out. A loud screech was his only reply. Then he started hopping up and down in place in front of me. I couldn't tell if he was being friendly or menacing. Before I could decide what to do next, a voice rang out, "Beevel! Get back here!"

"Samuel? Is that you?" I asked.

Samuel appeared just behind Beevel, looking a little ragged but otherwise none the worse for wear. "Yes, yes. It's me lad," he responded. "Is everyone all right then?"

"Yes," I answered. "We're all here and accounted for now."

"That's fine, fine," Samuel said enthusiastically. "I took Nestor on our usual wild goose chase and ran into Beevel here. He scared Nestor off into a briar patch not far away. He'll be quite angry when he gets home to see his meal has disappeared."

After introductions were made we all knew the next step was getting out of the Unfinished Lands. Besides the dangers presented there, we were running out of time to find any of the clues about Branwen's disappearance that may wait for us in Dyffryn Heul.

"I suppose you will be requiring my assistance to leave the Unfinished Lands and get you back on the trail of Dyffryn Heul," Samuel said.

"Well, yes," I replied. "We had thought that you would be excited about getting back to Gwerinatha."

"You have to come back, Samuel," Seren pleaded.

"I will certainly help you fine people... and animals out of this most dangerous of places," he said. "But after that I make no promises. I'm still unsure about my future and whether it brings me back to my people."

"Well, that's all we can ask for at present," I said. "We'd better get going."

Chapter Seventeen
In the Hands of Fate

Before starting out, we had a quick bite to eat in Samuel's cave. In spite of all that had transpired it still was a very nice place; we felt so comfortable there it was hard to leave. It was then that Gefell spoke with Samuel about his personal quest. "I am overjoyed indeed to find that the legends of your still being alive are true!" said Gefell's left mouth.

"I have been searching for you for quite some time you know," his right mouth added.

"And now you have found me, strange creature," Samuel responded. "You have something to ask me I presume?"

"Indeed I have," Gefell's right mouth said.

"I am on a quest for my origins," his right mouth continued. "And I was hoping you could explain to me why I have been made so strangely, with two mouths instead of one."

"Why do you think I could answer such a question?" Samuel asked.

"Because of the Orignators," Gefell's left mouth responded.

"It's been said that you were with them when they left," Gefell's right mouth said. "Surely they told you many things."

"They did impart to me much knowledge of this strange world they created," Samuel replied. "I had no idea that anyone would still remember the Originators in this day and age, let alone my meetings with them. I know a great deal of what they left behind here... but I am not sure what knowledge I could share with you that would aid you in your quest."

Gefell looked dejected. Samuel leaned over and put his arm around him. "You are a mule, are you not?" he asked.

"Yes. I am," Gefell's right mouth answered.

"To the best of my knowledge I am indeed a mule," Gefell's left mouth added.

"And it is very clear that you can talk," Samuel said pointing to Gefell's chest.

"That's more than clear," I chimed in. Gefell gave me a rude look.

"I don't know why that would be in question," Gefell's left mouth said to Samuel.

"You see Gefell," Samuel began, "the animals of Gwerinatha for the most part were gifted with speech. Most of the creatures who were begotten from the Abominable Ones and the unfortunate cursed members of my party cannot speak. They only mumble, growl, or moan, among other assorted noises I shan't discuss in mixed company." He nodded in the direction of Seren then continued, "What this tells me is that your origins, though still murky, are not those of the Abominable Ones and not likely to be of their ilk."

"This tells me little," Gefell's right mouth complained.

"I can't make sense of it," Gefell's left mouth added.

"Well, at this juncture, all I can do is guess from only the clues I see before me," Samuel said.

"Well, have a bash then!" an impatient Borb blurted out.

"All right," Samuel said, leaning back in his chair. "My estimation is that your parents were a Gwerinathan horse and a donkey that had descended from one of the ones I brought over myself centuries ago."

"That's all well and good, but why has he got the two mouths?" Borb asked.

"Well... it may be nothing more than a defect resulting from the odd coupling of animals from different worlds," Samuel guessed.

"Then I wasn't brought about by some Orignator curse!" Gefell's left mouth proclaimed.

"Probably not," Samuel said. Then he smiled and rubbed Gefell's head as if he were a family pet. Gefell seemed slightly amused by this and, from that point on, began to take on a different, more gracious attitude. He announced that he would continue with us on our quest, as we had become such good friends to him.

We headed out of the Unfinished Lands once and for all, with Samuel guiding the way. He knew exactly where to go, even though he hadn't been out and about for what could have been several decades. We managed our way east, far past the strange looking fence that first marked our entry into the Unfinished Lands. We could see the woods to the east that was called Adwyth Forest. Not more than an hour after that, we came upon the unnamed village Borb had tried to lead us to before our unfortunate detour.

I say unfortunate, but then on rethinking the matter, it was fortunate indeed that we'd found Samuel on our detour and, with him, a new hope.

The village was just outside the territory of the House of Fates. Like many of the unnamed villages outside the defined boundaries of government, this one had an air of secrecy and aloofness to it. The people were a little distrustful of strangers. However, with Samuel taking the lead, we were able to get some information from the otherwise uncommunicative locals. Though they did not recognize him as the 'father of their country,' he still had an unmistakable charm about him. Beyond that, of course, he commanded the respect of the elderly that one must give to someone over three centuries of age.

Samuel had been talking to some people near a large house while the rest of us waited in a less conspicuous location not far away in a small wood. "Over here, Robert," Samuel said as he motioned me forward. "I've learned there is a man in this village who knows quite a bit about the goings on of the Southern Guard."

"That's great," I replied. "Do you think he can lead us to where they've taken Branwen?"

"Not as yet," Samuel said. "He isn't here at the moment I'm afraid."

"Well, where is he?" I asked. "Can we go to him?"

"Quite possibly," Samuel answered. "He is only a half day's ride to the north at the Hot Springs. But like most of the people around here, he doesn't take kindly to strangers."

"Maybe you should go alone then?" I suggested.

"I shall take Gefell with me. He can act as if he is my beast of burden. I'll pretend to be a peddler. That way I can blend in with those taking rest at the springs," he said.

"Be careful, Samuel," I told him.

With that, Samuel took Gefell up to the hot springs at the foot of the Ochneidio Mountains. The rest of us headed northeast towards Dyffryn Heul with the intention of meeting Samuel at a point halfway between. We found a secluded spot where we set up camp for the evening. It was nice to be able to go to sleep and not worry about being eaten by a hideous creature or swallowed up by the very ground itself. There were just a few miles between us and the Unfinished Lands, but to our relaxed minds it seemed like an entire world away.

When we woke up the next morning Samuel had returned with interesting news. He had already a pot of tea brewing over our campfire and began pouring us each a cup. "Here you are, Robert," he said as he handed me the tea. "Let me tell you what I have learned. If my source is accurate, the Southern Guard does indeed have Branwen in Dyffryn Heul. But we must be very careful. Besides the obvious danger that the Guard presents with their physical prowess and weapons, they are also in possession of the blue orb."

"The blue orb!" gasped Seren, almost choking on her tea.

"Let me see if I can remember this," I said. "That's the one that gives people powers over emotion, right?"

"How did you know that?" Samuel asked.

"I have done *some* homework while here in Gwerinatha," I said. "But just the same, I'm not exactly sure what the extent of its powers really are."

"What it can do," began Samuel "is to give one the power to alter another's emotional state. For instance, a person who is calm can be made agitated or excited, while a person who is very sad can be made joyful. It allows the user to feel the emotions of another: and to take them away. He who wields the blue orb's power can even remove another's pain, or at least reduce it to the point where he doesn't feel it anymore."

"Sounds like a powerful drug," I commented.

"It's quite powerful indeed," Samuel replied. "The source of my information was a former member of the Southern Guard. He has long ago left them and has no love lost for the Lords of Wisdom, I can tell you that. But he did know some of the Guards' current members and, more importantly, knows their hideaways and other secrets."

"How did you get all that information from him?" Seren asked.

"Let's just say that anyone can feel comfortable talking to a harmless old man," Samuel responded.

"He can be quite persuasive," Gefell's left mouth said.

"I almost thought he was going to take us to the Southern Guard himself," Gefell's right mouth added.

"Now that's an exaggeration Gefell, to be sure," Samuel said.

"Nevertheless, what's our next move Samuel?" I asked, happily giving over any and all authority I had held as leader of the group.

"We need to get to Dyffryn Heul without the Southern Guard noticing us first," he answered. "Then we'll have to come up with a plan to separate Branwen from her kidnappers without her getting too upset."

"Too upset?" asked a confused Seren. "Whatever do you mean? Why should she be upset that we are trying to rescue her?

"We have to be prepared for the possibility that they've already used the power of the blue orb on her," Samuel said. "I believe whichever guard is bathing in the blue orb's light is using its power on Branwen to keep her in check. It may be that she will not want to leave."

"The fiends!" Seren exclaimed.

"Settle down Seren," I said. "We don't know for sure what happened."

"No," said Samuel. "But I needed to warn you just in case, so you may be on your guard should any of us begin to act strangely. If an odd change in emotion comes over anyone – or even yourself – make a note immediately so we can pinpoint just who is powered by the orb."

"What good would that do?" Borb asked.

"I can counteract any of the powers of one bathed in an orb's light with a device I have from the Originators. I need first to find which person that is before I can use it."

"Fantastic!" Borb exclaimed.

"I wondered what kind of odd things you had packed there in your bag, Samuel," I said.

"Yes," he responded dryly. "Your politeness in not asking about them is noted. The less some people know about certain powerful items the Originators created, the better."

Over the next hour or so we came up with the plan we'd use to rescue Branwen. The idea looked fairly simple on paper: divide and conquer. Executing the plan, however, would not be nearly as simple.

Chapter Eighteen
Saving Branwen

Dyffryn Heul was considered a sort of resort town. Or, at the very least, it was a popular vacation area. It benefited from its picturesque location nestled in between the foothills of the Ochneidio Mountains and the Hot Springs. Affluent people from the north enjoyed spending several days each year in Dyffryn Heul. It really was a great place to visit: serene and hospitable, like I always imagined a French Alpine town would be. Under less stressful circumstances I would have liked to spend some time there. Truth was, it was a destination we'd looked forward to reaching for quite some time. Of course we were looking forward to it for different reasons than most folks who journeyed there. We had finally gotten confirmation that this was indeed where the Southern Guard had Branwen. We were finally going to rescue her.

Or so we hoped.

I was getting quite nervous. I don't know which had my nerves more in a tangle: the prospect of confronting the Guard with their guns, swords, and blue orb powers, or meeting Branwen. You might think that in the excitement of finding Samuel, running from the lizard-man, and saving our friends that I would have forgotten my crush on Branwen. It was always in the back of my mind and, now that we were getting so close to her, it started taking center stage again. But I knew I had to focus, though, in order to carry out Samuel's plan.

Samuel had discovered that the Southern Guard was keeping Branwen in a cabin not far from the Hot Springs. This was quite clever, really; no one would think to look in such a well-traveled place. But it also supported the theory that she was under the spell of the blue orb, since she would be more likely to cry out for help in such a crowded place.

Samuel's plan involved us splitting into groups. Since Seren and I were already being searched for together, we joined separate groups. She went with Samuel and Gefell. The ancient man would once again pose as a peddler, with Seren going along as his assistant. Louie, Borb, and I made up the other group. Our job was to create a diversion to attract the Southern Guard after Samuel determined which cabin Branwen was in. Samuel and Gefell would yank her out, and we'd all make tracks out of Dyffryn Heul.

After getting Branwen away from the Guard's watchful eyes, the next step would be the most dangerous. Were we to take the most direct route back to the northlands the Southern Guard would surely overtake us. There were two other options. We could go over the mountains, which would be nearly impossible with our mixed group that included animals, children, and an old man. The other option was to go back the way we had come through the Unfinished Lands. We knew they would never think to take that route. The plan was hinged on Samuel's knowledge of the Unfinished Lands and the fact that he had friends there who could help us. We felt we'd be safe with him as a guide as long as we all stuck together. Then we'd head north to the Village of Idiots where we could send for help from New London.

We didn't know exactly which cabin that Branwen was in. We did know that it was one of twelve or so in the northwest corner of the town. So Samuel, Seren, and Gefell began there, knocking on each door and trying to look around for clues in each cabin. Borb, Louie, and I waited just out of earshot downhill. "You know I don't see how people are going to believe I am your pet dog," Louie told me.

"Just keep your ears folded down and stay close to my heels," I replied. "Everything will be fine."

"I still don't think this is very believable," Louie said.

"It will be," I hissed, "if you quit talking!"

Louie bit his lip and tried to play the dutiful pet dog role. He knew it was the best idea we had and, if it meant rescuing Branwen, he would've done anything. "We only have to have you pass for my dog for a couple of minutes," I assured him. "As soon as we get Branwen, we're out of here."

We waited patiently as Samuel and the others checked door-to-door, trying to find Branwen. In the meantime we had to act as if we were just tourists on holiday. Finally, after what seemed like hours of trying to look like we were having a good time just loitering about, we got the signal from Samuel. He waved his possum-topped walking stick in the air and circled it about. This was our cue to put our part of the plan into action. Borb grabbed Louie from near to my feet and ran off. I started after him screaming.

"He's got my dog! Hey you! Come back here with my dog!"

Since wolves can't bark, Louie started yelling "Arf! Arf!" just as I had taught him.

At first it seemed as if we weren't attracting any attention at all. A few onlookers sort of turned their heads and then acted as if they didn't see us. I chased after Borb, who was jogging rather than running. I had to "run" slowly so that I didn't overtake him too quickly. We finally got the attention of a couple of tourists who started after Borb. Then we doubled back towards the cabins with the tourists following closely behind. By this time they were yelling along with me. It was more than enough to stir a couple of the Southern Guard from their cabins. They came running out to see what all the ruckus was about. Since Borb wasn't going that fast, they easily caught up with him. The guardsmen grabbed him by the arms just as I caught up to them.

"Here now, what's this all about?" asked one of the guardsmen.

"This man," I huffed and puffed, "took my dog," I told them.

"Is this true, sir?" the guard asked Borb.

"No, sir," Borb replied. "The dog is mine. I took it back from this robber." Borb pointed at me and, when he did so, Louie playfully nipped him on the arm. Borb shrieked as if he'd been bitten for real and dropped Louie to the ground. Louie then took off with Borb, the two guards, and me in hot pursuit. Louie ran around in a zigzag pattern, partly to keep the guards busy, but also so I could keep an eye out for Samuel's signal that Branwen was safe.

Unfortunately that signal never came. After running about for a couple more minutes I saw Samuel out of the corner of my eye. Instead of the 'all's well' signal I had anticipated, he was waving both arms back and forth, meaning that we were to abort the mission. Something had gone wrong. I caught Louie's eye. He realized by my facial expression that something was amiss and allowed me to scoop him up. Then I took off towards the wooded area that was designated as the rendezvous point, leaving Borb behind. The plan was that he'd stay behind and make up an explanation to the Guardsmen that would keep them from coming after me. It was one of those 'seemed good at the time' kind of ideas that came back to haunt us.

Several minutes later Samuel showed up with Seren and Gefell. He explained how things had gone wrong. "We found the cabin she was in all right," Samuel began, "but when I went back in after the guards came out to follow you, we couldn't convince her to leave. It's clear she is indeed under the spell of the blue orb."

"How do we get her out then?" I asked.

"The effects of the blue orb should not last very long when she's away from the cad who is affecting her," Samuel replied.

"But you have a device to counteract the effect, don't you?" I asked.

"It will cancel out the blue orb-acquired abilities of the person who has the power," Samuel said.

"We've got to get them away from her!" Seren exclaimed. "It's the only way we can get her to come home with us."

"It seems that a plan B is required," Gefell's left mouth commented.

"Does anyone have a plan B?" Gefell's right mouth asked.

"Where is Borb?" Samuel asked.

"He's back in the town," I said. "Hopefully he's keeping the Guard away from us."

"No," Samuel said.

"What do you mean 'no?'" I asked.

"We *need* them to come after us so I can rid them of their blue orb abilities," Samuel replied. He reached into his pack and pulled out an odd looking device. "This is the orb nullifier," he calmly said while handing it to me. "I need you to run back into town with Louie and use this on one of the Guardsmen."

"Oh, that sounds easy!" I said, forgetting once again that Gwerinathans weren't used to sarcasm.

"Good," Samuel replied. "I'm glad you think that. You are the likely choice, since you can continue the subterfuge of Louie running away from you."

"Aw, you mean I have to go back to pinning my ears down again?" Louie said in a whiny voice.

Seren reached down to him and put her hand under his chin. "It's for Branwen, Louie," she said. "We've all got to do our part to help her."

Louie sat up straight and proud. "For Branwen I'll endure any humiliation!" he proclaimed. "It's more than worth it. C'mon Robert, let's go!"

"Hold on a minute, Louie," I said. "Samuel's got to show me how to use this thing."

Samuel took a moment to give me a brief introduction to the nullifier and how it worked. It looked like an aerosol can with a reflector on the top similar to the ones doctors used to wear on headbands. All I needed to do was to point it at the Guard and flip a switch in the back. His blue orb powers would instantly vanish. After that, our hope was that within minutes Branwen would come to her senses and be more than willing to take off with us.

Louie took off and I went after him. Borb was in one of the cabins that the Guardsmen were using and came rushing out when he saw Louie again. The guards came running out after him. "That's my dog!" Borb screamed. "And there's the man who tried to steal him," he said, pointing at me as I came running towards them.

"Hold on!" I yelled. "I told you. That man tried to steal my dog." Just then Louie began running around the feet of the guards. But I didn't know which of them had bathed in the blue orb's light. I could only hope to get them both with one shot. Then, as they were hopping around trying to get Louie off their feet, one of them reached for his gun.

"I don't care whose mongrel this is!" he shouted. "I'm going to kill it if it bites either of us." He then pointed the gun towards Louie, who froze in his tracks. But I had gotten close enough to make my move.

"Hold it right there, both of you!" I screamed. "Nobody's getting killed here."

As I said that they both turned to me, and when they did I pulled out the nullifier, which I had behind my back. "Say 'cheese!'" I said, and pointed it at both of them as I flipped the switch. A large white light went off, blinding them. It was at least three times as bright as any flashbulb I had ever seen before, maybe more. Fortunately, Samuel had warned me about it, and I closed my eyes, as did Louie. Unfortunately, the flash blinded Borb; there had been no time to warn him. I quickly grabbed the gun from the guard closest to me while he was rubbing his eyes. He swung around at me but still couldn't see. The other one was grimacing as if he were concentrating on something very hard. I assumed from his expression that he was the one who had the blue orb power and was trying to use them.

"Sorry, bub!" I said as I took his gun away as well. "No blue orb powers for you today."

"What? How could you know?" he asked.

"That's going to be my little secret," I said as I handed the other gun to Borb. "Can you handle a gun, Borb?"

"Shouldn't you have asked me that before you gave it to me?" he asked.

"Well, just point it at them for now," I said. "Louie, what do you say we get these guys back into their cabin?"

"Let's do it!" Louie exclaimed. He then began growling at their feet as I marched them at gunpoint back into the cabin where they had been holding Branwen.

With Borb followed slowly behind, we forced them to march with their hands over their heads back into the cabin. Strangely, the act of holding a gun on a person was more frightening to me than any of the encounters I had with monstrous creatures. I'm not sure if it was the fear of having to use it, or just the horrible feeling that I could end someone's life with just a twitch of my finger. Either way, I knew I couldn't back down. If I flinched and let these guys get back in control, Branwen wouldn't have a chance for freedom and I'd probably be killed.

We found some rope and quickly tied them up. Then I looked around but didn't see any sign of Branwen. After making sure the Guards were secure, I went into the backroom and found Branwen cowering behind a bed.

"Don't be afraid," I said. "I've come to rescue you."

"From what?" she asked. "This is the second time someone's tried to rescue me and I don't understand what's going on!"

Just then Samuel and Seren came rushing in. "Branwen! Are you all right?" Seren asked.

"Of course I'm all right," Branwen replied. "I told you I was all right when you and the old man came by earlier. And I don't want to leave."

"We have to leave, Branwen," Seren told her. "We have to get you back to safety."

"I'm safe here," Branwen exclaimed. "Why am I the only one who can see that? Or at least I was safe until this strangely dressed boy came in here with a gun."

"Boy?" I repeated hurtfully. "I told you I'm not going to hurt you." With that said, I laid the gun down and showed her my empty hands.

Samuel gathered us together and spoke hurriedly. "We must get out of here immediately," he said. "Even though they thought it safe enough to only have two guards on duty due to the blue orb, there will be more guards on us very quickly. We haven't much time!"

Seren grabbed Branwen's left arm and I her right. We pulled her out of the cabin to a waiting Gefell and Borb. This was not at all how I had pictured my initial meeting with Branwen. I was more worried about the lousy first impression than I was about the guards coming after us! Between Seren and Louie's efforts, Branwen finally calmed down enough to get her out of town without making too big of a fuss. By the time we'd gotten an hour away, the effects of the blue orb had worn off completely and Branwen was in her right mind once again. Additionally, we were far enough away by then that we could walk slowly without fear of being followed. Seren, Branwen, and I found ourselves walking behind the others.

"I'm sorry for the way I acted back there," Branwen apologized.

"That's okay," I told her. "You couldn't help it."

"I'm usually a lot more together than that," she said.

"So I've been told," I replied. She looked at me puzzled. "Seren's told me a lot about you."

Branwen looked over at Seren and smiled. "I bet she did. All good, I hope."

"You've got an incredible sister here," I said. "She really thinks the world of you."

"Here now!" Seren interjected. "Let's not get too fussy. I don't want her to go on thinking she's hung the moon or something."

Branwen laughed and leaned over to put her arm around Seren who was smiling warmly. It was good to see them both happy after all they'd been through. I walked ahead to let them have a moment alone, knowing things were about to get hairy again once we returned to the Unfinished Lands.

Chapter Nineteen
Back in the Frying Pan

It was great having Branwen free from the kidnappers. But, from her perspective, things weren't so rosy. She'd been rescued all right; but now she found herself heading to that most fearful of places, the Unfinished Lands. Having never been to that forbidding place and not knowing who Samuel was or why she should trust him, she was quite shocked when we told her where we were going. Fortunately, we had more than enough time to explain to her who Samuel was and why we thought it safer to go with him than to risk recapture by a reinforced Southern Guard.

We headed directly for Samuel's cave once we got to the Unfinished Lands. There we could rest and relax until we set out for the Village of Idiots. We arrived without incident and began making ourselves at home: which for Borb, Gefell, and Louie meant eating and sleeping, and for Branwen and Seren meant sisterly catching up. Not feeling particularly hungry or sleepy – and not wanting to interrupt the girls – I went in search of my ancestor. I found Samuel clearing out his cupboards. Not that there much in them to begin with, but he was emptying them completely.

"Samuel, why are you giving us all your food?" I asked. "You won't have anything for yourself when you return."

"I'm not coming back here, Robert," he answered. "At least not for a while. I've made my decision. I'm returning to Gwerinatha to make an attempt at rectifying all the damage my absence has caused."

"That's fantastic!" Seren yelled as she reached over and gave Samuel a hug. "Gwerinatha will welcome you back with open arms. You'll see."

"I hope you're right young lady," Samuel replied. "But like me or not, I am coming back."

We all sat around the table eating the last of his provisions. I watched the old man carefully. Samuel commanded attention whenever he spoke. He had a sort of masculine *presence* that you hear about but seldom encounter. Just the sound of his voice was captivating, even if you didn't know he was over three centuries old. It had a deep rich sound that reminded me of John Huston. It made me wonder if I would sound like that some day – *be* like that some day. A great man. It was something to think about.

Despite this, I still found myself still in the throes of a schoolboy crush, staring at Branwen while Samuel conversed. My attention wandered. She was incredibly beautiful. Even the travel's dirt on her cheeks and the wind-disheveled state of her hair made her seem more attractive, not less. I could have spent hours simply looking at her.

Perhaps I did.

Finally, Samuel snapped me out of it. I'm not sure what he said – in all honesty I hadn't been paying attention – but he got my attention when the conversation turned more serious.

"You see, I had a crisis of faith," he continued. "It started not long after I met with the Originators. I was amazed as everyone else when they revealed that they made this world. I'm still not sure how it was done. As I said earlier, I thought at first they might be fallen angels of our Lord, attempting to create a world in the same manner that he crafted our own. But later I began to think they could be... well, that they could have been from another world, like ours but very different. I began to question whether they were immortal beings at all."

"And this cascaded into waves of doubt about my own faith."

I was tempted to interrupt. I wanted to ask him for more details about his religious beliefs. All I knew for sure was that, like the pilgrims who came to America, he wanted to have the freedom to express his beliefs in his own way. What those beliefs were exactly I was less certain of.

Samuel went on while all eyes were directly on him.

"For a long time after the Originators left I thought that perhaps I'd been wrong all along. This may have been what caused me to be able to leave my people. Were I stronger in my faith, I would have surely stayed and worked with them through their time of rebellion. I had done it before with my own son, Artemis. I knew I could work with them, but something within me had closed off. That small, still voice had been quieted by doubt. That is what allowed me to become a hermit here in this horrifying place. I think I may have been testing God, or possibly even punishing myself."

Samuel's voice trailed off. "But that's all over now," he said, with his voice rising again to its normal base rumble. "I am going back to Gwerinatha and, come what may, I'll work to make things better. And I have you to thank for it, Robert."

"Me?" I said with shock in my voice. "What'd I do?"

"You said something that should have woken me right away when I heard it," he answered. "You said you and Seren came into my cave for a greater purpose than just your initial safety. You implied that our meeting was not chance at all but the work of Divine intervention."

"I said that?" I asked with puzzlement.

"You did indeed, lad," Samuel replied. "And with that, my small still voice began to speak up again and I knew what I had to do."

"That's wonderful Samuel!" Seren said as she took his hand in a friendly embrace.

Samuel smiled at her and everyone's spirits seemed to rise at that moment. I hated to change the mood, so I waited several minutes after we finished eating to comment on the fact that we really weren't all that safe, being in the Unfinished Lands and everything. We still had to get Branwen back to New London where she'd really be safe. I was also worried about Louie and getting him back to Serenity Forest. The city was no place for a wolf – and I knew his family would be even more worried about him than I was. It also bothered me that we had seen no sign of his family members who had been tracking Branwen.

"We need to start making tracks towards the Village of Idiots," I concluded.

"Yes. I am quite anxious to get home," Borb said nervously.

"Are you worried about becoming someone's meal?" Gefell's right mouth asked him.

"Well, that's only one of my many worries in this dreadful place," Borb replied.

"Don't fear, Borb. We've got Samuel with us this time," Gefell's left mouth said. "He can protect us from most any harm. You should have seen him earlier. He's quite spry for a three hundred year old man."

"Everyone, Robert is quite correct," Samuel said at last. "Though we need not worry about the Guardsmen tracking us here, they will be searching in many places soon enough. We must get to our rendezvous point at the inn Borb told us about and we should definitely not delay any further."

With everyone well rested enough, we took one final look around as Samuel packed the last of his things and said goodbye to his wonderful cave. "Maybe someone else here in the Unfinished Lands can use this place," he thought aloud. "But not very likely. It's a bit too civilized for this neighborhood. I've always thought it sort of an oasis."

And so he left his home of two hundred years.

I noticed as we marched away from the cave that Samuel did not look back, not even once. He was obviously resolved to his new future. That steely resolve of his came in handy on many occasions. Unfortunately, we would need it again very soon.

We hadn't gotten more than fifty paces out of the cave before Samuel stopped us all with a raise of his hands. He gestured for quiet.

"What is it?" Branwen whispered.

"Shh," Seren popped back.

"We must get back to the cave immediately," Samuel said.

With that, we all turned and began running for the cave. But it was too late. The noise Samuel had heard was a grumbling he'd encountered only a few times before. The Unfinished Lands were home to most of the descendants of the cursed peoples and the abominable creatures left incomplete by creation. These creatures, though of human descent, could not speak as such. They did have a crude type of communication, comprised of grunts, growls, and moans. Some of these creatures had even organized into groups which would sometimes raid the villages not far from the Unfinished Lands. This particular group was a collection of the crudest, nastiest, and most fearsome of all the Abominable Ones. They had no trace of morality whatsoever and were driven mostly by pure instinct. It was this group whose strange communications Samuel had heard before stopping us. Before we could reach the cave they had us surrounded.

The monsters surrounding us were diverse in their appearance. Some of them had overly large, bird-shaped heads. Others had more human-looking heads, though with massive amounts of scar tissue and odd hair placement. Some of them had no arms and some of them had an extra pair. There was one who resembled a bear but with more of a reptilian face and claws. One of the strangest creatures had a face where his stomach should be and, growing out from where his shoulders should have been, were two large and craggy horns. Most of them had no tails, but there were a couple that had large, rat-like appendages. They were dressed in ragged shreds of clothing much like Nestor, who now seemed adorable by comparison.

Some of the creatures had spears, others crude knives or spiked clubs. It was clear we weren't going to win a fight with them. Seren screamed as the creatures moved closer toward us. Branwen pulled her into a tight protective hug. Louie went right in front of Branwen's feet and began growling as fiercely as he could. I stood in front of Samuel who was in front of Gefell and Borb. We found ourselves back to back as the monsters moved in more closely forming a ring around us.

"What do we do Samuel?" I asked. "These creatures, whoever they are, are obviously not friendly."

"Yes, that is so," Samuel replied. "They are no friends of mine, that I can tell you. I am afraid we're going to have to go with them for now."

"Don't you have anything in that pack of yours that can help us?" a nervous Borb asked.

"Nothing I could get to in time to save us all," Samuel replied. "And I'll not risk trying to sacrifice any of us to save one or two."

"Well, this certainly is a bummer!" I moaned.

The creatures poked and prodded us with their weapons, forcing us to move in a direction we didn't want to go: further into the depths of the Unfinished Lands. We were headed into the unknown, far away from our destination and farther away from anyone who could help us.

We marched for what seemed like a couple of hours before reaching a large cavern sunk into the ground behind a large clumping of gnarled trees. The opening of the cavern was huge. I imagine you could walk a half dozen elephants through it side by side. Once inside, I was surprised by the intricacies of the decoration with which the Abominable Ones had adorned it. There were designs painted on the insides of the walls that looked very similar to Native American origin both of the northern and southern varieties. They also had all kinds of carvings made out of the trees that lined those painted walls. There was carved furniture made to fit the odd shapes and sizes of the strange beings. These creatures, though without the ability of speech, were nonetheless quite intelligent.

Unfortunately, they were also quite rude. They spat and belched and expelled gas from every imaginable orifice. They poked us some more with their weapons and some who had beaks even pecked at us. At first it wasn't clear what they wanted us to do. Then as we came around a corner we could see a large corridor at the end of which was what seemed like a jail cell. They herded us into it, closed the crude barred door, and locked us in. They took Samuel's pack as well as his walking staff and laid it in a corner opposite the cell. They'd already rifled through the food pack that I had managed to save from the horses. While going through that, they fought among themselves for each last crumb we had in there.

"What are they going to do to us, Samuel?" asked Seren.

"I'm not sure, lass," replied Samuel. "But I'm certain their intentions are not pleasant."

"This is awful," I exclaimed. "We came all this way and rescued Branwen just to be stopped by a bunch of monsters?"

"It's okay, Robert," Branwen said as she put her hand on my shoulder. "I'm sure everything is going to turn out fine."

"How can you say that?" I asked her. "We're locked in a cell by a group of monsters."

"They haven't harmed us yet have they?" Branwen asked. "If they had wanted to kill us they could have already done it. I don't know what they want, but as long as we're alive, there is hope."

"You're right, sis," Seren said. "We can lean on each other."

I was surprised to find that the girls were being the strong ones. Seren had always been the first to scream at any sign of trouble. But thinking back to all she told me about Branwen, it made perfect sense. Branwen was the firstborn of her family. She was always looking out for her younger siblings, as well as the animals in Serenity Forest. She had a remarkable, calming affect on Seren. To Branwen, this was just another obstacle to overcome. There was no need to act like we were doomed, even though we were.

Chapter Twenty
Possum Day

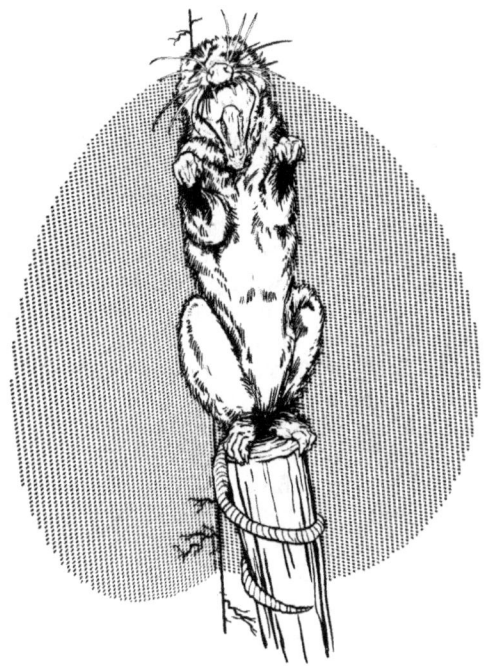

We were stuck in the cell all night. The strange creatures came and went, shuffling through and occasionally staring at us unnervingly. I worried that something would happen to us in the darkness, and tried desperately to stay awake while the others dozed fitfully. No one was able to sleep peacefully, at least not for more than a few minutes at a time. Not even Louie, who could have easily slipped through the cell's bars. He probably wouldn't have gotten far before the monsters would have killed him, of course, if that was even their intent. But he never would have left Branwen in danger anyway, and preferred to share her fate.

But there was a bright spot to being trapped in a dank cell in a large cavern by a group of grotesque monsters. I got to spend time with Branwen. Granted we weren't alone or anything and it was hardly romantic. But she and I did get to talk quite a bit during the night. I told her how much I admired her for standing up for what she believed in. I went on about how I'd visited her garden in Serenity Forest and how it had made an impression on me. I also told her that, through talking to her father and especially her sister, I'd felt like I'd known her for a long time. She told me that she was grateful for my sacrifice in rescuing her. She, like Seren, wanted to hear about my home in America and was as equally as fascinated. I have to admit the fact that she hung on my every word made me feel quite happy. As we talked through the night with the others going in and out of sleep around us, I'd almost forgotten that we were captives.

"Don't you miss your home and your family?" Branwen asked me.

"Of course I do," I said. "But you know, I haven't thought of them in a long time. I've had a lot on my mind as of late."

Branwen smiled. "Don't you want to go back?" she asked.

"Absolutely," I told her firmly. "But I'm not in any big hurry." I said, once again forgetting that I was locked up and didn't really have a choice in the matter.

"That's good," she replied. "I don't think you're going anywhere for a while anyway."

We both chuckled. Then we sort of just stared in each others eyes for a minute with neither of us having anything to say. The moment was priceless to me. Normally I hated awkward pauses in conversations. If this had happened to me back home with a girl, I would have gotten nervous and probably said or done something stupid to ruin it. But here, in this cell that no longer seemed to exist for me, I just sat there staring at her, and she at me. We probably would have stared at each other for hours had we not been interrupted by Seren.

"Hello," Seren said in a long, drawn out way. "Are the two of you at home? Anybody upstairs?"

"Oh, hello, Seren," Branwen finally said to her in a mocking tone. "Glad to see you're awake, dear. I'd been worried you were getting too much sleep."

"Aha!" I said. "So sarcasm *does* exist in Gwerinatha."

"The two of you need to do more worrying about how we're going to get out of here and less time off in dreamland," Seren told us.

"It's not polite to interrupt, you know," Branwen reminded her. "I'll remember this when we get home."

"You mean *if* we get home," Seren responded in an agitated tone. "And I don't see that anything the two of you are doing will help us get there!"

Her loud tones had woken Samuel who had been asleep for a good long while. "Here now, child. What's this all about?" he asked. "You'll wake the dead with all that loud talking."

"I think they're already awake," I said as I pointed out to a couple of the monsters who were playing some sort of chess like game just outside the cell.

"Clever," Branwen said. She winked in approval at my joke.

"Has there been any change in the guard's demeanor?" Samuel asked.

"No," I responded. "They've been mostly ignoring us for the last hour or so."

"How would you know?" Seren interrupted. "If the monsters weren't embedded in Branwen's eyes, you wouldn't know they were there."

I was embarrassed by her remark, knowing how much truth was in it. But at the same time I just couldn't get over how good I felt that Branwen and I had hit it off so well. I'd heard that difficult situations can bring people close together, but this was different. We were connecting on a level that was somehow deeper than that; and I was none-too-happy at Seren's interference. Sadly, I was too wrapped up in the moment to realize that jealousy played a part in Seren's ire. Her agitation ended up waking everyone.

"What's all the shouting about?" Louie said after an enormous yawn.

"Yeah," Borb added rather unnecessarily. "It's hard enough to sleep in this terrifying place without adding a lot of useless gabbing going on."

"Will you please keep it down, people?" Gefell's left mouth butted in.

"I'm having a hard time thinking you know," Gefell's right mouth responded.

"There's nothing wrong with my thought processes," Gefell's left mouth said.

"Oh, no," I said. "Gefell's reverted to conflicting personalities again."

"It's the nerves," Seren said. "They're getting to him."

"I'm perfectly fine," Gefell's left mouth insisted. "What in the heavens are you talking about?"

"Your sides aren't agreeing again, Gefell," I told him.

"Why that's nonsense," Gefell's left mouth said. "We got that all straightened out after my talk with Samuel."

"I'm worried, you know," Gefell's right mouth said after a long pause.

"Oh dear," Gefell's left mouth said. "You must be right."

"Then again..." Gefell's right mouth said.

"Don't worry, Gefell," Louie told him. "Take deep breaths. You'll be all right." Louie then leaned in and whispered to him, "I'm working on a plan to get us out of here, but it's going to take some time. No worries."

At this point the two guards had had enough. One of them, the one who resembled a bear with a reptilian face, got up from his game and sauntered apelike to our cell door. He hopped up and down and shrieked at us a few times. It was pretty obvious that he wanted us to be quiet. Everyone expect Samuel and Branwen retreated to the back of the cell when this happened. I couldn't help but be awed by their bravery. The mad creature huffed and puffed and then, as everyone had gotten quiet, he went back to his game.

Later that night, a disturbance of sorts began in the cavern. We couldn't make out exactly what all the excitement was about, but we could tell that a large party of the cavern's creatures was leaving. We figured they were going out on a raid. They left behind the two chess players to guard us. Like us, they were nodding off here and there. We'd stayed mostly quiet since the earlier incident and I spent a lot of time observing them. They honestly didn't look like they were the most powerful of the creatures. They didn't look all that fast, either, since they didn't have very strong-looking legs. I kept thinking if there was only some way we could get out of the cell that we could overpower them and free ourselves. But that was the rub. The bars were solid and the cell door was locked good and proper. We'd tried a time or two to shake it and it wouldn't budge. Of course, that had gotten us a good scolding from our guardian monsters.

Everyone had drifted off to sleep again except for me. I used the time to make what observations I could. Then I saw something strange. I guess with all that was going on I hadn't noticed it before, but there in the corner was Samuel's walking stick without the petrified opossum on top. I was pretty sure it was there before. I thought that one of the monsters must have tried to eat it and gotten a rude surprise when he tried to bite into it.

I nudged Samuel, who was only barely asleep.

"Mmm. Yes? What is it lad?" Samuel asked.

"Your staff," I said. "Wasn't the opossum on it when they took it from you?"

"Well, yes. I'm sure it was," he answered.

"So where is it now?" I wondered.

"He's probably running around here somewhere, I'm sure," Samuel replied.

"Running around...?" I stammered. "But how did it come to life?"

"Well, at a certain time of year, male possums seek out female possums that are..."

"No, no. I know all about the birds and the bees!"

"Birds and bees you may indeed know about. But it seems the possums have you puzzled," Samuel said.

"No. I mean how did he come *back* to life?" I asked irritably.

"*Back* to life?" Samuel echoed. "Oh you must have thought that petrified meant..."

"Dead for hundreds of years, then turned to rock," I interrupted hurriedly.

"Yes, I suppose it could mean that as well," Samuel supposed. "No, son, he was petrified of your party. Too many people frighten him completely, you know. But the pose does have certain advantages."

Once again Samuel had proven to be full of surprises. This turned out to be a very pleasant one at that. The opossum showed up minutes later after the two chess players had finally had enough of their game and drifted off into a snore-laden stupor. He scrambled up to their seat and grabbed the keys from off the hook on the wall next to them. He then ran over to us and gave the keys to Samuel. Samuel carefully opened the lock. Quietly as possible, we woke everyone who was still asleep and shushed them long enough for us all to get past the guards and out the cavern entrance.

Once outside the cave, Samuel and I went ahead and scouted the area to make sure there weren't any other monsters lurking in the early dawn shadows. When we were certain that we were no longer in any danger, I went back for the others. Within minutes we were away from the cavern and back on the pathway we had started on from Samuel's cave. The morning had started out with great hope. But as I knew from experience, hope was a very tenuous thing in Gwerinatha, no matter what the time of day.

Chapter Twenty-One
Betrayed

The next hour or so went by with relative ease. I say relative, because just walking in the Unfinished Lands can be hazardous, what with the ground changing into worms, large bugs lurking around every corner, and who knows what kinds of dangerous plants waiting to attack. Samuel sensed our fear of the place and tried to give us a bit of perspective.

"You know, what you are seeing now is really not so bad," he said.

"What do you mean?" I inquired.

"Well, you folks talk about the Unfinished Lands as if you should earn a medal just for walking through the place," he said. "What you're actually seeing just the tip of the iceberg."

"You mean it gets worse?" Seren asked incredulously.

"Absolutely," Samuel replied. "You see, we're just inside the border of the Unfinished Lands. Their full area, however, is quite large and it gets far more dangerous the further in you go."

"I can't imagine anything worse than what we've already seen," Seren exclaimed.

"Oh, yes," Samuel assured her. "For example, only seven miles southwest of my cave I've seen the earth moving like waves, crashing in on itself in a tumult. And I've seen storms rip large trees out of the ground and throw them for miles. The next instant the winds became calm and the sun shone brightly."

"That's horrible!" one of Gefell's mouths said.

"Yes. The closer you get to the middle of the Lands, the worse it gets… until you arrive at the City."

"City?" I asked, as I could not possibly imagine what sort of metropolis might lie within the Unfinished Lands.

"The City of the Originators," Samuel answered. "It's where I met them. They have an entire city built on a flattened mountaintop overlooking the Unfinished Lands, as well as almost all of the rest of Gwerinatha. That's where I met with them. They kept me safe in my travels there. Of course, it wouldn't be safe to get there now at all."

After hearing that, I felt a little better about our current situation, especially since we saw no signs of any of the Abominable Ones, whether the organized kind or the loners. It really seemed as if we were home free this time. I estimated we were just a half an hour or so away from the edge of the Unfinished Lands. The proverbial light at the end of the tunnel was just ahead.

I took advantage of the time to get to know Branwen more, even though it seemed to bother Seren. I was oblivious to that fact at the time, however, and went on with my conversations with Branwen, while almost totally ignoring Seren and the others. It wasn't as if I was ignoring them on purpose. I couldn't help myself. I'd been hearing so many wonderful things about Branwen and had been waiting to meet her for so long that everything else just had to take a back seat. I knew I was in trouble when I was facing hunger, imprisonment, and even death, and all I could think about was a girl I hadn't even met yet. Fortunately, she lived up to the hype. There are few people to this day that have impressed me as much as that sixteen-year-old girl. It wasn't just that she was cute or had a great personality or anything like that, though she was extraordinarily attractive in every manner conceivable. I just couldn't get over how someone so young could stand up to so many authority figures for principles that she believed in so strongly. She was willing to risk her safety and comfort for others. That, in my mind was, and still is, a very big deal.

As we headed over the last hill that led out of the Unfinished Lands I sensed something wasn't right. It was an odd feeling that's hard to describe, especially in such a strange setting. It was sort of like the feeling that you're being watched, but different. Then over the horizon I saw them. It was a group of men. I had no idea who they were at first, but it didn't take too long to figure out by the color of their uniforms that they were the Southern Guard. A dozen or so of them were lined up, just waiting for us. But how did they know where we would be? I couldn't imagine at the time that they'd have known we'd be coming from the Unfinished Lands. Not only did they know that, but they knew which path we were taking to get to the Village of Idiots. It was clear that they had been tipped off.

There were two directions we could go: back to the Unfinished Lands, or straight toward the Southern Guard. Well, I suppose technically there were more than two directions, but west to Anhysbys Forest and the east to the Village of Hollow Creek seemed like long shots to us. We couldn't let the Southern Guard take Branwen back. We'd fought too long and too hard to get her free. At the same time we had no chance against them in a fight. Samuel had an idea.

"Gather 'round, everyone," he said. "There's only one thing we can do. We must split up and give the Guard more than one target to follow. Some of us may get captured, but there's a good chance that least some of us to get help from the north."

"That's crazy!" I yelled. "We'll never get past them."

"Have you got a better idea?" Branwen asked.

"Well, no," I said sheepishly.

"I think I may have a solution to getting past them," Samuel said. He then pulled out the orb nullifying device from his pack.

"The nullifier!" I said.

"Yes," Samuel replied. "When we get just a bit closer I'll turn it on and blind them with the flash of light it emits. This should give us enough time to scatter in different directions. By the time they can see again they'll have to determine who to go after."

"And if any one of them has gotten another dose of blue orb powers, they'll be useless," Seren added.

"Bonus!" I exclaimed. "Let's go!"

We were still a little more than a football field away from them. We each had a preplanned direction in which to run once Samuel set off the nullifier. When we got about eighty yards or so away from them, we were on a level enough place for Samuel to start his plan in motion. We had been steadily separating from our tight cluster in anticipation of bolting away. Samuel stopped first, then we all stopped beside him. He quickly lifted up his hand and raised the nullifier. From that far away, the Guard couldn't see what he was doing. I wasn't quite sure but I think a couple of them drew their guns. Samuel flipped the switch, the flash went off, and we took off in varying directions as fast as we could go.

I wasn't sure exactly which way the others were going to go. I believed Samuel and Louie to be heading far west, while Gefell and Borb were bound to head toward the Village of Idiots. Branwen, Seren, and I would head east. We hoped to run into somebody that wasn't too unfriendly to northerners. It seemed reckless to head back toward the location where Branwen had been held prisoner, but it was the closest place with any kind of population.

It seemed logical. Or at least it seemed logical at the time.

Unfortunately, it wasn't. Oh, we ran pretty fast for three young teenagers and we had a pretty good lead on them. But the Southern Guard are trained and conditioned soldiers, and the four that decided to take off after us seemed to be even better conditioned than most. We'd hoped to get far enough away during the initial flash that they wouldn't be able to see which way we went but, we were still in their line of sight by the time the retina burn wore off.

We made them work for it though. We ran as hard as we could for as long as we could, but after five minutes or so they caught up to us. They fired off a couple of gunshots which scared Seren, causing her to trip. I stopped to help her, and that was that. By then they were close enough to hit us. I didn't know enough about these guys to be certain they wouldn't kill us. One thing was for sure: I wasn't going to take that chance. They might not have harmed Branwen or Seren for fear of repercussions from the Gwerinathan government, but I knew there was nothing keeping them from harming me. And being unarmed, there was nothing I could do to keep them from taking us captive.

"It's all right, Robert," Branwen told me. "We still have hope. Look back." She pointed past our oncoming antagonists. I could see the rest of the Guard coming from behind. This indicated that they had not gone after the others. There was still a chance that they could get help and rescue us. After all, Branwen's father had a group of men out looking for us. And the wolves were out looking for us. Our friends were bound to find help sooner rather than later. Maybe we weren't in such a bad predicament after all.

Then the Guard caught up to us and I lost that shred of hope. "Thought you'd get away from us, eh, stranger!" one of the Guard yelled at me. "You never had a chance of escape! We're too damn tough to be beaten by an old man, a young boy, and a group of freaks."

"Okay, so you've got us," I relented. "Don't harm the girls. They've done nothing to you."

"Harm the girls?" the first Guard mimicked. "We've no intention of harming them. You, on the other hand, are quite another matter."

"Don't you touch him!" Seren shrieked as one of the Guard reached over to me.

"It's okay, Seren," I said. "Everything will be all right." I looked into Branwen's eyes as I said it and, for an instant, I actually believed it.

The Guard grabbed my arms from behind and cuffed my wrists. They did the same to Branwen and Seren, and then pushed us ahead for several yards to a wagon with four Gwerinathan horses. They put us all into the wagon and we took off for parts unknown.

The bumpy ride was made all the more uncomfortable by our hands being cuffed behind us. We winced and moaned a bit but the Guards didn't seem to notice.

"Where are you taking us?" demanded Branwen. "We have a right to know."

"You are being taken to New Wellington where your fate will be decided," the Guard answered.

New Wellington was the capital city of the House of Fate and it was where the Southern Guard's headquarters was located. It was about a two-hour ride east from where we were at the time.

"You're going to be in a great deal of trouble with the government of Gwerinatha," Seren told them.

At that the Guard chuckled. "We answer to no one, save ourselves and the inner circle of the House of Fates – which is the true heart of the Gwerinathan government."

"I must ask," one of the Guard said to Branwen, "why is it that you don't leave the north and join us in the south? Your ideals are far more akin to that of the House of Fates rather than the old-fashioned notions of your Lords of Wisdom."

"The Lords of Wisdom are my family," she replied. "Not that it's any of your business, but I believe I can fight for change and what's right within my own land. I don't need to leave my people just because I may disagree with them. I'm not going to turn my back on my family. I love them and would never leave them."

"You are a fool then!" The Guard shouted back, seeming genuinely angry.

"You can do far more for change within a group of people who think differently than you than you can within a group who all think alike." She paused. "The problem with all of you authority figures, whether in the Lords of Wisdom or the House of Fates, is that you aren't open minded enough to listen to other people's ideas. Try listening to what other people are saying for once instead of running around like a horde of huns."

I was quite proud of Branwen's retort and couldn't have put it better myself. It must have hit a chord with the Guard, too. They didn't speak much after that. It was of no use talking to this bunch anyway. They were as hardheaded as could be.

A lot went through my mind during that trip. I needed to know how the Guard knew where to find us. I wondered if Samuel and the others were okay, but most of all I just felt bad for Branwen and Seren. We had been through so much together in such a short time and it seemed to be all for nothing. Seren kept tearing up, but Branwen stayed calm through the whole trip. She even smiled at me a few times. She had amazing confidence, even if I didn't. Just the same, I couldn't let her down. So I matched her smile for smile, keeping my chin up the whole time. I think it eventually rubbed off on Seren, who bit her lip and choked back her tears. She, like us, didn't want the Southern Guard to have the satisfaction of seeing us miserable.

Eventually we arrived in New Wellington. We were taken to the headquarters of the Southern Guard and put in a cell there. At least they took our cuffs off before putting us in. Seren began yelling at the Guard, but they ignored her.

"Don't waste your breath," I said. "These creeps are all the same. The only one who was worth anything was the one that tipped us off to Branwen's location. And he had sense enough to leave these jerks a long time ago."

"I've seen worse cells," Branwen said. "Just yesterday, in fact."

We chuckled dryly her comment. She was right, of course, and it just illustrated the point that you should always have perspective. As bad as things were, they sure didn't seem as bad as the fate we had just escaped. There certainly was no need for sulking, despite the fact that there would be plenty of time for that.

After a few hours in the cell, we noticed some people milling about in an office we could just barely see around the corner. There was a man with our captors who looked somewhat familiar. Then I realized that it was Borb Feargrinn, only cleaned and tidied up a bit. We turned and looked at each other in amazement. With what little we could overhear, it had become clear to us that Borb had tipped off the Guard to our plan. That's how they knew exactly where we'd be.

"It can't be!" said Seren. "He must have been under the effect of the blue orb. That's it. He couldn't have turned us in otherwise."

"I don't think so, Seren," I said solemnly. "If he were under the effect of the blue orb, then why didn't he shoot me when I gave him the gun? And why didn't he warn us after the effects had warn off? No. Something else is going on here, and I sure would like to find out what."

"Does it really matter?" Branwen asked.

"What do you mean?" I asked back.

"We're here now. Captured. Whatever reason Borb had for doing what he did doesn't change that fact. Any reason you find may only make you angrier. And what purpose would that serve?"

I realized that Branwen was right. We needn't work ourselves up into a rage at Borb's betrayal. It would do no good. I also realized that Branwen was far deeper than any other sixteen-year-old I had ever met. Besides all that, we had enough to worry about trying to figure out what the Southern Guard was going to do with us next.

Chapter Twenty-Two
Judgment Day

We heard a great deal of discussion from the other room. After it had died down, Borb and one of the Guard came over to our cell.

"Borb!" How could you?" shouted Seren. She rushed forward and shook the cell bars in impotent fury. She was so mad I wondered if she would spit at him. Branwen and I remained seated on the bench in the back of the cell.

"I'm sorry, Miss Seren, but really it's for the best," Borb told her.

"How can you say that?" Seren replied. "Don't you know what they're going to do to us?"

"Oh, they're not going to hurt you. They promised me," Borb said.

"And you believed them?" Seren responded.

"Oh, yes," Borb replied. "They're nice people, they are. I'm sure you'll be free to go once everything gets settled with your father and all."

"Why Borb? Why?" Seren cried.

"Like I told you," Borb said, "They're nice people. Because I'm overweight and slow everyone outside of the Village treats me like I'm a pariah. They don't act like anyone from the Village of Idiots are really people. But these fine chaps here treated me with all kinds of respect. I feel like I have some dignity when they talk to me."

"Oh, Borb. They were just using you to get at us," Seren said. "Don't you see?"

"Let it go, sis," Branwen said. "It's all over now. There's nothing can be done about it."

"She's right, Seren," I said. "Sit down here with us. It's probably going to be a while before we're freed."

"I'm sorry," Borb said to all of us. He looked down at the floor as he walked out. Seren came over and sat with us.

"Can you believe that?" she asked. "I'm seething and there's nothing I can do about it."

"You can't stay mad at Borb," I told her.

"I know," she responded. "That's why it's so frustrating."

It was a sad situation with Borb Feargrinn. He really was a trusting sort. Unfortunately, the Southern Guard took advantage of that fact. I couldn't tell if he felt it at the time, but I imagined Seren's words would get to him eventually and he would understand that she was right. I just didn't want to be there when that happened. Of course, I didn't want to be locked in a cell either, and that's precisely where I was. But at the very least I had the company of the two most wonderful girls in all of Gwerinatha. All right, so they were pretty much the *only* girls I knew in Gwerinatha, but they were pretty terrific all the same.

With all that time to think in the cell, we figured out at least one thing for sure: they didn't have the blue orb close by. Or, if they did have it close by, they weren't using it – but I imagined at this point the jig was up as far as they were concerned. There was little need for subterfuge. We gleaned a little more information from what we could overhear. Soon the Guard would contact Governor Baylies and inform him that they had his daughters, and the cat and mouse game would begin. It seemed there were some prisoners they wanted released from a Gwerinathan prison in the north. If we were to be returned, those prisoners had to be freed.

Branwen was certain that her father wouldn't go for anything like that. Seren pretty much agreed. Our worries now were not so much that they would harm us, but that we'd be stuck in a cell for a very long time.

"Are you sorry you came to Gwerinatha now, Robert?" asked Branwen.

"Are you crazy?" I answered. "If I had never have come here I would never have met you," Seren looked at me with waiting eyes. "...and you, of course, Seren," I added as an afterthought. "This whole trip has been a life-changing experience for me. If I never get back home..."

My voice trailed off as my thoughts began drifting from them.

"What is it, Robert?" Seren asked.

"Home," I said quietly. "I hadn't actually given any thought to the idea that I might *not* get back home."

"The feeling is hard for you isn't it?" Branwen asked.

"Yes," I answered softly. "I don't know *what* I'll do if I don't get back home."

"You'll stay with us in the governor's mansion," Seren quickly responded.

"And you'll take frequent visits with me to Serenity Forest to visit Louie and the wolves," Branwen added. "You'll be part of our family."

"After all, you *are* part of Samuel's family," Seren said.

I knew they were doing their best to make me feel better and their words did put a smile on my face. Those two were truly something else. But I couldn't get it out of the back of my mind that I would never get home again. My friends and family would never see me again. I'd already been gone ten days. They had to be completely insane with worry. I imagined the cops were out looking for me, my name all over the news and all kinds of fuss being caused by my disappearance.

Before I could sulk about it too long, one of the Guards came over to the door. He opened it up, struck me a solid blow across the face, took me out of the cell, and dragged me into a room around the corner. Branwen and Seren protested, but to no avail. I was thrown into a chair and was hit with a barrage of questions by two other Guardsmen. Somehow word got down to the Southern Guard who I was and that I came from another world. It was pretty clear they were disturbed by the idea that I could poison their world with my knowledge of technology. I tried to explain to them that I meant no harm, and was only visiting. They accused me of being an advance scout from some sort of alien invasion. I couldn't believe my ears. It was preposterous. But they wouldn't listen to anything I had to say in my defense.

"Look," I started, "I'm trying to tell you: I mean no harm to your society here."

One of the Guards slammed his fist on the desk and shouted, "That's enough out of you! It is clear to us from your strange clothes and the intelligence we have received from our spies in the north that you have come from another world with advanced technology. That is more than enough reason for us to believe you a spy!"

"I am not a spy!" I shouted back.

"You *are* a spy and you are going to be treated as such," the first Guard said.

"Just what does that mean?" I asked.

"Silence!" the second Guard shouted back. "You will speak only when spoken to, *spy*."

"You deserve no information about your fate!" the second Guard said.

And then I was taken back to the cell, where they shoved me hard towards the back wall. "And no talking to the other prisoners, spy!" the Guard said as he walked off.

"Spy?" Seren said quizzically. "What are they talking about Robert?"

"They think I'm a spy from my world," I responded.

"That's crazy," Branwen said. "Who would believe you were a spy?"

"Apparently *they* do," I said. "And from their tone they aren't going to sit still about it, either."

"What do you mean?" Seren asked. "What are they going to do to you?"

"I don't know," I answered. "They wouldn't tell me. But I get the feeling they're not going to throw me a surprise party."

"We've got to get you out of here," Branwen said with a worried tone I'd never heard in her voice before.

"Well, yeah," I said. "We've all got to get out of here."

"No. It's not just that," Branwen said. "If they really do think that you're a spy, then they are more than likely going to execute you."

My heart sank. Branwen's voice had always been full of hope, but now it was desperate. Seren screamed. A Guard ran in, told her to be quiet, and read me the riot act for talking to them. I'm sure they wish there was another cell to keep me in, but that was the only one in their little Mayberry jail. So we were stuck together. A Guard was assigned to watch us from that point to ensure I'd do no more talking to the girls.

The rest of that day and on into the night we did no more talking. The Guard watching us was all business, never moving a muscle in his face the whole time. I remember thinking he'd have been good for duty outside Buckingham Palace. Even though we couldn't talk to each other, Branwen and I said plenty with our eyes. I was pretty certain she knew how much she'd come to mean to me, even in the very short time we had been together. And though I could never say for sure how she felt about me, I do know she was heartbroken at the thought of my fate. Seren cried herself to sleep that night. Branwen and I eventually fell asleep, leaning on one another and hoping against hope that Samuel and our friends, the wolves, Governor Baylies, or simply *anyone* would come to save us.

Chapter Twenty-Three
Saved by Branwen

The next morning didn't start out so bad. I woke to find Branwen's head on my lap. She looked so peaceful and beautiful I hated to disturb her. I'm not sure I had ever felt so content up to that point in my life. There was something about her there that just seemed so right. I stroked her hair and smiled. Then I closed my eyes tightly and prayed as hard as I ever had that this moment would somehow not have to end. It wasn't so much that I was afraid to die, but now that I had found Branwen I couldn't bear to be apart from her. The thought of my life ending now when everything was just starting to come together was more than I could bear. I began to cry and the tears that trickled from my cheek fell on Branwen's face and woke her.

"Wha-what's that?" she said as she rubbed my tears off her forehead. "Robert? Are you crying?"

"I-I'm sorry Branwen," I told her. "I didn't want you to see this. I'm not as strong as you are. I wish I was. I love that about you. In fact... I love everything about you."

"Don't be silly, Robert," she said. She sat up quickly and brushed away the remaining tears from my face. "I'm not as strong as you make me out to be. I'm all torn up on the inside. I just met you and now you're being taken away from me. It's horrible."

"But you hardly know me," I said to her. "How can you be all that upset?"

"You think you know me so well and you have to ask me that question?" she said with a hurt tone. "First off you're a human being, aren't you? Any person about to be killed would cause me to be horrified. But more than that, you helped my sister to rescue me. I owe my life to you, Robert."

"I'm sorry Branwen," I said, looking down at the cell floor. "I certainly didn't mean anything by..."

"Hush now," she interrupted. "I know you didn't mean to upset me. You're just scared and confused. Anyone in your shoes would be. There's something about you that I can't explain, Robert." She looked around the cell stopping when she came upon Seren, still sleeping. "I know I haven't known you much more than a day, but I can tell you're very special. It may be that I'm simply infatuated with the fact that you're from another world. It might be that I am just so flattered at the way you've done nothing but go on about me since we met. I don't know."

"It could just be that you think I'm really cute," I added immodestly.

"That's all it is, I'm sure," she giggled. Then we stared into one another's eyes until I thought I might begin to cry again. She leaned in to kiss me and, just before our lips came together, there was the sound of a door slamming. Seren awoke with a start.

"What's going on?" she said loudly.

"I don't know," I said. "I think we have visitors."

Then two of the Southern Guard came around the corner, one with a couple of trays of food and the other with just one. They were bringing us breakfast, but they added no hospitality.

"Here comes your last meal sonny boy," one of them said with a smirk.

Just as they were about to open the door, I noticed Branwen and Seren exchanging glances. I didn't know what was going on, but they obviously had something in mind. The guard opening the door carefully balanced his trays as he began to unlock it. Seren jumped over to the left front corner of our cell and began moaning and crying. She kneeled over as if in pain. The guard with only one tray of food went around to see about her and then, faster than I could even think, Branwen rushed past me and slammed the door back on to the guard as hard as she could. The food trays flew though the air as the guard closest to us fell back over the guard who was looking after Seren, pinning him to the ground. I reached around and helped Seren up as the three of us rushed out of the cell. None of us were really thinking far ahead at this point. It was suicide running away like that, but they had no qualms about risking their lives when they thought I was about to be killed.

It was still quite early and, fortunately for us, there were no other guards on duty yet. We simply looked around and picked a direction without thinking, running as hard as we could. I don't think either girl had been to New Wellington, before so none of us had any idea where we were going.

We rushed through what seemed to be the center of town. There were only a few people milling about, none of whom had a friendly face. We knew they'd be more than likely to tell the guards which direction we went, so we kept running harder and harder. Finally, we came upon a busy stable. We knew we'd only have one chance. So we grabbed a few horses and took off. With no plan in mind, we kept riding until we got out of town and began heading back to the northwest towards Dyffryn Heul.

We couldn't believe our luck. As far as we could see there were no guards chasing us. We saw no one behind us at all. We were running the horses too hard and, against my better judgment, we had to stop and rest them. Branwen cared too much about animals to sacrifice their health just to give us a better chance at getting away. Besides, she figured like Seren and I did that we were safe, since we seemed to be all alone. In order to be more certain of our safety, I suggested we try to find someplace where we could hide the horses while they rested.

In the distance we could see the foothills of the Ochneidio Mountains. In front of them lay a small patch of farmland. There were large stacks of straw piled up like some kind of native huts. We decided to leave the horses behind them and rest ourselves.

We sat around and just felt grateful to be alive. Picking at the grass and straw we made plans for what we'd do after we got back to the north.

"I can't wait to get back to Serenity Forest and see the looks on the wolves' faces when you return, Branwen," I told her.

"That will be special," she said. "I wonder who's been tending to my garden?"

"I can't wait to get home and have a bath and put on some decent clothes for a change," Seren said.

Branwen laughed and threw straw at her sister. It was great to see them happy again. Branwen then told Seren to go look after the horses, as they might be hungry.

"What are you talking about Branwen?" she asked, "There's plenty for them to eat all around us."

"Just make sure they're eating the tall grasses and not the little short ones," she replied.

"Why would they..." Seren paused and then, as if a bolt had suddenly hit her out of the blue, she knew what was on Branwen's mind. "Oh, right. We can't have them eating the wrong grass now, can we? We don't want them to cramp up just when we need them again."

Branwen laughed at her as she left. We walked in the opposite direction and just over a small hill we sat down again.

"What was all that about?" I asked.

"Just this," she said, and reached over gave me a peck on the cheek. "That's for being my knight in shining armor and coming to my rescue." I began to blush a little. Then she gave me a long stare and we kissed each other long and slowly on the lips. "*That*," she said, "was because I think you're really cute."

If there were a top ten of moments I could freeze in time forever that would certainly be one of them. It was the happiest I'd felt since I had entered Gwerinatha. Actually it was the happiest I'd been since I could remember. I wished we'd had more time, but knew that we weren't out of the woods just yet. We weren't far from Dyffryn Heul and we knew we could get help there. The horses were likely ready to go again, so we walked back towards them. Before we had taken more than four steps in that direction we heard a scream.

It was Seren. She was screaming like her head was about to come off. We both ran to her as fast as we could. Once we got there our worst fears were realized. She had seen the Southern Guard. They were coming down on us faster than rain. We had no chance to mount our horses and get away. There was nowhere to run. It was our final stand.

Knowing it was probably the end, I turned to Branwen and gave her a long embrace. Then I pulled her away from me and held her arms. Tears were streaming down her face. She too knew that the end was near. "Listen," I told her, "you are the strongest person I know. I don't want you to change that. Don't let them see how upset you are." By this time Seren had run behind us, and the Guard were just seconds away from us. "I want both of you to look after Louie for me," I told them. "Other than you two, he was my closest friend in Gwerinatha. He needs a lot of guidance, but he's really a good kid." At this point both of them were now crying buckets. "And tell Samuel I was proud to be his descendant." Before I could add any other words the Guard had us surrounded.

"It's the end of the road for you, lad," the lead Guard said. The other guards began chuckling at this point. "There's no need to take you back into town for execution. We can just as easily handle it here."

"No!" screamed Seren. Branwen was doing her best to hold back her tears.

"C'mon now," I said. "Why not be civilized about this? Don't I even get a trial?"

"Trial?" the lead guard mocked. "You really *don't* know us, do you? We don't need to put you on trial. Your fate has already been decided. You're a danger to our way of life and you cannot be allowed to go back and give a report to your fellows in America."

He said that last part with such disdain that I wanted to bust him upside the head with a Louisville Slugger. Unfortunately, I didn't have one, and he had a gun in any case. Still, right then I wouldn't have even minded the other guards shooting me dead if I could have just gotten one good whack at him. But he had the upper hand and continued his grandstanding while trotting his steed around us.

"My comrades," he announced to his fellow guards, "could it be that this spy has already begun to spread his virus to these poor Gwerinathan girls?"

They yelled in the affirmative, mainly to egg him on. "Well then," he continued. "The time has come. This spy must be purged from our great land."

I could hear something in the distance, but I didn't know what it was just then. My concentration oddly wavered. I knew I was about to get shot, and not knowing exactly what that would feel like, I wasn't sure how to take it. I thought about cringing into the fetal position, but I knew I couldn't do that after my speech to Branwen. Then I thought about standing my ground with my fists clenched, my chin up, and my upper lip stiff. But that was a bit more then I could muster. I settled for something in between. I just looked him in the eye and said, "Go ahead. Do what you have to do."

He never even got off his horse. He just raised his gun and pointed it slowly down towards me. The barrel seemed huge: like a cannon. I knew I couldn't run. I also didn't want to take the chance that they might hit one of the girls. I could hear Seren screaming close by. I simply closed my eyes and waited. Then I heard it. The loud gunshot, so deafening I thought my ears would explode. But I felt nothing. Then I heard something drop on my feet. I opened my eyes and saw Branwen lying there with blood oozing out from under her. I dropped to my knees and began screaming her name.

Seren was inconsolable. Her screaming drowned out my own. I knew that this was not the way Branwen should die. I blanked out all the other people. I just concentrated on Branwen and I could see she was still with us. I picked her up and rolled back and forth with her in my arms. I kept repeating to her, "Everything's going to be all right. Don't worry." She looked up at me and I could see the terrible pain in her eyes. But she didn't wince. She didn't even blink.

Then her dark blood flowed down my arms and I knew the wound was fatal.

I could see the light fading from Branwen's eyes. It was terrible to behold. But she just looked at me and smiled. I tried to tell her one more time that everything was going to be okay, even though I knew it wasn't. I couldn't get the words out. Her death was too sacred of a moment for lies. She whispered, "I know," and closed her eyes. With that she was gone. I held her tightly for God only knows how long as Seren wept.

Once I could finally open my eyes again I looked up to see all the Southern Guard standing around in shock. They were more surprised than Seren and I that Branwen had jumped in front of the gun like that. They didn't know her like we did. Although they were intent on seeing me dead, at that moment all they could do was stand in awe. Most of them stood motionless. All of them were quiet. The lead guard who meant to kill me dropped his gun.

And then behind them in the distance I saw something else. I couldn't quite make it out, but it seemed like a large number of figures moving down from the direction of Dyffryn Heul. They were the source of the sounds I had heard just before the shot rang out. Whoever they were, I was certain they were about to be just as shocked and saddened by this horrifying scene as the rest of us.

Chapter Twenty-Four
Too Late, the Cavalry

As the group in the distance got closer, I could tell there were familiar figures with them. I saw Samuel in the center. He was leading a group of governor Baylies' security forces. Branwen's cousin Urien was with them, as was Gefell, Louie, and even some other wolves. Any other time it would have brightened my heart to see the wolves and humans working together. It was obvious they had heard Seren screaming, because at that moment they sped up, ridding their horses even harder.

Urien was the first to get to us. Upon seeing his cousin's corpse he became enraged. "Who is responsible for this?" he screamed, rage seeming to radiate off of him.

The lead guard stepped forth. "I am," he said. "But it was an accident. I was aiming for the boy but she... she took the bullet for him."

"You Southern swine!" Urien yelled back. He then drew his gun and the guard lifted his hands in the air.

"I am unarmed, sir!" he pleaded. "This does no good to anyone."

"It will do me good to see you pay for this hateful deed!" Urien said, still on his mount.

By this time Samuel had reached us. He got down off his horse and came over to where I sat, obliviously cradling Branwen's lifeless body in my lap.

"Oh dear," Samuel said quietly. "This is most tragic. How could I have let this happen?" He fell to his knees beside me and began praying.

Louie and the other wolves had gotten close to us by this time. They circled us and began howling mournfully in the manner of their kind. Seren reached over for Louie and held him close as they cried together, each in their own voice.

During all this I just kept rocking very slowly back and forth with Branwen. I was in denial. Just hours earlier I'd been lamenting how I wouldn't be with Branwen very long because I was about to die. And now she was dead and I had to go on living without her. It's something you can never prepare for and, as such, I had no idea how to deal with it. I'd never cried so many tears in so short a time. It thought my eyes were going to break. It was painful beyond belief.

I don't remember anything coherent about what happened in the minutes after that. It all seems blurry to me, like the moments just after an automobile accident, comprised of all sorts of strange memories that may or may not have happened. I remember seeing a flock of birds flying off from the trees on the horizon. I had yet to see even a single bird in all of Gwerinatha. To see an entire grouping of birds was amazing and I vaguely recall the others staring up at them in disbelief. I think someone, I can't even recall who, came over and pulled Branwen from me. I faintly recall struggling and possibly even shouting at this time. Then the next thing I remember was sitting under a tree with Seren and Louie who were crying and howling respectively. The sound must have jolted me back to reality. I reached out and hugged them both, sharing their tears.

During that time period where everything was a bit fuzzy, Samuel got in between Urien's security team and the Southern Guard. He singlehandedly stopped a scuffle that would have most certainly ended with more bloodshed. Once the Southern Guard realized who he was, they, like everyone upon learning of Samuel's identity, gave him the utmost of respect. It was like there was some kind of power in just his name that made people stop fighting and pay attention to him. I suppose living for over three centuries has some advantages.

I was glad he was able to stop the fighting. However, it seemed pointless. They would only start up again. But this wasn't the time to worry about such things. This was a time for mourning. Whoever had taken Branwen from me had covered her with his jacket. I looked over at her lifeless body and the phrase "she's gone to a better place" hit me. I had heard it so many times before: to the point it made me mad, even. After all, I used to think: if death led to a better place, then why weren't we all in a hurry to get there? But I realized then that no matter what you believe, pretty much everyone agrees that you are only in the life you have now just this once. You have just one life to be you and you must live it to the fullest, with as few regrets as possible. That's how Branwen lived. I vowed to myself then and there that I would live the rest of my life no matter how long it may be to its fullest.

I gave Seren a big hug, tighter than I'd hugged anyone ever before. I looked at her and told her that everything would be all right again. I knew it would, and I knew that's what Branwen was trying to tell me. She knew her work wasn't going to stop just because she was gone. She knew there were lots of others to carry on in her place. She knew that life would move on without her. And she knew she would not be forgotten. She'd left a powerful legacy.

The next few hours went by in a blur. I know we moved on from that farm and gathered together a large caravan that left for New London. I remember being scared to death at the reaction from Governor Baylies when he heard the news. Fortunately, I wasn't there when he got the news initially, as word got to him long before we arrived.

It was late in the evening when our carriage stopped near the governor's mansion. Seren and I had sat on one side, with Samuel and Urien riding on the other. We all stepped slowly out of the carriage, dragging our weary, mournful bodies out step by tearful step. I was the last to get out and I could see that Branwen's parents were already surrounding the carriage that had carried her body. Branwen's mother sobbed uncontrollably and her father stood stoically, but I could tell he was broken inside. Seren ran to them. I stood back near Samuel and watched the sad reunion. The whole scene just made me begin to cry even more. It seemed the pain would get worse long before it even pretended to get better.

Samuel and I were given rooms near the governor's mansion to stay in overnight. I was told I was welcome back in the governor's mansion, but I didn't feel it would be appropriate right then. I knew the family needed to be together and I certainly didn't want to intrude on that. Also, though it was selfish, I was sad enough as it was and didn't want to have the added burden of seeing someone crying around every corner.

Samuel and I managed to talk a little before retiring. It was almost impossible to sleep and having someone to stay up and talk with was therapeutic, to say the least. We spoke of our future plans. He meant to work hard to gather the people of Gwerinatha back together. I wished him well, and then the topic turned to what I might do.

"Are you planning to stay in Gwerinatha then, Robert? You could stay with me and help bring the people together," Samuel told me. "You could become a great symbol of hope to the people."

"Well, I certainly don't know how I could do that," I said. "But as far as going home, I don't really think I have a choice."

"Why, what do you mean, son?" Samuel asked.

"Well I don't know *how* to get home," I told him.

"You still have the key don't you?" he asked.

"The key?" I asked. "Why, yes. I'd forgotten all about it. Yes, I still have it. But I don't know how to use it."

"Well, that's not a problem lad," Samuel said with a smile on his face. "After all, who do you think discovered how the doorway works and made the key in the first place?"

I felt embarrassed, but smiled anyhow, because I knew for the first time that I actually had a chance to make it home again. "That's fantastic!" I said. "I need to get home now more then ever," I said.

"Does Branwen's passing make it that much harder on you?" he asked.

"Yes," I answered. "Any thought I might have given to staying here died with her."

"That is a shame, then," Samuel said quietly. "You're a large part of the reason I came back, you know."

"I know what you said before," I reminded him.

"It's not just that," he said. "Once I thought about the fact that I had a direct descendant here in Gwerinatha, I had hoped I could pass on everything to him."

"That's more than generous," I told him. "I have a pretty good idea of what an honor that really is."

"And you still want to leave for your home?" he said.

"More than ever," I answered quickly. "It's not just Branwen. I've been gone for over a week now. My family has to be extremely worried."

"Oh, yes," he mused. "I hadn't actually considered that. I'm sure they are worried, son. I think I can help there as well."

"How?" I asked.

"Gwerinatha and the old world are not separated by merely space, but time as well," he said. "I think I can arrange your reappearance to be just a twinkling after you left."

"You can?" I said with excitement. "That would be awesome!"

"Well, you have to promise me one thing," he said.

"Anything," I said.

"You must keep the location of Gwerinatha a secret. We cannot risk others following you back here," he said. "From what you told me about your society, it seems to have progressed much further than ours, technologically speaking. I worked hard to keep this a peaceful society and, though I have my work cut out for me to get it back to what it was, I don't need anything to make it harder."

"I think I know what you're saying," I told him. "Believe me, I understand. Some of the people from my world would want to take over your land by force. Others would want to rape its resources, while still others would ruin it unintentionally through overpopulation and commercialization. It's not worth the risk. But you don't have to worry. No one will believe me anyway."

"Be that as it may," he said, "I'd feel better for as long as I have left here if you promise not to tell anyone in your world of this place."

"It's a deal," I said.

We then both retired to sleep. We knew there was to be another hard day of mourning to get through once we'd awoken. I wasn't at all looking forward to my last few days in Gwerinatha.

Chapter Twenty-Five
Aftermath

The morning was like a slap in the face. While asleep, I could dream I was back at home or that I was with Branwen in Serenity Forest or anything but this. The cold hard fact was that Branwen was gone, never to return. After waking, we went right away to see Seren and her family. As much as I didn't want to disturb their first night as a family together without Branwen, I also didn't want them to be alone too long. Everyone handles grieving differently, but it's always nice when you have others around you to help you along in the process. As you would imagine, the governor's mansion was somber. The help staff hadn't fixed any breakfast, as the Gwerinathan custom is to fast for five days after a death in the family. Most of the family was sitting around in a large room that was mainly used for receiving guests. The governor was pacing back and forth in the hallway. Seren was on the couch with her sisters. I walked over to her and put my hand on her shoulder. Without looking up she grabbed my forearm and clenched it tight.

I never know what to do in these situations. At that time I had very few relatives that had died and had little experience in grieving myself, let alone with helping others. I just stood there for a moment without moving. Seren begin to sob. I couldn't help but start to cry myself after that. Crying is far more contagious than yawning, especially when everyone is sad about the same thing. Which was obviously the case here.

The morning flew by at an incredible pace. People came by in large numbers, one after another. There were leaders of the government, both the House of Fates and the Lords of Wisdom. There were business people and kids that had gone to school with Branwen. And there were the family members, mostly from Baylies Crossing. Most stayed, but some just stopped by for a moment and then left. It was obvious that Branwen had a lot of friends and had made an enormous impression on everyone she met.

Of course some of the visitors were just there for the governor. You could easily tell which ones were friends of Branwen's and which were just making an appearance. But I guess that's the case in most deaths, especially those where a family member of a government official is involved.

Samuel and I milled about with the guests most of the day in the receiving room. Despite the fact that there was a wake going on, the scuttlebutt got around both that Samuel was who he was and that I was who I was. People couldn't help but pull us aside to talk. I imagine it was like going to a wake and finding out that George Washington, who had come back from the dead, and an alien from another planet were both in attendance. It was impossible to just blend in with the crowd.

The attention was unnerving. Any other time I might have enjoyed it, but my grief was too raw to be able to think of much anything else. Every time someone began to talk to me, my mind would wander back to Seren, and I'd look around to make sure she wasn't out of my sight. On a couple of occasions I had to remind people that I was grieving too, and I couldn't really pay attention to them. I may have sounded rude, I don't really remember, but sometimes you have to state the obvious for people.

Word finally got around about the funeral proceedings. I learned that since Gwerinatha wasn't such a large place that the practice of burial had been supplanted by cremation. Some of the old timers still hated this option due to their religious beliefs, but the practicality of the thing overruled them long ago. It was decided that Branwen's ashes would be spread over her garden in Serenity Forest. Initially Branwen's parents hated the idea. Her father fought it tooth and nail. But Seren, who'd suggested it, was very adamant. She eventually won over her mother and with some prodding, the governor finally relented.

So it was that on the third day after her death that Branwen's funeral began in New London. Flags were at half-mast all over Gwerinatha. Many spoke at her service. I can't really remember too much about what was said. Mostly, it was the usual things you'd hear at a funeral: what a wonderful life she lived, how much she cared for others, and how much she would be missed. I didn't really pay attention. I was in a daze most of the time, lost in my own thoughts about Branwen. I only looked up every once in a while just to check on her family, who were trying desperately to keep up a brave face.

Then after the formalities of the public funeral were over, the trek to Serenity Forest began. This trip was just for the family and a few close friends. I was honored to be among them. Seren insisted that I come along and, because of my involvement in her last days, her father thought it appropriate. Other than Samuel and me, the only non-family members were a couple of the members of her wildlife defenders group. We spoke little on the long journey to Serenity Forest. Everyone was too upset.

I couldn't believe that I'd actually gone three days already without eating. In the past I had tried to fast for spiritual reasons, but could barely get past the first twenty-four hours. I have a high metabolism and going even a minute more than three hours without eating usually causes me to be very grumpy and weak. I get dizzy after going four hours without food, but this was different. I'd never grieved this hard before and the grief was so strong that it vanquished any hunger pangs I might have had.

Eventually we got out of our carriages and walked the rest of the way into Serenity Forest. We found our way to the garden. The other members of the wildlife defenders had kept it up in Branwen's absence. They, and Seren and her sisters, would be taking care of it from here on out, I supposed. It was the first time Branwen's parents had seen it. It was very clear that Branwen's mother was moved. She had only heard about the garden and why Branwen had started it. Upon seeing it, she fell to the ground weeping. As usual, Governor Baylies was less emotional, but even he became misty eyed during the brief ceremony.

Overall he seemed a bit perturbed at the whole thing, and was especially irritated when Branwen's friends were speaking. I believe deep down the governor resented them for putting the ideas into Branwen's head that caused her to become a wildlife defender. But they could not be blamed for such a thing. Branwen was the most independent person I had ever met. She was a free thinker who prided herself on being an individual. Had governor Baylies spent more time with his daughter, he may have realized that. As it was, he only got misty eyed when Seren spoke.

I have to admit, that was the part that got me too. Seren was so young and to imagine her speaking at a funeral only a week earlier would have been incredible. Now here she was, the one that put the whole thing together and was the one to sprinkle the ashes over the garden. At that moment we heard the mournful howls of the wolves that had been watching from hiding nearby. It could not have ended more beautifully.

Of course, everyone handles the whole process differently. I think Governor Baylies was well on his way to getting past his daughter's death before the carriage returned to New London. I, on the other hand, wouldn't have fully processes it for many weeks to come. I had dreams of Branwen even after returning home. And as the years went by and I began dating, I couldn't help but think of her every time a pretty girl smiled at me. I'm pretty sure I'll carry a piece of her with me until my own death.

After we got back to New London the conversation eventually turned to having Samuel back. News of his return spread through Gwerinatha like wildfire. Some in the government were clearly nervous about his return. He assured everyone that he wasn't about to take over the government, but to do what he could to assist them in governing themselves. I wished him a lot of luck with *that* job. I hoped it wouldn't be too much for him to handle. But if anyone could do it, it would definitely be him.

After the final day of fasting, Samuel held what basically amounted to a press conference where he laid out his plan on bringing the government back together. It got a mixed reception. Obviously, the folks in power weren't excited about it. But the populace at large was more than eager. They'd waited for someone like Samuel to come along and shake things up for generations. The rift between the Lords of Wisdom and the House of Fates had grown in recent years, and it was taking its toll on the people. The problem with the dam in the Village of Idiots was just one example. There were lots of issues that infighting within the government had caused. Now it seemed that at least there was a hope of a brighter tomorrow.

That night there was a large feast. In their custom, after the five days of fasting for the grieving family, a feast is held in their honor. I spent much of the time talking with Seren. She was my closest friend in Gwerinatha and I had to tell her first that it was time for me to leave. She didn't take the news as well as I'd hoped.

"No Robert!" she yelled. "You can't leave me now. I've just lost Branwen. I'll be heartbroken if you go too."

"I think it's best now, Seren," I told her.

"But you told me that Samuel could bring you back to the precise moment in which you left," she said "You could stay here for years if you *really* wanted. Your family would never know the difference."

"C'mon now Seren," I said. "Do you really think they wouldn't notice a fifteen year old changing into an eighteen year old overnight?"

"I guess you're right," she said begrudgingly. "But why do you have to leave now? Can't you stay just a few more days?"

"I've thought about it Seren," I replied. "I think the longer I stay, the harder it will be to leave, and the worse you'll end up missing me."

"Maybe you're right," she said. "But I don't want you to go. I'm not as strong as Branwen and I need someone to lean on."

"You've got your parents," I told her.

"Yeah, right," she responded curtly.

"And your sisters..." I added. "You've got to be strong for them. You need to teach them all the things Branwen would have and be the kind of role model she would have been."

"That's too much responsibility," she lamented.

"It'll get easier with time," I assured her.

"Are you leaving tonight?" she asked.

"In the morning," I answered.

"Well, in that case stick close to me for the rest of the night," she said.

I did as she asked. We didn't talk much more and spent the evening looking up at the Gwerinathan sky. I wondered for a minute if these were the same stars I saw at home or if they were altogether different. At that moment my homesickness flared up stronger than ever, and I knew I had made the right decision. Seren and I hugged and said our goodbyes. I told her that I would be gone before she awoke and that spurred another tear from her eye. We hugged again and I left for my room.

The next morning I quietly got up early and woke Samuel. The two of us journeyed alone to Serenity Forest. It turned out that I could have left from anywhere in Gwerinatha to get back home, as long as Samuel could figure out the coordinates. I thought Branwen's garden would be the most appropriate place for me to make my departure. I also wanted to say my last goodbyes to Louie, who was the first friend I had made there. That wasn't easy. I don't think he understood why I had to leave, but he knew it was what I wanted to do and he respected my decision. Saying goodbye to him was in some ways harder than it was saying goodbye to Seren or Samuel. I wasn't sure if or when I would come back. Samuel had explained that while it was certainly possible to come back to Gwerinatha, he was concerned that too much traffic back and forth eventually would cause someone from my world to learn the secret of the interdimensional travel (though that wasn't what he called it). And, though he was too polite to say it, he was still worried that I might bring back some negative influence from my world into his.

After my goodbyes to Louie and the other wolves, Samuel had worked out all the details of my trip back on the dimension key. There was a panel in the back that slid open which Cameron and I had never discovered. It was there that the settings were adjusted and I was ready for my trip back home. I probably should have asked Samuel how he had worked it all out, but I assumed the math was way over my head, and didn't bother. I was just happy I was going to be getting back home.

Soon the familiar doorway was opening up in the middle of nowhere and I could just make out the park I had left so many days before. I thought I could even barely glimpse Cameron through the blurry haze. I turned to say goodbye one last time and smiled. And then as I held tight to the key I walked through the door and stepped into the park in the other side.

Cameron greeted me with astonishment. From his perspective, I had gone for a brief moment rather than some seventeen days.

"Wow! That's cool! You just disappeared and then reappeared," he told me.

"Well, not exactly," I responded.

"Let me see that," he said, quickly grabbing the key out of my hand.

"No wait!" I yelled.

But before I even finished that exclamation he turned around and walked through the portal, just as it was closing. I couldn't go back in after him. I was stunned. I stood there, my head spinning. And then it hit me. Samuel could fix it so that he could come back at the last second, couldn't he? He would be back in another minute or two, I figured. So I just sat down on a rock, made myself comfortable, and waited. But nothing happened.

I waited an hour and still nothing. I couldn't understand it. Something must have gone wrong. It couldn't all have been a crazy dream. I knew where I had been and all I had seen. I also knew that Cam was gone. After several more hours of wondering what in two worlds could have happened to Cam, I decided to go home. I didn't know what to tell anybody. I had hoped that maybe it was too late for that portal opening and Cam would have to wait until the next morning on my end to come back home.

But the next day went by and no word from Cameron. More days went by and there was all the usual fuss surrounding a missing person that I had expected would happen for me: the pictures on posters all around town, the story in the papers and on television, and the like. And I was caught in the middle. The police questioned me several times, as I was the last person to see Cam. I didn't know what to do. I couldn't tell them the truth. Besides my promise to Samuel I knew that no one would believe me. And so I've kept silent until now. The story of Branwen's garden needed to be told, not just because it explains Cameron's disappearance, but also because it deserves to be heard by people here and around the world.

Epilogue

With this telling, my conscience becomes somewhat clearer. I hope that those in Cameron's family to whom this is mainly directed can understand why I kept silent and can respect that decision. I will certainly understand if they cannot.

Directly after I came back through the portal I coughed quite a bit. It took me several days to get used to the polluted air of our world again. I didn't notice it as much in the park, but when I got back home to the suburbs it became obvious. I mention this only to highlight why I think it is so important to keep the world of Gwerinatha clean from our tainted, modern touch. In many ways it is a pristine world, and Samuel was right to keep it a secret. I don't know how much longer before a modern scientist discovers its whereabouts, but I can tell you I now know that there are those who will fight like crazy to keep Gwerinatha the way it is. And deservedly so.

As for me, my life was completely altered by this event. Many close to me believed that the disappearance of Cameron was what caused me to grow up so quickly. But of course, it wasn't. The events with Branwen and my friends in Gwerinatha were responsible.

I have since grown up and become an art teacher at a middle school. I'm also a husband and father. In my spare time I help with animal causes, especially those that help out wolf relocation. My family has been raised in a vegan fashion and, though I do not proselytize about such things, I am more than willing to help any who want more information on the subject.

These are all things that came from my Gwerinathan experience, but that's not all. I learned a lot from Branwen about getting the most out of life. I no longer live in the shadow of my siblings. I don't care about many of the things others find important. To some people, being a teacher isn't such a big deal. That's fine. In some people's minds, helping out animals in no way compares to helping people. That's fine too. But I realize it's no good living your life by others' standards. You have to live the kind of life that is right for you. That's what Branwen did, and I know she died with no regrets.

One day I will do the same.

About the Author

Brad Parnell was born in the mid-'60s into a quasi-nuclear family. He became interested the comic books handed down by older brothers, he began copying the art and drawing things out of his head. Receiving top marks in every drawing class from first grade to college, he decided to follow the path of art wherever it led.

Bored by mundane opportunities in the business world, he sought out work to stimulate his creative side. Fortunately, those in the science fiction and fantasy worlds liked his work well enough to give him the occasional illustration jobs.

Besides creating artwork, he's written some self-published comic books and his own comic strip, *Nuthouse*. Now at an a age where he can sit still for a bit longer, he has finally been able to write a fantasy novel with hopes of more to follow.

He lives with his wife of twenty years in their hometown of Louisville, Kentucky. Although currently just the two of them, they have been blessed with some wonderful cats over the years and hope to be able to open up to a new life to join them soon. Like many fellow Louisvillians he is totally caught up in college basketball and an avid U of L fan. He is a science fiction fan who loves *Star Wars*, *Lost in Space*, *Battlestar Galactica* (the original), and *Smallville*.

He is also a Beatle-maniac who was inspired to pick up the bass guitar by listening to Paul McCartney – his all-time favorite musician/songwriter.

Also from BlackWyrm...

by Jason Walters

At the edge of the known world, two desperate armies struggle for the right to siege a city that has never been taken. Terrible magics are unleashed and the fate of empires hangs in the balance. Highdome and his crew of cutthroats, monsters, and mutants don't care. They just want to stay alive. But when sorcery backfires and the fury of the Vast White desert is unleashed, the men and women of the Red Regiment must look inside of themselves to find the strength to survive.
[Dark Military Fantasy, ages 14+]

by Ian Harac

One FBI agent
One geekette
One dead munchkin
Parallel worlds galore
An interdimensional conspiracy.
When Matt Anders stumbles across the body of a dead munchkin in a suspect's apartment, a conspiracy begins to unravel that leads him on a reality-jumping adventure to the magical Land of Oz... and beyond!
[Snarky SciFi Thriller, ages 14+]

AFTERTHOUGHTS
by Lynn Tincher

Detective Paige Aldridge was found beaten and without any memories of the previous few months. When her nephew is found dead a year later, she begins to have terrifying flashbacks, plus visions of the murders of her own family! As her loved ones begin falling prey to a serial killer, Paige believes that she must be going mad. With her family dying around her and dark suspicions forming in her mind, Paige has to pull the pieces together before it's too late.
[Psychic Crime Thriller, ages 14+]

Albrim's Curse
by Trevis Powell

All young Albrim wanted to be was a master bowman like his father. Then a savage attack on his home cost him his family, his arm, and his humanity – all at once! Crippled and contaminated by the Curse, his beloved Gran leaves him in the care of Mute, a giant warrior dedicated to protecting humanity from the depredations of the Quarg. Albrim does what he can to assist his master and redeem himself. But can a werewolf ever really recapture his humanity?
[Epic Werewolf Fantasy, ages 14+]